A Journey to the Interior

A Journey To the Interior

P. H. NEWBY

DOUBLEDAY & COMPANY, INC.

GARDEN CITY, N. Y. 1946

FIRST PUBLISHED, 1946, IN THE UNITED STATES

TO JOAN

Contents

A Journey to the Interior

CHAPTER I : *Death at Sea*

ON THE THIRD DAY THE LAND ROSE OUT of the sea.

Winter walked over the coiled ropes to the blunt bows and for some moments looked full into the eye of the sun; and then the land, when he turned his face towards it, was an oily indistinctness between the glitter of the waves and the deep brilliance of the tropic sky. 'Rise and fall, energy and rest, labour and repose,' he allowed his mind to think. 'Sparkle and gloom, day and night,' for there was a sudden release of spirits within him. He stood at the extreme prow of the boat listening to the ripple of water as the waves were divided, really the inland sound of brooks, here imposed on the deeper sighing of the ocean. Winter stretched out his arms. He knew that there was a smile upon his face but he was not ashamed to be smiling at nothing. 'Ripen and decay, flower and fall, ripple and smooth,' he was content to allow himself to think now that after his dark cabin he had come up into the light and the rhythmic pitching of the boat had set his own pulse beating faster.

The sterile land showed itself to be in echoing distance. An Arab sailor, naked save for a pair of torn shorts, dropped a heavy metal pin on the deck: the clank surely must have come

back from the two-thousand-foot precipice that fell almost
sheer into the sea: but the constant washing of the waves, that
here set up a complicated web of movement over barely concealed crags, was all the sound that the glaring day could hold.
The sun looked searchingly into the face of the cliff, destroy-
ing colour and shadows. For a hundred feet or so up from the
point where the surf came licking respectfully in, there was a
yellowness in the strata. But it was a lifeless colour, like the
colour of a melon flower long preserved between the pages of
a book; above the strata the pitted face of the cliff, which
would have been rose-red in the sunset, was an anaemic colour
wash in the blaze of noon. The crest of the precipice was a
ragged edge against the sky. It was a vision of the earth before
a cloud had arisen from the sea and scattered water over its
desolation.

The Arab sailor picked up the fallen pin and stood for some
moments looking at the land. He was as unmoved as though he
were regarding the back of his hand, no curiosity, no purpose-
ful searching with the eye, for he knew that there would be no
life or any movement. It was the very least that nature could
do in the way of land and as such he was not interested. His
idea of land was black earth and palm trees amongst the white
houses; about such landfalls he could have strong feelings for
he knew that the sea was bad. That is all that he would say
about the sea. It was bad; and this lunar cliff was bad too, but
there, a man could at least feel the sand crunching between his
toes and sit under the shadow of a rock, like a lizard, dozing
and then wake to rattle his knuckles on the pebbles, knowing
that the earth would not open and swallow him. The Arab
sailor had been wrecked three times along this coast for it had
not been charted since the first rough survey made by a naval
sloop a hundred years before.

The sky was all light. Behind the shoulder of the cliff there might have been a hint of positive colour but otherwise the whole sky was incandescent, and the many-faceted waves mirrored such a profusion of glory that the eyes ached to look at them. Between the cliff and the sea there was the fiercest opposition. The tawny land was as unmoving as the back-cloth of a theatre: the sea swirled in front, claiming that it and it alone had life and reality, and indeed, by its very steadiness on the sight the cliff became more unreal. There was no depth in that faded rose and yellow. A giant hand raised to knock against its powdered face would destroy it. The cliff could be torn down and crumpled up like so much rice paper. At least, that is how it appeared at high noon but when the sun had moved farther down the sky and the small coasting vessel had made its way gingerly between the reef and the shore and could once more think of deep water, there was depth in the shadow on the land and fissures showed up like jet. Then the cliff was no longer a background: it was a presence capable of bodying forth groans and concealing thunders, a land of giants.

A rock fell. It was falling a long time. It struck against the face of the cliff in its flight and a crumbling landslide went leisurely after it to the narrow strip of sand that fringed the sea. It was as though the cliff had grunted. For some moments a cloud of dust hung before the face of the rock, then disintegrated and disappeared. The land, now, was at least as real as the sea, and as though having waited for some such assurance before manifesting themselves, a caravan of a dozen camels strung themselves out along the little shore. Like large silver insects in a decorative frieze, contriving to look enormous against the khaki-coloured rocks, for the camels were alive and the rocks were dead, the animals went unregardingly along between the cliff and the sea. There were men, small creatures

perched like dolls, looking down at the snake-like necks leading eastward to Rasuka. A long white wave curled up at the
very feet of the patient beasts.

All this could be watched from the deck of the small boat.
Winter had slept a little during the afternoon and now he came
up to clear his head; and he opened his eyes a little wider than
usual to see how close they were to the land. He was alone on
the deck so there was no one to ask the reason for their going
so close inshore. He stretched his arms and watched the line of
camels going in the same direction as the boat.

'Ahmed!' he suddenly shouted, annoyed at being alone.

The Arab sailor came forward immediately though it was
obvious that this was a mere coincidence. He scarcely looked
at Winter but said patiently, as though to a peevish child, 'To-
morrow, Rasuka.' Then he went to the rail and stood in the
red light of the sunset, swinging a piece of lead on the end of a
length of cord.

It was all right, thought Winter. These people knew what
they were doing. He told himself that he would rather trust
himself in a native boat off this shore than in any craft manned
by Europeans. This was to comfort himself. But the very reflection reminded him that he was European and all the others
Asiatics, the cheerful-looking captain in the white turban, Ali,
the consumptive cook, and the naked men he saw working in
the throbbing interior of the engine-room when he looked
down the short flight of steps that took one from the sea air
of the deck to the exhalation of machines. It was such a tiny
ship. But these men knew where they were going, had made
this voyage before, were unafraid. Yet it was not that entirely.
They knew about themselves in a way that Winter felt himself
unknowable. The captain in his white turban had a perpetual
smile of self-congratulation on this account. 'Look,' he might

seem to say, 'you can criticize me, you can say what you will.' He had the almost unheard-of habit among these people of taking snuff, placing the grey powder carefully on the back of his hand, snuffing it up first one nostril and then the other, replacing the leather box in his pocket, all gracefully, self-assuredly. He seemed to know that it was right to take snuff. These people could never be caught out in mistakes. They made none. There was such an accord between the inner coil of their thoughts and feelings on the one hand and the machinations of the workaday world on the other that there was no such thing as a mistake. All was as conceived in the Mind of God. No hesitations, then, no doubts, no questionings. Only the perpetual backward and forward flowing of the tides of love and hate, of lust and fear, washing over them almost non-committally, so that they could roar in temper, shaking out their hands in front of them while in their eyes was a look of startling indifference. 'See how this thing takes me,' they might be saying. They were so terribly sure of themselves.

Winter was still a little dazed with sleep and had lost his lightness of heart. The woman had been crying again and as his mind cleared it was to a realization of his detestation of that animal misery. She was in the next cabin and the wooden partitions were thin. Even now her sobbings seemed to palpitate inside him, opening and closing a hand of suffering beneath the diaphragm. What was it, after all, to be a widow? he thought. The captain would know for he had not stopped smiling and neither had Ali, the cook, ceased coughing; the wind had not ceased nor the sea rising and falling. It would pass, they were saying, men and elements. They did not deny that the pain existed. Only Winter would wish to deny that. The sobbing seemed to follow him.

So Winter drew his thoughts together and thought of the

morrow. There would be no formality about the landing for
the Company would have made all the necessary arrangements.
There would be the Company's launch and three times as many
men to carry his baggage as were absolutely necessary, great
servility, everything made easy. But that was how it should be.
He wanted no responsibilities or cares. Everyone knew that
when the Company bestirred itself and sent one of their men
down to Rasuka for a change it was because a prolonged stay
in the delta area had necessitated a change of air. Men came
here for their health. Naturally there was work to do—of a
sort—for the Company would never have maintained an installation out of mere sentimentality. But there could be no comparison with the great installations in the delta where the
cherry-coloured wooden buildings and the meccano derricks
covered square miles. The Rasuka well produced a few hundred barrels a year and if that represented any loss there was a
corresponding gain in having somewhere where one could send
sick employees. In addition to being good for the firm's repu-
tation it was also good for the health of the European members
of the staff. In winter the climate was dry and sunny, so crisply
cold at nights that a man's breath could be seen as vapour in
lamp-light, a cold that furbished the stars and stirred the blood
which had gone sluggish in the humid delta. Rasuka itself was
a native town presided over by a Sultan but the Company had
built a small wharf and a jetty to take the pipe-line out to sea.
Periodically a tanker would come and suck at this pipe.

When Winter landed he felt that people would ask after his
health for that would be the natural thing. This he would detest. He made up his mind to detest it immediately. People
naturally hated disease and invalids and all pretensions to the
contrary were morbid. It would be impossible for him to pretend that he was perfectly well, otherwise he would not have

been sent. But he was in the convalescent stage, almost cured; just a few more weeks now and then it would be all over. How one hated seeing a man sick in bed, he thought.

It was pleasant to feel that he was going to have a holiday. Not a complete holiday, Rixon had said, but—'You know . . .' Perhaps he would go into the office two or three times a week and look at the installation once in a way with Ford. He was only going to be there in an advisory capacity. Tranquil days and cold still nights, he thought, with a mental rubbing together of the hands. Yes, that was good. All would be well.

He was at once restored to his good humour and as though his irritation with the weeping woman had been a bandage over his eyes of which he had now rid himself, he could once more look about him and see the land rising and falling and the Arab sailor with his back to him, swinging a piece of lead on the end of a length of twine.

So I am going to Rasuka and so are you, he thought, looking at the Arab's back. But then you return and I do not. You are a different being from me. By some enormous chance I am I and you are you. He could think now, easily and a little jocularly, along these lines and perhaps it was a trifle patronizingly.

Those rags might be my rags, he thought. The half-naked figure leaned over the side of the boat and looked into the clear depths. Around his head a woollen strip that might once have been a European vest clung dirtily: scars on his back were shellfish pink. His hair was dirty; it hung in dirty knots; his face was scored with wrinkles of grime; his feet were scaled and callused, the large toes at an angle of thirty degrees with the rest. If he were more elaborately clad he would be more wretchedly clad. But this man had some little dignity in his semi-nakedness. He was not pitiable as the European tramp is pitiable in his torn bowler, his ragged trousers, the newspapers

that he has bound around his feet for boots. The Arab sailor
had not those pretensions and therefore none of that humiliation. But one could be no poorer nor eat less.

And these might be my scars, thought Winter, looking at the
rosy weals. This sailor had some object in his mind, it was true.
He was doing a job. He was not purposeless. At that moment
he was swinging a piece of lead on the end of some twine and
screwing up his eyes to look into the glassy depths.

Winter looked at him with a warm feeling that might almost
have been affection. It was an affection that would never be expressed. That brown skin with the blue vein, he thought, that
winks in the sun—why isn't that my arm and my vein? Why
am I not he? In what way am I better or worse?

The Arab sailor spat into the sea. It was an unnecessary spit
by way of being a luxury of indulgence. When the Arab at
last turned his head on the sea and grinned back as though
aware of being under observation, Winter could understand all
that. But why was it that spitting was no luxury for him? The
extraordinary, the inconceivable, the profoundly moving
chance that he had not been conceived in the womb of this
man's thin-bellied mother to whimper in some gutter with the
flies at his eyes and mouth until the time came when he could
wade in the shallow water, casting his net, could likewise take
a wife and conceive others in his own image. It was enough to
make a man feel guilty to look at such a creature. Winter felt
moved to look at him. He would go over and touch that arm
and look down into his eyes. As human beings they had more
in common than they had differences. Flesh, muscle, bone,
joint, nerves, brain, living and breathing in this hot air; the
sun was looking down on them, two specks on a floating shape
between earth and sky, and the disposing of their respective
faculties carefully or casually done, one knew not which. Why

had there been any choice? Why had it been necessary to choose?

The man said something in Arabic and showed black, jagged teeth in an unrestrained grin. He appreciated the interest taken in him and wanted to be friendly. He flung out one hand to the pulsating land and moved closer to Winter as though to tell him an intimate joke. Winter realized immediately that there was something else about this man that he had not taken into account. He stank abominably. The sailor went on talking in a low encouraging voice, his head on one side and the light of calculation in his eyes. He was telling Winter about Rasuka. He approached closer. Winter stiffened. The wretched man plucked at Winter's sleeve. Being so much taller, Winter could look down on to the crown of his head and see that it was scored with ring-worm.

It was too much. Winter shook himself free and stepped across to the other side of the deck. He feared that the Arab would follow him. He did not dare to look round in case it were interpreted as so much encouragement. The merest look, the hint of a smile, the slightest relaxation was enough for these people. They were vigilant for the slightest sign of weakness.

'St'aas,' said the low voice as a shadow fell across the rail in front of him. Winter swung round on the Arab in sudden temper.

'Go on—be off with you! 'Y'Allah! Imshi!'

He was trembling with fury.

'Backsheesh.' A filthy paw in front of his face, the leaded cord in the other, dripping water.

''Y'Allah!' Winter pushed past and went down to his cabin.

The small coasting vessel had not really been constructed to carry passengers and the three small cabins were makeshift affairs in which a man could lock his baggage and sleep on the small bunk, the porthole open on the hot evenings. The bunk was much too small for Winter and he had slept awkwardly on his side, his legs bent painfully. There was little difference between day and night temperature on this tropic sea and he would wake in the middle of the night to find his light pyjamas clinging to him, wet with perspiration. The water in the glass jug was always warm and he had bribed Ali, the cook, to lend him one of his clay pots which could be stood on the shelf at the side of the porthole: here the sea-wind would beat upon the porous pot which glistened and was as damp as a skin. Waking in the night, he would see the damp pot in fine phosphorescence, but the water it contained was always sweet and cool. There was a small electric fan glued up in one corner of the cabin. It did not work. The cabin had been painted specially in Winter's honour and the native painter had been as careful to cover the blades of the fan with his cream-coloured paint as he had been neglectful to work his brush well into the angles of floor, wall and ceiling. Sometimes a gout of spray would whisk in through the open port and fall saltily on his face. It was pleasant because it was cool. But after the first night it had been impossible to sleep because of the lamentations of the bereaved woman who occupied the cabin next door. The partition was so thin.

It was her husband who had died, suddenly and mysteriously on the second morning. The two of them had come on board some time after Winter, who, after seeing his baggage well bestowed in the cabin, for it was safer that way and in any case there was no separate provision on the boat for baggage, had come up on deck to shake hands with Bennett. The embarkation of the woman and her husband had every sign of being a last-minute decision. They had come on to the quayside in a two-horse arabiyeh, from which the man was already

springing before it had come to a halt, and running up the gang-
way to engage in furious conversation with the snuff-taking
captain. He waved papers in the captain's face. Apparently
they were all in order for the captain did not even deign to look
at them and was seemingly communing with some interior
being of his own and smiling all the time. The newcomer gave
the appearance of being a man of some position. A brown turban was wound tightly round his head and his long white
gown was drawn to his body with a tooled leather belt. He
was not a young man. His long yellow face was moulded
closely round his bones, cleanly and purely, and there was a
cluster of curly grey hairs on the extremity of his chin in symbol of a beard. There were two large gold rings on the fingers
of his left hand and his feet were thrust into a pair of fine
sandals, more sophisticated than the ordinary native variety,
but consisting of two great flaps that folded over the foot and
left the big toes peeping out at the end. He produced a purse
and there was a chink of coins. The captain seemed genuinely
surprised and raised his hands in the merest of delicate gestures
but the two of them moved away to a more secluded corner
and Winter thought he had discovered the interior dream that
the captain had been smiling.

Such a fine, powerful, self-possessed man to die so suddenly!
It was the woman who had looked ill as she came up the gang-
way, slowly following their one servant who carried apparently
what was all their luggage in a pot-shaped basket. She was
rather a plump woman in middle age, dressed in the customary
black cotton cloth, but she went unveiled, so that Winter could
see her pouched cheeks and gross, thick lips. She mumbled pet-
tishly to herself as she walked and gave the impression of being
the kind who will eat sweets impatiently for an hour on end
and then drink two or three cups of black coffee, all with an

air of fierce self-indulgence. Her cheeks, rather heavily rouged, quivered as she passed. And then her husband had died in a few minutes, almost as soon as they were out of sight of land, and this same woman was lying alone in her cabin helpless with her grief.

The body had been thrown into the sea. It would have been impossible to keep it even for a day in this climate. Winter had not seen the actual consignment to the sea but he had come up from his cabin immediately afterwards and found the widow standing a little apart from the small group of men who had performed the last offices. How could she cry and wring her hands? Winter had thought. How is it that she knows so soon what has happened? She is as vehement as though it were an old grief. Why isn't she stunned and helpless, the nerves shocked beyond all feeling? She cried loudly looking back at that spot on the waters; the wind got between her and the enveloping black gown so that her form was grotesque, then fluid, then straining to fly out above the waves to the point that her eyes were watching, all by turn. She beat her hands on her bosom. Her face was blubbery with tears. Good-bye, my fine gentleman with the brown turban and the great gold rings, thought Winter. This is your grave and this your mourning.

She had cried in the night so that Winter could not sleep and now she was crying again as he levered himself into position on his bunk after the encounter with the Arab sailor. For a while he listened to her, the painful drawing in of breath and then the spluttering, rending sob as it was exhaled. It was imperative this misery, all the misery that had ever been, drawing in and breathing out in the next cabin, on the other side of that thin partition. Winter found himself breathing to her rhythm and holding his breath when, for the moment, there was silence. The fat woman snivelled quietly to herself.

Winter sprang angrily out of bed and slammed the thin cabin door behind him, exultant to hear that the sudden noise had startled the woman into silence. Were there not worse things than the death of her husband? Could he not, for example, enter her little cabin with a drawn knife and murder her? The act would in no way be extraordinary. Her husband had been just as much alive as she twenty-four hours before. Speculatively he felt himself capable of the murder and the woman, living in a half-civilized society, would not regard being murdered as outside all ordinary possibilities. She would know immediately what the drawn knife meant. Probably she had seen knives drawn in that way on other occasions. She would not be bewildered as a European woman might. She would fall silent in fear immediately and forget her grief before puckering up her inflamed, bloated face into a scream of terror. She would forget her husband lying two-thirds of the way down the ocean in his white sheet, plucked at by the tides in the bottle-green light.

Winter found the captain on his bridge. The ship was intimidated by the frowning bluff of land, solid and dark now that the sun was getting behind it, but before them the sea, in the middle distance, had a transparent vacancy. Here the boat would float on air. Farther out, towards the horizon, there was purple again, and above that a bright star had come out.

'Look here, you must do something for that woman. Go down and talk to her—comfort her. I can't say a word.' He spoke in English. The captain's English was much better than Winter's Arabic. In any case, he did not reply for a while. 'Woman crying, yes, husband dead, yes. Well?' he seemed to be saying.

'I can't get any sleep for the noise that she is making,' Winter added.

The captain's smile deepened. He understood this more clearly. He knew that Winter was an important passenger and this woman, after all, had been only a last-minute passenger with her husband.

'Yes,' he said, 'she can be moved.' A boy whom Winter had never seen before was standing at the wheel and the captain turned to say something to him in Arabic. 'Yes, she can be moved. After all, the nights are warm. After all, there is only one more night.' The captain had learned his English in Basra; he was careful never to use a phrase that he had not heard previously used by an Englishman. He was not inventive. He knew how extraordinary foreigners sounded when they talked Arabic and he did not wish to talk English in this way.

But Winter was still angry. It was expected of Europeans and the captain looked at him with all courtesy.

'Crying like a . . . howling like . . . She can't feel like that. It's—it's impossible!'

The captain did not argue with him. 'She is happy in doing that. If she did not grieve she would be frightened.'

'Can't something be done to comfort the woman? Why don't one of you go down there and talk to her in her own language?'

'She is not so—' began the captain, and then, searching for a word, worked his lips. 'She is not so unhappy. How do we know, for example, that she did not murder her husband?'

'Murder?' Winter was not surprised. Nothing could surprise him.

'He died very quick, that man. One moment he jangles his purse and then . . . who knows, yes?'

'The very fact that the woman is crying like that—no, it's absolute nonsense. That bellowing is too real. She's making herself ill.'

'She could have murdered him and still—cry. She could be sorry for example.' The captain said something more to the boy at the wheel. 'Nevertheless, I will send some coffee. A man does not jangle his purse one moment and then be thrown into the sea the next. Something happens, yes?'

And it was suddenly night. The night sky was rich with large stars and the ship swam like a fish through the luminous sea. Specks of phosphorescence, some as large as half-crowns, went milling past, the souls of those of the Faithful drowned on their pilgrimage to Mecca.

'You've got another place for her, then?' asked Winter. His anger was subsiding. Evening had come.

'But certainly, there is plenty of room up here on the deck. That woman you see, she is not really a lady. I can tell. That trash, when they travel, almost always on the deck. Something strange, a cabin. I can tell you, for her.' There was the full measure of oriental contempt in his voice.

Winter made up his mind immediately.

'No, it is I who will sleep on the deck.'

At eight o'clock his evening meal was normally sent into the cabin on a tray but this evening Winter asked for it to be placed on the bulkhead. The evening was still, the sea calm. He would eat in the open air, for it was the last night of travelling before arriving and he could not go down once more to his cabin and hear the woman crying. A bronze wing of cloud, catching the last light of a now remote sun, was lightly attached to the dark mass of land. All sounds fell softly upon the ear, the thudding of the engines, the cough of the boy at the wheel, the ripple of waters under the bow. They were summer evening sounds when in an immense shell of quiet every particular lapping wave was caught and quietly emphasized, and yet all, all was muted and there was no remoteness and nearness of sound but only a dream-like middle distance of vibrations that were rather felt than heard. The stars burned clear.

There was bean soup in a little blue plate, grilled mutton with lentils, white cheese that had a lemony bitterness, and fruit.

Impossible that the man had been murdered. It was the captain's excuse for his lack of sympathy. It was the easiest way. Say that the sympathy is undeserved. But when the woman had come running up on deck some few hours before her husband had died she was in a kind of terror. Winter had been with the captain and to them she had poured out incoherently whatever it was she had to say. Winter had even gone down to the cabin with them and felt the sick man's pulse. It had been rapid and shallow like a bird's. Impossible to say what colour his face was in that yellow electric light, but his pillow was under his neck instead of the head and his chin pointed at the ceiling, a curious angle with his throat. Impossible that it could have been a murder. Some kind of stroke, perhaps. Winter knew nothing of medicine.

Winter would have carried his mattress up on to the deck himself but when he descended to the cabin the lad who had been at the wheel was already rolling the sheets into a bundle and coiling the mattress around them. He was a cheerful boy with large white teeth and Winter felt grateful for the sight of him. The boy knew just where Winter should sleep, in the lee of the bulkhead and where the morning sun would not be a nuisance. He explained all this with many gestures and when they were up on deck in the luminous night Winter found himself watching the boy's white teeth with curious concentration. When the boy closed his lips they disappeared. But Winter was obeying those teeth. They showed him the spot where the mattress was to be spread out, they assured him of a quiet night and a happy awakening. And then the boy was gone and Winter merely removed his shoes and stretched himself, clothed as he was, upon the sheets. He lay on his back and looked straight up at the stars. The warm night enfolded him.

Misery, misery, pain, his thoughts said to him. The sobbing of the woman came back to him and the sound was louder than the present washing of the seas. He saw her distorted face and it shut out the stars. That was the sound and picture that his mind brought back to him but there was something almost physical in the way that he brushed them away. It was as though he had raised an arm and torn down gossamer. How he hated it, this animal misery! The salty hotness of the emotion rose up from his stomach. It was its unproductiveness, he told himself, it was its unnecessariness that he reacted against. It was death and contempt. It was uncreative for the mind turned in on itself. It was nothing active, but passive. All these thoughts and others like them he drew out of his own mind in his attempt to thrust unhappiness away from him. For him it was an old struggle. There was nothing new. He knew the way of negation, recognized the scenery as he advanced, the familiar rocks and the expected resting place. He forced his way along the path. He would not grieve. He could not afford to grieve.

The evening was warm but it was cooler here on the deck than down in the cabin. Blood heat. To open an artery in a bath of warm water, they said, was a sinking into a sleep. He could imagine the flowing out, the sense of dispersion, the attenuation, for now, in flinging his arms out on either side of him, he felt the bright night worlds pressing down on him and the blood-hot flowing in and out through his mouth, his ears, the pores of his skin, the orifices of his body. The stars were close and he felt attenuated on Orion, his limbs on the limbs of the star-man, the golden belt around his waist and the sword upon his thigh. The stars are not impartial. They were aware, they took sides, they had the awards and rewards, the gifts and the punishments. The planets gave up their wheeling and the comets fired their furious path through the recesses of his brain: fires and star dust descended in perpetual rain within the hollow of his eye. The purple of night was his own darkness and calmness, but there was no within and without, no objects or subjects, no star music, for it was all there within the intricate labyrinth of the body. The body rose and fell in the womb-warmth. He was there. The reaching out was over, the incompletion, the idea of God, the broken arcs, the bitter crying from the cavern within the body to the blue sky-body above was quieted. He was rarefied. He was between sleeping and waking. Let the weepers and the beggars gather, then, and the sound of their lamentations would be a star creaking on its axis. The virgin's withered pap knows no milk but does not it flow through the veins of the earth? The fires of volcanoes are human passions. The baby sucks its mother's breast in tears, while the river, sucked by the same power from its grotto source, whimpers between the dove-grey pebbles.

Winter was dazed by the multitude and splendour of the stars. In his half-awareness the thought of the mourning woman came to him with a sense of obligation. It was to him that she was stretching out her arms. So clean cut was the vision and so searing the pain that he was startled into complete awareness and sat up to find his clothes soaked with perspiration and clinging to him. The boat was rocking through an almost silent sea, and to-morrow, he told himself, to-morrow, the sun would be as bright as ever and each wave would be a polished mirror and they would come to Rasuka and a holiday would begin. Was there no anticipation for a holiday? Think, think, of the holidays there have been in the past, the eagerly anticipated departures, the holiday sands and the freedom from responsibility. But he could find no eagerness or anticipation now.

The woman, if she were still weeping, could not be heard up here on the deck. Perhaps she had fallen asleep. She would be exhausted by her weeping. How was it that he had not wept when his own wife had died? He had loved his wife more deeply than—he did not know how he loved her, in what way. And sometimes it was as though she had never died, so clearly was he conscious of her presence. In the six months that had passed since her sudden death there had been time for grief but no grief had come. It was all too incredible for grief. Was this, then, his mourning, with the woman in her cabin wringing her hands and waking him out of his sleep to a desolation of unanticipation? He could envy the woman the spontaneity of her grief. She, at least, had recognized the enemy immediately and had known no confusion. Her tears were washing away that which still remained in Winter's breast as an obstruction.

I loved my wife, he almost breathed aloud. When he could think quietly and connectedly about her as now it was to regard her as the reality and himself as the illusion. He rubbed his hand over the deck at his side. Intangible, unsolid, he thought. It is the dream curtain behind which I shall suddenly come upon her in a burst of sunshine. All was a dream and the ordinary chances of life had no impact.

One day he would awake, he knew—to what? He would awake and take up his position at the side of the weeping woman, a year, eighteen months, two years too late, and she perhaps would have moved on. She could not grieve for ever. When the time came, Winter thought that perhaps he might.

And in the morning they came to Rasuka. Winter rose straight from his bed in the hot morning sunlight to find the

houses of the town huddled in an exciting white between the
water and the mountain. The sea was waveless. He could look
down as through air itself, only more tangible, colder, flowing
air, into great depths. Although the surface might lie calm there
would be a flurry, a stain, some five, ten, fifteen fathoms down,
and the shadows that were the fish rippled under the keel. The
land had been volcanic, had been tilted like a board, and the
sea off the coast was sometimes correspondingly deep. Then
suddenly the sea floor came up to within five fathoms of the
surface and it was easier to see the shadows than the fish. The
sand had a few large pebbles, then a rusty spar at an angle of
thirty degrees and finally what appeared to be the remnants of
a small boat's timbers, and these were almost engulfed. The
water flowed silkily back from the blunt nose of the boat as it
swam to the Company's landing-stage.

The houses might have been cut out of the white Arabic
cheese. The façades looked coolly out at the ocean symmet-
rically studded with windows, many of which were glassless
and as a result no more than soft shapes on the cool expanse
of wall. The eye could start its journey with the boat-builder's
shack and run along the nervous line of windows belonging to
a stone house whose very foundations were stone piers running down into the water. The eye continued. It found the
decorated roof-line of the whitewashed mosque; it leaped to a
tenement where a large orange carpet was hanging out like a
tongue from an upper window. There was a movement
amongst these houses, an artistry in their disposition that led
the eye from the water front by way of the lines of socketed
windows and a wave of green that marked a garden to the grey
hem of the mountain itself, and there, because the eye naturally
recoiled, one went back to find the minaret of the mosque insolently vertical where the quality of the town had been hori-

zontal. Then one realized that the mosque was the nerve centre. For this tall finger the windows were staring out to sea; they had been actions that were inexplicable, but now the minaret had been marked, the motive understood.

It was as though the town had given a start to see the boat coming in from the ocean. Winter was aware of figures moving among the houses. A boat suddenly fluttered up a sail and came bearing proudly out for all its tinyness. A canoe shot out from the wharf and there was a naked black boy flinging his arms up in the air, rocking it crazily from side to side. He was singing for sheer delight, for a boat had come in, out of the immense blue ocean a boat had turned in to the land, and with the singing black boy in the foreground, the ham-shaped sail of the fishing-boat in the middle distance and the windows of the houses producing coloured carpets and the wharf that suddenly had a group of men in white robes, all Rasuka was awake in the early morning to see the sight, to see that the ocean had opened its hand and disclosed a boat with a plume of grey smoke.

CHAPTER II: *The Ingenious Machine*

WHAT!' SAID FORD, COMING OUT ON TO the balcony. 'Already? I had no idea! The first time for . . . and this of all times!' He was a small man with a round, womanish face, an almost blossom-like complexion. He was still dressed in his pyjamas, which were open to the waist, revealing a hairless chest and plump breasts.

'Don't agitate yourself,' said Winter shortly, 'on my account.'

For Ford seemed so overcome by the unexpectedly early arrival of the expected man that he had no words for the ordinary exchange of civilities. His dark round eyes were quite taken up by the sight of Winter. He took in every detail, loose-fitting cotton suit, long thin face with hollows behind the jaws, hands that looked obviously strong and capable with their long fingers and prominent veins. Winter gave Ford only a short glance and then turned to watch his luggage being handed down from the back of the arabiyeh that had brought him up from the harbour. He had been met by no one and although he pretended to himself that this was a relief he was secretly annoyed.

'This man said he knew where you were, so . . .' He left

the sentence unfinished when he turned once more to the manager of the well. In his eagerness Ford had come down the steps from the balcony and was counting the packages, the large wooden trunk and one or two other smaller cases and boxes, although this was obviously not of the slightest value, for he did not know how many there should be there. 'Eight, yes, that's right. Up! Up! What a beautiful box this . . . you should see my old travelling-chest. Although the ants! I warn you they get at everything. The extraordinary thing is that you have come so soon. I can hardly believe it, yet here you are.' So eager was he that he had come down from the balcony in his bare feet and he began to raise them one after the other now, rather hastily, as he became aware of the heat of the ground. He touched the trunk with his open palm. The Arab who had brought Winter up the rocky road grunted and then protested. No, it was too big for one man to move, he declared. Was there not another man about the house? All this in deep-throated Arabic that Winter found hard to follow after the lighter, more nasal speech of the delta. Even as the conversation went on two Arab boys came down from the bungalow.

'But then,' Ford suddenly shot out, 'you must have come up all by yourself. There was nobody . . . Oh, but you know. This is the first time. Yes, yes, I can see the boat myself, now.'

Actually that was not true for the boat was hidden behind the mass of the wharf-side buildings but there was a pall of smoke over the white houses and that, in Ford's estimation, passed for a sight of the vessel itself. The tired-looking horse that had dragged the arabiyeh up the rocky track had drooped its head and occasionally drew its hoof back over the shards. The grunts that the boys made in lifting and carrying the boxes were enormous in the still, sunlit morning. Winter paid the driver and preceded Ford up the wooden steps to the veranda. If he had not taken the initiative Ford out of excess of politeness and deference would, he felt, have ceremoniously insisted and he wanted to avoid that oriental ritual.

'Excuse me, please,' said Ford and darted to the open door in front of which a bead curtain was hanging. 'Yvonne! Yvonne! Would you believe it? He's come, you know!' He parted the beads and trotted through, waggling his fat posterior, but immediately he was back again.

'Please, this way.' He can't be English, thought Winter. To the English mind there was a quality of over-ripeness about the well manager; it was expressed in an elaborate courtesy and desire to please. Winter removed his pith helmet and passed into the cool interior. There was no sign of the woman Ford had addressed, but Ford was walking about the large untidy room, dressing as he went, pulling on a shirt and knotting a tie while still in his pyjama trousers.

'What sort of a trip did you have? But then it is always quiet and just a little bit uncomfortable.'

'As a matter of fact a man died.'

'But do sit down. Here—let me . . .' He pushed a brown cardboard box and some papers off a chair. 'Died, you say? Really! Well, of course—I mean we all have to . . . I say, you must be terribly hungry. You haven't had any breakfast, have you?'

'This man died very suddenly and then there was his wife.'

But Ford was not interested. The subject passed right over him and he could not even find a question to ask. He continued to fuss round the room. There were sounds of activity from the inner room.

'Things are going very well here just now. Like clockwork. Arvanitaki is a very good foreman and, of course, that takes work off your hands.' By now he had pulled on some grey flannel trousers and thrust his feet into a pair of native sandals. 'I go up there in the morning and then the rest of the day I have my own work. I'll show you later. Any news from . . . ?' He had a way of finishing a question by a raising of the eyebrows and opening his eyes just a little wider. The suggestion was that he had come to the end of that particular breath and, in any case, what was the point in bringing out proper names that were realized in the hearer's mind before they were uttered.

'In that case,' nodded Winter. The case was out on the veranda where the boys had left the rest of the luggage. He made no move to go and open it. There were letters, circulars, some newspapers, magazines. The truth of the matter was that Winter was exhausted. He had been up soon after sunrise as a result of sleeping on the deck and the coming and going on the dusty quay-side, the inquiries, the blank and apparent idiocy with which his questions were greeted, the voracious flies, and then the long and painful climb up to Ford's bungalow where it stood at the entrance to the ravine that cut across the edge of the escarpment and so gave access to the interior of the country, had all tired him. The sun dazzled on these rocks as on liquid. He reminded himself that he was still convalescent and must not over-exert himself. For some reason he wanted to avoid at all costs Ford's realizing that he was exhausted. Also, he would have liked to talk about that man who died.

'Good morning, Mr. Winter. I'm afraid that you have caught us a little unawares.' A woman whom Winter took to be Ford's wife came sweeping suddenly out from the back room. The precipitancy with which she had launched herself upon him with its rather self-conscious enthusiasm suddenly

put him in mind of a play. Why, of course, the dramatic entrance. Vivacity! Humour! The husband looking round for
something and slapping his pockets. Winter rose to his feet.
He took the hand that was offered him. Perhaps it was unfair to come suddenly upon a woman so early in the morning,
but she was shapeless under her blue wrap. She had cheeks
that circled out grandly and long white lashes to her eyes. Her
hair was hidden under what might have been a large red handkerchief. She was almost as tall as Winter and correspondingly
big in her bones. Too big for Ford, he thought. He stood swaying on his feet.

'How are you?' he said.

'Why, what a quiet nice-looking man you are! We'd imagined a—I don't know what! You see we've heard all about you.
The murder case, for instance. Quite the model white man,
we all thought. Of course, there are some who are jealous.'

Ford came over and stood at his wife's side, grinning up
into Winter's face. 'Of course, we only get bits and pieces of
news here. We pretend to have the greatest contempt for news
of the outside world. But that trial . . . phew!' He whistled.
'Now that is something you're going to tell us all about.'

Winter felt the room spinning.

'It is so nice to have a fresh face to look at. Tell me, Mr.
Winter, do you dance?' asked Mrs. Ford.

'But of course, it's breakfast, breakfast, breakfast,' her husband suddenly muttered, racing out of the room as if this were
his province and not his wife's. Winter put his hands back and
lowered himself into the chair. Now that Ford was out of the
room he did not mind showing his weakness.

'Not feeling too good, are you?' the woman said with no
note of sympathy in her voice. She was still smiling. She might
have been commenting on the colour of his tie.

'I'm a little tired.' Yes, certainly he was tired. Fatigue had seized upon his limbs and yet there was no weariness about his eyes. He had the curious feeling that he was about to sleep with his eyes open. The woman was still standing in front of him but he had no more consciousness of her than he would have of a thing inanimate. She was a statue, and he looked at and through her. The room was soundless and the chink of a plate coming from a distance was soporific. Yvonne Ford looked down and saw that he was asleep, his chin sunk on his chest, his whole body somehow shrunk into itself, his hands long and loose over his knees.

At this moment her husband came hurrying in from the kitchen, rubbing his hands together and talking as he came. At the sight of the relaxed figure in the chair he stopped short, his hands out and his fingers spread as though they were wet and he was searching for a towel.

'What, asleep? Poor fellow, must be exhausted. His wife, too. You know, it's a lot for a man. You're sure he's asleep? I mean . . . Looks absolutely worn out, doesn't he? Poor fellow. We must do what we can to look after him, Yvonne. Leave him for the time being. Yes, that's it, leave him for the time being and he can have his sleep out. The sleep will do him more good than the breakfast.'

'I think I'll wake him.' She moved her foot as though to give him a prod in the calf.

'He'll be furiously angry. No, leave him.'

'Why should he drop asleep the moment he arrives? Doesn't he know that he's come here to entertain us? Very selfish of him to go to sleep.' And she would have touched his leg with the toe of her shoe if Winter had not suddenly opened his eyes and looked up at her, moving his head a bare two or three inches.

'You were asleep, you know. Breakfast's ready. You can sleep after breakfast if you like.' She was in no way abashed at the thought that possibly he had heard what she said. There was something very cool and ironic about her. Take it or leave it, she seemed to be saying. I don't really care what you think but on the other hand I know that I am beyond criticism. That is what gives me my confidence.

'Look, what would you like? There are eggs, and we've even got some bacon this month. Plenty of fruit, you know. The usual things really. We don't make much of a meal at breakfast time. I think it was too bad to wake you. *Ya Karima!*' Ford didn't even look at Winter as he was talking but moved round the room, looking out through the window, gazing through the bead curtain, weighing up the cases in his mind's eye once more. But so far as he was able, he was giving himself over completely to Winter. He was extremely embarrassed.

Not so Winter. He yawned, stretched himself, and looked up at Mrs. Ford who was still watching him with a soft smile on her lips. Winter said not a word. He made no reference to his having fallen asleep. 'Not so much to eat. If there is any coffee . . .' Physically he felt very light, as though his flesh were distilled of all its grossness and his bones hollowed and fluted like a bird's. It was a very pleasing sensation for there was nothing more physical in it than the soothed paralysis as when a gentle hand is drawn repeatedly upwards over the short hair at the back of the head. But the nerves linking spinal cord and muscles had lost their tension, or the very grip of the muscles on bone had slackened their hold, or the bones themselves had become so brittle as to be unable to respond without the stirring up of a hundred fears. He had moved his head and could look directly into the smiling face of the full-bodied woman before him but he had no power to stimulate his body to further action. It was a pleasing, gentle paralysis. He spoke. 'There are all sorts of curious after effects from this disease. Sometimes there is a tremendous sense of well-being. A fortnight after I recovered I felt better than I had ever felt in my life before. I still get moments like that occasionally. I can put back as much alcohol as you like one night and there will be no hang-over in the morning. You get a new lining to the stomach too. It sets you up in fact.' There had been the slightest difficulty in starting to speak. But once the first two or three words had been pronounced then he could proceed quietly and without emphasis, taking no strain on himself, talking for the mere sake of talking, for the pleasure of pouring out the words, sensing the emanation, the giving out of sense and sound. He felt completely relaxed and reposed.

'You'll like it here, I think.' Mrs. Ford snapped out of the fixed regard that she had been giving him and walked round her husband towards the kitchen. 'You'll fit in. Everybody's a bit queer here. Take my husband and his machine. But I hate it. I'd give ten years of my life to get away. Yes, I do, do, do!' She went out.

'You know you don't mean that, darling,' said her husband a little absently. And then to Winter: 'It never does to take much notice of what a woman says. They don't know how to use words. I understand my wife, you see! Coffee, of course, is excellent here. *Ya Karima!* That girl is—ah, here it is!' The servant girl placed the pot of coffee on the small table at Winter's side.

During the course of the meal, as Ford told him about the well and his wife drank coffee and stared at Winter, he felt his strength coming back to him. He knew that this was delusory and the moment he got to his feet the dizzy feeling would

come back again, but he was going to stand up, he was going
to walk across the room and push through that bead curtain,
take a look round with Ford. He was curiously ashamed of
his weakness and more particularly anxious to conceal it from
Ford than the woman. Ford seemed to avoid making reference
to it. Winter's awareness of this stirred him.

'I'm still convalescent, you know. Typhoid.' He hated saying it and almost dared them to derive any satisfaction from
what he had said.

'Ah! Well, this dry cleanness of air here . . ..' said Ford.
He did not drift over the subject as he had over the subject of
the man who died on the voyage. There was a little uneasiness in his eyes.

'You look thin. Like a rake,' said his wife.

'I never was fat in the face.'

They continued with the meal. Ford took refuge in facts
about output and labour problems. 'That was just downright
ingratitude, of course. Do you know what I said to him? I said
that if he wished he could leave! I knew that would fetch him.
I wanted to show him that he was not indispensable. Arvanitaki is a jewel!'

'I've got romantic ideas about Rasuka,' said Winter. 'That
was why I came. Not so much because of health.' It was not in
his nature to talk so freely and openly especially to people he
had so recently met, but the mere framing of the words and
the resonance inside his head was a physical pleasure. 'You
see, there is the bare desert and the sea, the ascetic and the
austere. Just a little fringe of human beings with their town,
I thought, and in the cool of the day you can walk behind a
sandhill and step out of . . . out of, well out of the world
of men. No, that's badly expressed. But I thought that in bare-
ness and nakedness there would be some sense of . . . primi-

tive origins. I thought that I could get hold of something simple and essential in myself. But, even though I've only been here a few hours, I see that it is all different. There's the sound of the Diesel. You can hear it now. And once behind those hills, I know that I should be walking with all my awareness on the side towards houses and other human beings.'

'I know what you think. You think we don't understand that.'

Winter looked at Mrs. Ford in surprise. Her indignation seemed so strong. It is not false, he thought, this is genuine. She is not teasing.

'I should think that everyone must feel the—pull of deserts.'

'Yes, and it's all hooey! Take it from me, a man who goes out in the desert for the fun of the thing is—well, he's unpleasant, if you want my candid opinion. The whole thing just reeks. When I was a child I used to get a beating if I went into the corner to sulk.'

She had got over her indignation already and by way of compensation gave Winter a round-cheeked smile that suddenly, by some strange trick, some tilting of a mirror or facet, showed her as he felt she must have been at sixteen. He saw round, red cheeks, well fed and shiny, moist lips and dancing eyes. They were the eyes of a girl who has just come in from playing hockey in the frost.

'I've not come here to sulk,' he said quietly and feeling more friendly towards the both of them than he had done at any time since his arrival. He had made up his mind not to allow the fact that he was going to be brought in close contact with the Fords to dispose him to like them. He had intended to enjoy the laziness of an isolation to which no one was to be admitted, but he felt himself being drawn to these two. He liked Ford's muddled amiability.

'Really,' said Ford hurriedly, 'I don't see that that's of any importance.' He was, of course, making reference to his wife's statement. 'I'm sure that we're happy enough here. I like it.'

'I don't,' she said.

'I think you do, really,' he said. She made an impatient gesture. 'But I must show you my machine,' he went on, turning to Winter. 'It's in the cellar under here, though you have to go outside to find the door to it.'

Yes, thought Winter. I will get to my feet and walk, unaided, to that door and out into the sunshine and round to this door.

'What sort of a machine is it?' he asked.

'It's a machine for binding copper wire with cotton.'

'It's an improvement then? Such machines already exist.'

'No, it is probably not an improvement. It is probably worse than any other machine, but you see, I made it all myself from first principles.'

They had come to the end of the meal and Winter had even drained the last of his coffee. Then it was that he realized that this is what he had feared. He had drunk an extra cup of coffee merely to postpone having to get to his feet. In the sudden silence he thought that Mrs. Ford was smiling at him. She was. She was indeed, surprisingly, laughing out loud and wiping the corner of her loose mouth with her handkerchief. She was in a kind of girlish excitement.

'So serious and—and—there's egg on your face!' she gasped. 'There! That's off. Oh, you mustn't mind me. I don't need anything to make me a bit . . . drunk. It's my sense of humour.'

'Your sense of humour?' said Winter wonderingly, looking at her.

She went off into another hoot of laughter. 'Yes, my sense of humour! Oh, dear me! Oh dear!'

Ford was gathering the crockery together. He too was quietly shaking with laughter. 'You mustn't mind my wife. She's very jolly.'

The woman looked at him with tears of laughter in her eyes. It was enough. She made off immediately and Winter knew that the moment had come. Flies buzzed at his face. He brushed them away and though he had moved suddenly he felt quite steady, no jelly-like quivering of the control nerves. He would rise to his feet now, pushing the chair back as he did so, and then Ford would lead the way out on to the balcony from where he said the Sultan's palace could be seen. He would also see the bungalow on the other spur of the hill which he himself was to occupy.

'You will really be my nearest neighbour. That is delightful.' Ford was already out on the balcony. He would rise, Winter insisted, and he would walk. He would even talk. He would look about him. The flies were at his face again and this time he made no movement to brush them away. He gripped the chair. Perspiration broke out on his brow. He was on his feet and the wooden planks were passing under him.

'See, the Sultan's palace,' said Ford, standing aside so that he could pass.

'That white building? Looks—cool.'

'And now this way. Down here. Steady now. That step is not too safe. The wood just rots into powder.'

'I'm perfectly all right.' But who had suggested that he wasn't? He clumsily caught himself up. He was dazzled by the brilliant light and closed his eyes, concentrating all his awareness on to the hard pebble under the toe of his right shoe. With one hand he held on tightly to the veranda rail.

Strange, he thought, that the cicadas should be lively so late in the morning. Did they not know that the sun was up? Their shrilling vibrated at the back of his eyes. The earth was tilting slightly.

Ford's voice was as irritating and as irrelevant as the conversation of one's neighbour at the theatre. It came from some incredible and remote place, so incredible and remote that whatever it said would be without significance. 'Yes, yes!' Winter said loudly in order to soothe it. The voice impinged ruthlessly.

'Of course, I don't suppose this is in your line at all. I don't suppose you're really interested. It is kind of you to show any interest, I can assure you. What I would like to explain is the principle and what I think it stands for.'

Winter opened his eyes and saw in the distance the unreal mass of the Sultan's white palace. He looked down in the direction from which the voice was coming. Ford was looking out from the door of the cellar, a smile that inquired on his face as though he were on the point of releasing some fabulous animal into the golden air, a unicorn with a silver horn perhaps. There was sufficient anxiety in the smile to show that he did not wish any of the significance of the sight to be lost on Winter.

'Come on. It's awfully good of you really.'

Winter realized that he was not going to be sick after all and had an access of joy at the thought that he was not going to collapse or faint. He could smell the air and feel the earth again. He went down the steps into the cellar and Ford switched on the electric light although it was in no way necessary.

'There you see! Now, what do you think of it?'

As it lay there idle on the top of a large trestle table the

machine was merely wheels with loaded cotton bobbins round
the circumferences, a greased axle that gleamed like glass,
and steel feeders that led the cotton strand to a copper wire
that passed from the final roller on to a winding drum. But
when Ford threw over a switch the small room palpitated and
the wheels with their bobbins were whirling arms, continuously and precisely covering the copper wire that passed between them with the sleeve of white cotton. By the touch of
the switch Ford had given it a kind of conscious life like one
of those Eastern goddesses, many-armed and exuding an atmosphere of intense absorption.

'Here,' said Ford, 'is the copper wire.' He touched a large
drum on which the folds of naked wire were gleaming. The
drum was slowly turning as the wire was drawn into the heart
of the machine.

'And here is the cotton.'

Winter was suddenly aware that in addition to himself and
Ford there was a third person in the room. An Arab youth in
white cotton drawers was sitting quietly in the corner sifting
his hand through a quantity of raw cotton. But Ford was calling attention to dozens of neatly loaded spools standing in a
tray on a corner of the trestle table. 'And here.' He stopped the
machine. 'Feel that covering. There are three layers of best
sea-island cotton on there. It's as neat as any European job.
Touch it. It's perfect, isn't it?'

Then he started the machine again and the bobbins disappeared into a liquid whirl.

'You're going to cover a lot of this wire here?'

Ford laughed excitedly and sat on the corner of the table,
swinging his leg. 'No, you see it is very impracticable. But
please sit down. I beg you to sit down. Because I want to explain the idea to you. You know the story of the man who shut

himself away from society and devoted himself to the perfection of a particular mechanical invention. At the end of thirty years he emerged with his life's work—it was a bicycle! And of course he found that the world had passed him by and that bicycles had been in use for the last dozen years or so. That's a funny story, I know.' He laughed quite delightedly. 'And really I am the same as that man. But there is this important difference.' And here he became unusually grave. 'I know that the world has passed me by. There are better machines than this doing the same job. I know that, economically and all the rest of it, my machine is useless. But you see, it is my own machine, every bolt, wheel, spool, pulley, the conception and modifications. There is nothing I looked up in a book. And do you know how long I've been working on this idea? Two whole years! Now it goes perfectly. Not a flaw. See? The cotton goes on like a silk glove. On top of that it needs a rubber sleeve. But that's not my job. That could be anyone's job. Your job, if you like!'

Winter was quite steady now. He had got up from his chair, walked across the balcony, down the steps, through the intense white sunlight, down here into the cool cellar. Ford had stopped the machine and was looking at him eagerly in a silence that seemed to tick. The Arab boy stopped sifting the cotton and looked at Winter placidly.

'And your first idea for this machine?' Winter was not in any way surprised by Ford's eccentricity. He was indeed strangely excited by it now that his head was clearing.

'You are interested? Yes, I thought you would be.' He was so pleased that he got to his feet and stood looking down on Winter with a blaze of triumph on his face. 'It's a process of deduction. I did it this way. By examining the finished article, the wire already bound in Europe, I could ask myself the question, "But how was this done?" I found that there were two layers, see? And each of those two layers consisted of three strands, always crossing one another, not going the same way at all. Now, the question was, "How was this done?" You could do it yourself, with your hands, I mean, by very carefully winding. Round and round your hands would go, and what I had to devise was some mechanical substitute for those arms. It took two years. The feeling, the feeling, when you first realize that those arms can be wheels! And then, beyond that, the light that comes when you know that the "hands" are really bobbins.'

Yes, Winter could imagine all this. Ford and he were understanding each other perfectly now, smiling into one another's face.

'Your brain,' said Ford, 'just expands.' He opened his fingers spasmodically to show what he meant. 'Lines, wheels, forces! Do you know what, beyond its utility—the thing is beautiful.'

Turning round, he suddenly caught sight of the Arab boy sitting idly by his heap of cotton. Ford's hands jerked out and forward in query and censure. He shouted at the boy in Arabic. 'Why do you think that you are paid? I do not keep you for your looks, no!'

Very gently, as though awakened from a light sleep, the boy began to feed the strands of raw cotton on to a wooden frame that he kept revolving with an occasional push of his right hand. In the face of such calm, Ford's uprush of irritation was ludicrous.

Winter had been sitting on the bottom step and now because he wished to say something which would please Ford, he got to his feet and ran his little finger over the green glass feeds through which the cotton thread passed before becoming part of the enveloping fuse.

'Even this little item must have cost I don't know how much thought.'

'You see,' said Ford, delighted once more and immediately forgetting the boy. He spoke as though he had just clinched an argument by an incontrovertible fact. 'Even these glass feeds. I knew that you would understand. But no, as a matter of fact these two came to me in a flash. Almost in the same moment as the bobbins. What delights me, my dear fellow, is that I feel I am talking to a man who understands. Look! We must make you feel at home. We must get your things carried across to your bungalow and the whole place put neat and tidy. If there is anything—anything at all, you must let me know.' It was almost as though all this had been dependent on the approval of his machine. 'I am so happy to see you, really. I feel, well—lonely. Of course there are quite a few people. You will know them all by name already, but you don't know them like I do.' He shook his head. There was a wry expression on his face. There was a bitter taste in his mouth. 'They are not really people you can get friendly with. Frankly, I don't like them much. I'm talking about the Europeans all the time, of course. But you and me, I think . . . Of course, there is one point about this machine. The strands must not fall on the wire in a straight line. They must fall just one behind the other, by the thickness of the thread. That I've not really solved. I shall though.'

He broke off suddenly. 'There's somebody outside. There's somebody coming.' He looked round quickly and Winter had the momentary impression that he was looking for possible means of escape.

'Ford! Are you there, Ford?' said a voice peremptorily. It was a cultured voice spoken from the back of the throat. Winter rose to his feet and moved to one side to allow the newcomer to enter. 'Your wife told me that you were here.' An elderly man in a grey flannel suit and a shirt open at the collar came down the steps, talking as he came. 'Ah! There you are.'

'Dr. Plunkett,' said Ford.

'Eh! What's that?'

Because Winter was standing on one side his first sight of the doctor was in profile. It was a face of great dignity and strength. It was a hawk face, a full rounded nose and a rat-clamped mouth, but when he turned and Winter saw him full faced it was obvious that the hawk was old and almost certainly degenerate. The firm lines were gone. The nose was seen to be fleshy and there were those lines round the mouth and capacious pouches under the eyes.

'Who are you?' he asked bluntly.

'I've just come. My name is Winter.'

'For the moment,' said the doctor after Ford had made the introduction, 'of course I can't see you. My eyes are not adjusted. Often heard about you and, on the whole, admired you. You are a man of independence. You saved that man's life, of course. Though I'm not sure that you weren't lying. Were you lying?'

'No,' said Winter.

'Ah!' The old man peered at him. 'That's better. I can see you now. Typhoid?'

'Yes.'

'But what I really came to do was to tell you that that old fool's house is on fire.'

'Good heavens! Not—not . . .' Ford had read some terrible significance into this. Winter knew immediately it was more than a simple fire.

'Yes, it's Rider's house. If you come up on the bank you can see the smoke. Just the sort of thing . . .'

Ford scrambled out of the cellar with surprising rapidity. The old man stood back politely for Winter to follow. Within a couple of minutes they were all three standing on top of the sand bank that rose to the height of the top of the bungalow's windows. Winter had no sense of dizziness or fatigue now. At a point roughly half-way between where they were standing and the Sultan's palace a column of black smoke was going up from the roof of a small bungalow. The fire was very localized and there seemed every opportunity of saving a great deal of the building, but even from that distance it could be seen that the small crowd which had gathered to watch the spectacle were making no attempt to put the fire out. There was a deserted air about the bungalow. The windows were shuttered. The black smoke was a desecration, like the soiling of a corpse.

'That's oil smoke,' said Ford. He seemed strangely agitated and after taking a glance turned and ran back to his own bungalow.

'Let him go,' said the doctor to Winter. 'Look!'

More men were beginning to appear. A small group in white gowns came out of the main gate of the palace and stood wavering. Although as yet there were no flames, only this thick black smoke, the heat must have been growing more intense for the small crowd of spectators was slowly withdrawing.

'Why don't they do something? Is there no water? Who is the owner?'

'There is no water. And there is no owner.' Winter wondered where the doctor had appeared from out of the middle of the morning in this way, merely it seemed to inform Ford of the fire. In what way did it concern Ford?

'He will go there,' said the doctor with a note of contempt in his voice, 'and when he gets there he will not know what to do. He will just stand there like the others. You see, there he goes.'

Ford had gone into the bungalow merely to collect his topee and even as the doctor spoke he reappeared and went trotting away over the sand, kicking up tiny clouds of dust and dogged by an irritated shadow. He turned and waved to the watchers on the bank and then fell into a more steady walk. Apparently he had not expected that they would wish to accompany him.

'I wanted him to know about this,' said the doctor.

The roof of the bungalow suddenly and silently fell in and they heard the roar some moments afterwards, like the rapid opening and closing of a furnace door. A sheet of flame was suspended over the black shell like an orange-coloured flower. A murmur arose from the crowd. Ford had not gone a hundred yards on his journey before the walls blazed up like celluloid and then the crowd began cheering, yes, it was distinctly cheering, and Winter could even see some men indulging in an exaggerated dance.

'I thought he would want to see this,' muttered the doctor. 'I suppose he has been telling you about his machine, saying that he invented it all himself. It's lies, lies, lies! He copied it all from a blueprint. God blast it, man, does he think we're fools? He couldn't invent a—a mousetrap. Pah! His own clerk told me that he has seen him poring over those blueprints. He gets them from London. He's the laughing stock of the place. What does he think we are, I ask you?'

At that moment Mrs. Ford came out of the bungalow and climbed the bank towards them. She was still wearing her blue wrap but now it was gathered to her form by a green silk girdle round the waist. The doctor's indignation had been so loudly expressed that she could not but have heard it but she gave no indication by her languorous progress up to the position they were occupying. She stood between them and looked out towards the burning bungalow, but the glory was now almost over. The woodwork was highly inflammable in this dry climate and where had once been the shuttered bungalow, and then the column of smoke, and then the spirit-like blaze was now a heap of black ruins, barely breast high, that passed grey smoke up into the brilliant morning air and would occasionally produce a pale flame. Ford himself was still more than a hundred yards from the site and now that he saw it was all over he came to a halt and then began walking uneasily about, rather like an ant that has been picked up out of its track and deposited some yards away. His agitation was expressive of pain and distress.

'How dare you talk of my husband like that?' the woman shot out. She did not look at the doctor.

'You're not angry,' said the doctor contemptuously, 'so it's no good trying to kid me. You don't feel anything honestly. You've got to think it all out first. See this, Winter,' he went on, turning to him, 'this woman is the most cold-blooded creature God ever created. She loves no-one, not even herself. She is lazy and self-indulgent. She is a Lady Macbeth. Though Lady Macbeth loved her husband. It's true, every word of what I said. Ford is an ignoramus. He is incapable of . . . of . . .'

'Hate, hate? Why it's you who hate . . . mean-spirited and jealous.' All these words came from the surface of her mind. The doctor had not troubled nor could not trouble the inner woman. Winter was reminded of the Arab way of flying into a passion and committing violence with a look of other-worldliness in the eyes, the inner man untroubled.

'My husband is a noble man,' she went on, 'and you fear him because of that. He would not have gone over there if he were not a good man. And how did it get alight, that's what I'd like to know.'

'A light, a bit of glass, anything acting as a lens.' The doctor had calmed down now and his manner was icy. The three of them stood side by side looking out over the desert. The woman tried to catch her husband's attention by waving her hand.

'Strange that it should happen now of all times. And strange that it should burn down so quickly and with that pall of black smoke.' She pointed. The black smoke had risen and formed a black pall like a rook's wing against the blue sky. 'You have no right to talk of my husband like that, doctor, and I notice you never say anything of the sort in his presence. In any case, what does it matter, whether the machine is his or not? What business it is of yours I can't imagine.'

'Business!' the doctor spluttered. 'Look here, my good woman, when a man sees anything bogus it is his duty to expose it. The machine is bogus. Your husband is bogus.'

'Why is it his duty?' She might have been a priest putting the catechism questions, all a little absently and mechanically.

'Winter, here, naturally believed all that . . .'

'I still do,' said Winter shortly.

'What!' The doctor was so incredulous that he swung round and confronted Winter, blocking out his line of vision. 'You mean to say that after what I told you, you still think—that's as good as calling me a liar!' He gobbled his mouth.

Mrs. Ford tinkled with laughter. One had the impression

that she had demonstrated something with considerable deft-
ness.

As Winter made no further remark but looked calmly into
his face as though it were an object of scientific interest, the
doctor began to shout. There was a look of extraordinary intensity on his face, almost of desperation, for his eyes were
open very wide, the whites showing clearly around the pupils. 'You know nothing about Ford. You have only seen his
name on official reports and now for a few hours here. Why,
I thought you were a man of intelligence. I know all about
you, when you came, how you came up here, everything.'

'I am not interested. If it is a question of believing you or
Ford, I will believe Ford.'

'But what does it matter? That's the point,' broke in Mrs.
Ford, now quite decided upon her laughter. Her face was very
merry. 'I don't care. I don't know whether he made the machine himself or not. The machine is there, it keeps him quiet
and undoubtedly he thinks that he made it himself. He's not
going to put it on the market. He's got no illusions like that
about it.' She looked from one to the other of the two angry
men.

'That's just the sort of thing a woman would say. And as
for you, Winter, I'm just disappointed in you, bitterly disappointed! There is nothing more to say.'

'Look,' said Winter, 'I'm sorry. I lost my temper. I think
Mrs. Ford's attitude is the wisest. Let's forget about it. I don't
want to start off by making enemies here.'

Looking back towards his bungalow, Ford could see them
standing close together on top of the dune. He felt himself to
be in an arena where much was expected of him, but the
enemy had been destroyed and there was nothing left but the
charred ruins. He had no wish to go closer for that would

have meant mixing with the crowd who were in a good mood
because of the diversions that they had just enjoyed. There
was nothing to be done. He felt dispirited like a man who
has come to some point in his life, the birth of a grandchild
perhaps, when he feels the finger of time and change upon
him. Something inside him was grieving terribly. Looking up,
he was suddenly aware that the bystanders had begun to
search amongst the ruins for any articles of value that there
might lie concealed.

'Hi!' he at once shouted and started off towards them, waving his arm in the air. 'Leave off there!' He would have to get
a posse of soldiers from the palace, he thought, in order to
guard the ruins. These filthy Arabs! He felt that they were
violating a personal privacy as they kicked amongst the
charred remains. He would stop them!

And then he stopped. This is my anger and my own feelings, he thought. They would not have been his. I am being
stupid once more. If Rider had been alive to see he would
have been cheered to see the way the people were salvaging
a few of his poor belongings. That is the way that he would
have wished it. The thought came to Ford like a revelation
and he realized that any further act on his part would be pure
selfishness. But it was hard! He had no right to be grieved
but when a man in a yellow turban lifted a blue water jug in
the air and triumphantly waved it backwards and forwards
Ford had to turn away quickly and make a determined path
back towards the bungalow or he would, he thought, have indulged himself in some foolish and sentimental gesture.

He came up to the group just as the doctor and Winter
were shaking hands. 'Yes, yes, of course. Mind you, there is
a great deal we shall have to discuss. But I see that funda-
mentally you are a civilized man and because of that I can for-

give you much. You must allow me to take charge of you medically. You are still in a sick state, I can see that. We must make some tests.' He was all benignity and enthusiasm. 'What, Ford! We saw you! We were watching you and thinking what you were thinking.' He could even laugh and smile into Ford's face. 'What, come cheer up, man. But I knew you would want to see it.'

'You are a good, good man, doctor. Thank you, thank you. But you see what is happening now. Like vultures over a corpse. There should be some soldiers, I thought, and then that that is how Rider would have wished it himself.'

'Who is Rider?' asked Winter.

'Who *was* Rider?' the doctor gently corrected. His eyes had amusement in them. He had interpreted Winter's speech of a few minutes ago as a handsome apology and was prepared to be generous himself.

'Well, in many ways, Rider was a good man,' said Ford dreamily and looking out over the sand towards the group of men working like maggots on the black stain of debris. 'I suppose,' he added a little helplessly.

'Perhaps, he meant well. Winter, I'll tell you all about Rider. He is not an easy person to understand but I can put you in possession of the facts, so to speak.' As the doctor spoke they were moving down the side of the dune towards the bungalow. 'One could say that he had intentions.'

'I think I ought to tell you that the doctor has been insulting you again,' said Mrs. Ford to her husband.

'Oh, yes; well, he means nothing. One has to live and let live. The doctor is a good man.' He spoke as though the doctor was not there and the subject of his remarks smiled a little consciously as he continued his conversation with .Winter.

CHAPTER III: *The Palace*

THE SULTAN'S PALACE STOOD IN ITS
palm gardens like some enormous iced cake, well buttressed at
the four corners. The whitewash shone like fondant. Near the
ground the palace was austere and sombre in honest mud brick
but progressively it grew in frivolity from the level of the second floor where the whitewashing of the exterior began. Even
at this height the windows were simple rectangles with bevelled
lips; but from this chasteness of line to the topmost rampart of
the palace, where odd pyramidical and semi-human shapes
were wittily perched, there was a gradual progression of ir-
reverence. The third-floor windows, for example, were re-
cessed under a characteristic stalactite decoration: the fourth-
floor windows, in addition to this refinement, wore a ram's
horn at each corner: the fifth-floor windows, the harem windows, had a painted eyebrow raised in perpetual astonishment over each one of them. A yellow flag hung from the flag-
staff. From this point, the flat roof of the palace, there was not
a movement in the harbour below that could pass unobserved.

The third day after Winter had been installed in his bungalow across the valley from Ford's he was received by the Sultan. During those three days, Rachid, the youth in his early

twenties who was to be Winter's servant, had unpacked the
bags and spread their contents rather untidily about the four
rooms of the bungalow. Winter had sat and watched him with
a curious apathy. Somehow it did not seem to matter that his
books should be stacked in one corner underneath the window and one suitcase left with the lid flung back on the table
in his bedroom. He felt that there was a great deal of time in
front of him and these matters could be arranged later. He had
inspected the plant in the company of Ford and Arvanitaki,
an enormous Greek who was a very quiet-spoken man in
whom Ford placed much reliance. Everything was in perfect
order. Two years previously the Company had insisted that
the native employees should live in a compound close to the
well mainly as a sanitary precaution. Men living in Rasuka and
coming up the valley each morning were liable to bring con-
tagions with them. But up here in the compound the Company
had a stricter control over them, vaccinated them, inoculated
them and saw to it that the huts of concrete were always sweet
and clean. There were few flies in this area. Here Winter met
the Rais, the head man of the native labourers, Ahmad Ghaith,
a severe man with a cast in one eye. To Winter he was most
undemonstrative and even eager to get away.

'A good man!' said Ford. 'A strong man. Great understanding.'

This was not the way that he had struck Winter. There had
been a certain amount of uneasiness and unwillingness to meet
one's gaze. Winter realized that it was very hard to get into
Ford's bad books. All men were a little larger than life size in
the manager's eyes, and any bad qualities that they had which
were too glaring to be overlooked were excused as irrelevan-
cies. 'They don't mean it.' He did not take the doctor seriously,
for example, though Winter was by no means sure that that

very changeable gentleman was all that he appeared to be.
Winter thought that the doctor had a great *will* to be warm-
hearted.

'This is Mr. Cator,' said Ford when they reached the administrative block. Winter shook hands with a thin, nervous
person, a little shorter than himself, with restless eyes. 'Mr.
Cator is the head of the clerical side here. He has his wife.
You've not met his wife yet? But of course not! How nice it is
to be out on a morning like this, Cator. Good to be alive. What
happy days these are, to be sure.' Ford really was happy.
He had been dancing about all the morning and seemed to have
quite got over his upset on the day of the fire.

'Happy to meet you,' said Cator. He was standing up but
he was not standing in a natural position. His body was bent
just a little to the right at the hips and there was the sort of
tension about him that would arise if he were holding his
breath. It was almost as though he feared that any relaxation,
any assumption of a normal position, any deep breath would
be offensive in the eyes of his visitors. Yet there was no weakness in this tension. Winter felt that the man would be capable of flaring up into the most uncontrollable of tempers and
then committing some act of unheard-of violence. But in everything he said on this occasion there had been nothing that was
not matter of fact. He was glad to see Mr. Winter and hoped
that the change of air would do him good. He hoped that
within the next few months Mr. Winter would completely re-
cover his health, and what is more, if he could be permitted to
say so, he had been looking forward to meeting Mr. Winter
for some time. He had heard a great deal about Mr. Winter.
They, that is Cator and his wife, would be happy to receive
Mr. Winter.

It was in Cator's company that Winter went to the palace on the third day after settling in at his bungalow.

'The natives are, for the most part, very dishonest,' said Cator suddenly. They were crossing the soft sand of the wadi bottom and the whole valley, the cliffs, the broad ocean before them all lay in a silence that was all the more marked because of the throbbing of a single Diesel engine. Everything was pale in the sun, the occasional polished pebbles with their small shadows, the thin mantle of sand over the rock and even the ragged palm trees that grouped round the palace. Cator's voice was human and thin in this impersonal landscape.

'All men are liars,' said Winter. He was a little surprised at the turn of the conversation.

'A lie,' said Cator quaintly, 'is a false statement meant to deceive.'

'You mean it isn't only telling lies?' Winter was aware of a great antipathy towards the man.

'They don't make false statements. They are false statements.'

'You can excuse a lot of a man when he is really poor.' He was annoyed with himself for having delivered this sententiousness but Cator was the sort of man who made one talk that way. Winter decided that he wouldn't say another word.

'How I despise them. They have no honour even among themselves. And what is more they are not punctual. They've really no idea of time. What they want is to be drilled and controlled like soldiers. That's the only sort of treatment they understand.'

'I disagree entirely,' said Winter shortly, in spite of his resolve.

The entrance to the palace was through a mud gateway which rose suddenly out of the sand some thirty yards from

the front door. The entrance was rather watch tower than
gate for there appeared to be a soldier stationed on top of the
arch but the construction was really too small for any real
service as a vantage point. A soldier who was wearing a khaki
jacket with no buttons was leaning against the mud wall as
they passed through but although he followed them carefully
with his eyes he made no move to stop them. His rifle, which
Winter saw to be of British make and a recent pattern, lay
on the sand in front of him in a dirty condition. The soldier
was smoking.

'You see,' said Cator in disgust. 'No idea.'

Rixon, way back in the delta, had spoken of the Sultan before Winter had left for Rasuka. 'Of course, you understand
there is no political control over Rasuka. The maintenance of
law and order is entirely the Sultan's affair and when you meet
him you will be meeting the head of the state. As far as he is
concerned he does keep order. As far as we are concerned
. . . well, in spite of the climate it'll probably not be healthy
out of doors alone after dark. Fifty years ago Rasuka was an
impoverished place. Its great glories had been in the sixteenth
century and before when it lay at one end of a spice route and
the Portuguese boats would put into the harbour. I'm interested
in this part of the world, you know. After that there was a
decline and the harbour fell into disrepair. Lot of emigration.
The Sultan has a lot of Indian blood in him, as you will see.'

In Rasuka itself the Sultan's word was more or less law between sunrise and sunset but this control did not extend very
far inland. Out of the sight of the sea the rulers were the tribesmen who, because they lived in a state of permanent destitu-
tion, were bandits when the opportunity offered. A bandit was
a well-respected person in this part of the world, for after all,
the chiefs, and the Sultan himself, were only the sons and

grandsons, the descendants of the most successful bandits in the past.

As Winter and Cator approached the doorway of the palace a white-robed porter jumped to his feet, gave them one glance, and disappeared without a word into the interior. The eyebrows above the fifth-story windows seemed arched in greater surprise than ever, there had been a feeling of urgency conveyed by the porter's twinkling legs and then there was complete silence. Two camels were kneeling amongst the knobbly trunks of the garden palms with their noses towards the crumbling wall of the palace well. The palace seemed oblivious of them and Winter was beginning to wonder whether it would have been better, after all, to have formally requested an audience of the Sultan instead of coming along like this without any warning, in the manner suggested and even recommended as best by Ford. The two visitors stepped across the threshold and entered the reception hall where at least a dozen small chairs, all covered with white cloth, looked in at a small blue carpet in the middle of the stone floor. The walls were quite bare save for a framed inscription in Arabic over the small doorway opposite and the plaster was here and there peeling off and showing the skeleton of the building.

'Fad'l,' said the white-robed porter, suddenly appearing at this door.

It was all right then. Winter felt surprise but apparently their visit was accepted as being in perfect order. The porter did not presume to meet their eyes as the visitors passed into the dark interior but bent his head forward so that he had to look at the floor.

'Must and decay,' said Winter quietly. 'They don't seem to live in their houses. They camp out in them.' On the right was a large room into which they could see because the door was off its hinges and lying awkwardly across the threshold. There was a mass of blue cloth untidily piled on a chair in the centre of the floor and around it cardboard boxes, small pieces of wood, two knitting needles stuck into a ball of yellow wool and a small, portable sewing-machine.

'Fad'l,' said the porter once more and without further ceremony Winter and Cator walked into the Sultan's study. 'Here we are,' said Cator just before they entered, so Winter was prepared for the dark-faced, grey-headed man in navy-blue lounge suit and orange tie who was sitting behind a glass-topped table rather as if he were only doing this for the sake of effect and the article of furniture embarrassed him. On his head was a white, close-fitting turban in the Indian manner.

'Good morning, gentlemen,' he said, smiling and not moving an inch. 'I beg you.' They understood that they were to be seated.

'I feel I owe an apology for coming so casually,' Winter began.

'I beg you,' repeated the Sultan once more, still smiling.

'I understood that Your Excellency is a man who dispenses with ceremony. I have just arrived in Rasuka and have come to pay . . .'

'Cigarettes—on the table at your side. I had been attending you, so you see I know something of you.' Winter guessed that the Sultan spoke better French than English.

'My name is Winter.'

'I have already had the privilege of meeting Your Excellency,' said Cator from the edge of his chair. The Sultan ignored him completely. He had large fish-like eyes set in his expansive face and a moustache of fungoid whiteness on his lip. He spread his hands on the glass-topped table and because of his smile and his immobility at once put the ramshackle palace beyond all criti-

cism. The room in which they were sitting may indeed have
conveyed the impression that it was part of an unfinished house
and that the decorators would at any moment come in and remove the Sultan's glass-topped table, the few chairs and his
ornamental spittoon which comprised practically the entire
furnishings into another chamber that they had long been pre-
paring. But the Sultan's complacency was an imperative direction that all was befitting the private apartment of an inde-
pendent sovereign, and after the first glance round Winter
found himself looking at nothing else but the Sultan's eyes.

'I don't smoke, thank you, Your Excellency.'

'There was no trouble of being admitted?'

'We walked straight in.'

'I always wish to be—I wish it that men can get to me easily.'

'Accessible?'

'Ah! That is the word.' He clapped his hands. For the
moment there was a shade of annoyance on his face and then
it immediately cleared. 'You are ill, Mr. Winter? I am so sorry
but then on the other side I am so very glad. Sad for you and
happy for me. If you had not been ill I should not have the
pleasure of . . .'

Coffee was brought in, again by the porter who seemed to be
the only servant inside the palace.

'How much money do you earn, Mr. Winter?' The Sultan
sucked his coffee noisily and even glanced at Cator who had
subsided into a silence that seemed to say that he had been
through all this before.

Winter told him. He was not at all surprised by the question
for the Sultan had said it as easily and naturally as an Englishman will ask the time. It is an oriental conversational gambit.

'Your Excellency must be a wealthy man.'

'Thank you! I sometimes go to Switzerland in the summer. A

beautiful country, Switzerland. And then I once went to London. I stayed in the Ritz Hotel. A very clean hotel. The table-cloths always clean and proper.'

'Yes, the Ritz Hotel is a clean hotel.'

'It is very pleasant to meet you, Mr. Winter. I wonder, very often wonder, what white men here do for—for . . . women.' This remark was addressed more to Cator as being an old resident than to Winter. 'That is those who are without women —wives.'

'I am married, Your Excellency.'

'Are you married, Mr. Winter?'

'No. My wife died two months ago in childbirth.'

'The child?'

'Was still-born.'

'Yes?' This was still a question. The Sultan had not understood.

'The child was dead too.'

'Would it have been a boy or a girl?'

'I don't know, Your Excellency.'

The Sultan had come to the end of his coffee and he put the small cup down regretfully. 'I am sorry to hear it,' he said, though whether this was a reference to the death of Winter's wife, the still-born child or even an oblique expression of sorrow that there was no more coffee was not clear. 'Fortunately I have four sons, but two of my wives have died. Now if your child had been a boy—it is not prejudice that makes us prefer sons, Mr. Winter. A son is courage and defiance. A daughter is weakness and regret. There are some of us who need courage when we get older and it is good to have a young man to go red with anger for you.'

'It was my wife, Your Excellency. That was the thing.' Still the Sultan looked at him with those cold eyes and Winter felt

fear creeping over him at the realization that he was using
words that were poor things by the side of his emotions. He
feared himself and would have given much to get to his feet
and walk abruptly out of the room. To his amazement he even
thought that he might burst into tears. The poor, threadbare
words still echoed inside his head and mocked at him with their
pitiableness. He and the Sultan were not talking about the same
subject. Behind the fish-like eyes there were thoughts of young
men with like fish-like eyes and the wombs that produced them.
And inside Winter's head there was just a poor word knocking, knocking, knocking: wife, wife, wife.

'What the white men do without wives I do not know—I do
not know what they do. They live up there, alone. Dr. Plunkett,
for example. There is Mr. Flynn. They are both without
women. Of course, there is Miss Leader. That is a problem
that I often think of. It must be that white people are different.'

Although Winter and the Sultan were looking directly into
one another's eyes they gained no greater understanding of one
another. The Sultan saw the long, fixed face of an Englishman
in whose eyes the odd light might be embarrassment, pleasure
or pain. Winter saw the Sultan complete and solid like an
apple. If the Sultan were a selfish man or a cruel man Winter
had the feeling that the Sultan would be aware of these qualities. Compared with himself—and Winter felt himself to be a
tangle of unresolved emotions—the Sultan was a completely
realized individual. 'I am a man, no better, no worse, but in
any case you cannot criticize me,' is what he seemed to be saying. For this reason Winter forgot that the palace was dirty,
forgot the air of makeshift, the musty odour, the curious ease
with which he and Cator had penetrated to the private apartment of the constitutional monarch of Rasuka. And then there
came a point where he could even forget the Sultan, and those

large, fish-like eyes were pale pools in which he was bathing himself, losing himself, sinking slowly to the bottom. My wife would have laughed, he thought. She would have giggled suddenly, like a kettle on the hob that will suddenly bubble water from its spout. The desperate fit was on him again. At any moment his wife would walk through the entrance hall, past those watching chairs, and into this very room. He could almost smell her fragrance: no bought fragrance but the perfume of her sweet-smelling body. He was shocked at the intensity of his emotions. One moment he had felt tears behind his eyes and now it was almost as though he could laugh at the absurdity of his wife's being dead.

The Sultan and Winter were still watching one another.

'You are amused?' the Sultan said with a faint smile on his own lips. And Winter could not find it in himself to answer.

In a strange moment he had broken through into an inexplicable world of sphinx-like beings that could not explain themselves. One moment he thought that he had realized the Sultan but now he was only a shell of a man sitting behind a desk, representative of God knew what! His smile might represent complete knowledge. He might even have Joyce concealed about the building and the ease with which Winter and Cator had come into the palace explained by the fact that it had all been arranged. There might be a joyful reunion at any moment. The glass-topped table, the view of the palms through the window were not of the world he had known before entering the palace. In fact nothing was knowable any more. A terrible solipsism!

But actually the Sultan was still talking about sex. He went on to explain that it was a problem that troubled him much for it was not natural for a man, even a white man, to be without a woman. But what could one do? A white man would not marry a Rasuka woman.

Cator seemed to have withdrawn into himself. All the lines of his body were relaxed. There had been a point up to which he had followed the conversation but there had been a noticeable reaction when the Sultan began talking of women. Well, I've brought you, he seemed to be saying, to Winter, and if you want to talk about things like this please do not expect me to take part in your conversation. He became non-human.

'We are all very happy in Rasuka,' said the Sultan suddenly. 'We are all—how do you say it?—I do not know all the words. We are all united. You see, there is Rasuka and there are the people of the well. Even my own people when they go up and work at the well, when they leave the town and live in the compound, for example—well, then they are different. They become people apart. You may say—"Ah! he thinks that because he no longer controls them." No, Mr. Winter. I am not like that. We are all—we are a simple society and everyone obeys the rules. What is terrible is a rebel!'

Cator seemed to take a sudden interest once more. He even sat up a little when the Sultan used the word 'rebel' but he said not a word. Although Winter did not look at him he was conscious of all this.

The Sultan continued, speaking more loudly. 'There is no crime here. A thief loses his right hand immediately. You could leave your money on the sand and no one would even pick it up to bring it to you for fear of being taken for a thief. There are no thieves. You are safer in Rasuka than in—London. Day or night.' The Sultan was boasting, of course. 'But once you leave this coast area, then I can do nothing for you. Up there you will be destroyed. Because of that I forbid you to leave the coast area, Mr. Winter.'

'Why, do you think I might want to?'

'I think it very probable. You look an uneasy man. If your

guilt should drive you into the desert—you must not go! You don't answer.'

'I can't promise that.' It was not that he had any desire to travel into the interior. It was just that he felt it impossible to engage himself in any way when he felt so much possible and impossible. Anything could happen.

The Sultan continued to smile but by the way he agitatedly fingered his coffee cup Winter knew that he was angry.

'Mr. Winter, I forbid you. I am Sultan, you understand. If too many Englishmen wander up into the hills and get their throats cut there will be inquiries. Think of my position if you think not of yours. We do not want English soldiers in Rasuka.'

There was a note of pleading in his voice, even, but Winter could not find the words that would have comforted him. There was too much behind those words. The Sultan was using words to hide, not to reveal. Then Winter had an idea.

'Too many Englishmen?'

'Is there some devil in Europeans? We say that they have done some sin and their demon punishes them by driving them to the desolate places of the earth, among the stones of dead cities and old tombs. Mr. Rider, for example.' This last was said almost explosively.

This was the man that Dr. Plunkett had said he would tell Winter about. So far he had not done so. He was the owner of the bungalow which had been burned down.

Cator was now quite alive and even leaning forward in his chair.

'Mr. Rider was most troublesome. He was uncivilized. Mr. Winter, to tell you frankly, he lived as though there were no laws except those he made himself. He would come here and go there. Ask nobody's permission. Never once came to visit me. He was quite an individualist. We must not have such

people in Rasuka. This is a happy community—we all co-
operate.'

Surprisingly Cator decided to speak. 'You never saw him,
Your Excellency? He was a dirty man. He never seemed to
wash. One of the "have-nots." I think he was a miser.'

The Sultan and Cator, between whom there had previously
appeared to be no sympathetic contact, now struck sparks off
each other. Both of them sparkled. They both voiced their indignation, speaking directly to one another so that for the first
time Winter found himself moving out of the centre of things.
What the Sultan and Cator were saying was without importance for their emotion was jointly so strong that it kept them
ballooning heatedly. No single hard fact emerged. Their dis-
like of the unknown Rider was something so deep and instinc-
tive that any concrete instance they might give of his odiousness
would have been feeble by contrast. They maintained their
line of angry ambiguity.

'But of course, he's dead too.' Winter was hardly aware of
what he was saying before he had interrupted them and they
were staring at him with something like annoyance.

'Irrespective of that fact,' Cator said testily, 'and after all he
brought it on himself, he really was an embarrassment around
the place. He didn't even act like a European. One can be
realistic even if he is dead.'

'I see what you mean, Mr. Winter,' murmured the Sultan,
suddenly gentle and even smiling once more. 'You feel that we
are being hard on a dead man. But then perhaps he is not dead.
Who knows?'

But that is not what Winter had meant. The moment that he
realized that Rider was dead, in the same way that Joyce, his
own wife, was dead, the unknown man became more real to
him. And he even came alive. The Sultan and Cator had spent

all their conversation in bitterness and never once had they said anything that could conjure up an idea of the physical appearance of Rider; nothing, that is, save Cator's outburst that he was a dirty man. But as soon as the significance of the fact that the bungalow had been allowed to burn down without anyone's lifting a finger to save it, the fact that he was always spoken of in the past tense, now that these words and signs added up and framed the simple statement that Rider was no longer an animate being capable of walking and talking but bone and clay like his own dead wife, it was almost as though Rider was capable of showing himself at the window. Winter could see him so clearly. He was a tall spare man, of indeterminate age, but somewhere between thirty and forty-five, with a slight stoop as he walked. His clothes hung on him slackly. Although he was close shaven his beard was so black that his chin had always a bluish tinge, and then his large dark eyes were, as often as not, seemingly expressionless. His hands were large, hairy on the back. There was black hair on his chest, over which his shirt was tightly buttoned, even up to the throat. Yes, even this small detail could be clearly seen. And he came to life as soon as Winter realized that he was dead.

'What if he were to say something through my own lips?' Winter thought in horror. 'He might wish to defend himself.'

'Mr. Winter,' said the Sultan, looking straight at him once more and folding his hands together over the table. 'At all costs, if you should insist on going perhaps I shall be able to give you a bodyguard. But there is nothing. Just the empty wadi and the bones of camels. Stone forts.' Both he and Cator had a glow of satisfaction as a result of their conversation.

'Why didn't you give Rider a bodyguard?' No one had told him that Rider had gone into the interior. He just knew this now.

'It was on his own head. He was not a man to be interfered with. We all assume that he is dead. Perhaps that is not so. Perhaps he is still alive.'

'This is the position, you see, Winter,' Cator broke in. 'Six months ago he bought a horse and—believe it or not—in spite of everything we said, and in spite of His Excellency's excellent rule about people not being allowed into the interior, he slipped off one night. No guide, nobody. Well, he's not come back and the obvious thing is that somebody has cut his throat—oh, just for his horse, just for his clothes, just because of force of habit.'

'No one went after him?'

'That would undoubtedly have cost more lives. He was told not to go. Why should other men—ordinary soldiers, it doesn't matter who, have to put themselves into an ambush for his sake! Now that is merely an example of his selfishness. He would realize all this before he went. He is the sort of devil that would even arrange it so. Just to make us feel guilty, you see, by feeling that someone should go and look for him. Oh, I know that he left a message behind saying that no one was to follow him whatever happened. But that doesn't mean anything under the circumstances. You are probably not aware of it now, but the whole business is weighing upon people. It is almost a—a crime that he has laid at our doors.' Cator stopped and looked deferentially at the Sultan. 'I beg your pardon, Your Excellency, but I feel very strongly about it.'

The Sultan raised his hand. It was easy for him now. He could smile at Winter and disassociate himself from all this bitterness by that small gesture which seemed to say, You and I understand one another. We must not take this man too seriously.

This was a betrayal of Cator that annoyed Winter curiously. And what is more Winter was now delicately sensitive on this subject of Rider. He wanted to change the topic or better still leave the palace entirely, because what he particularly wished to avoid was either the Sultan or Cator giving any more details which would be so revealing of Rider that they would change the mental picture that Winter had of him: and especially he did not wish to hear either of them attempting to describe the dead man.

For the first time the Sultan got to his feet and if Winter did but know it this was a great honour. He came ponderously round the glass-topped table and Winter felt it necessary to stand up. He found that they were of a height. Cator sprang suddenly to his feet and if he had had a hat would have been twisting it in his hands.

'I trust that our climate will re-establish you, Mr. Winter, but not too quickly. I hope to have the pleasure of your company for a good time.'

'Your Excellency is very kind.'

'And let us leave it like that. If there is anything that can be done to make you more comfortable, I am your servant. The palace is your home and my servants your servants. It is yours.'

How sure and complete you are, thought Winter. There are no dark corners. You have resolved everything, your capacities for good and evil, the situations that make you laugh, those that give you distress. You are completely realized and as a result completely uninteresting. All the others, Ford, his wife, the doctor, Cator were all patch-work by comparison. These people did not even know themselves. Ford, for example—what a vacuum there was in the heart of him! The man who had been so enthusiastic about the machine and the almost bewildered man who had wandered on the sand—where were their common heart and brain?

The Sultan even came as far as the door with them. Everything now became stiff and ceremonial. There was a great deal of shuffling because Winter did not know whether the Sultan intended to leave the room, in which case he would have to be given precedence. Cator thought that Winter was hesitating out of politeness for him. At last Winter stepped into the corridor, feeling that he had destroyed something by his peremptory action.

Cator trotted along at his side.

'He's taken to you all right. Don't know how some people do it.'

CHAPTER IV : *Time in Crystal*

Rachid, the lithe young servant with a broad nose and crisp hair, was anxious to please Winter, and would go out of his way to bring up flowers from the town and set them in the earthenware jars which stood along the veranda: but there was never any water in these jars and after a few hours' sun the flowers would wilt and die. Rachid was a cheerful person and willing to do all the work that was asked of him, but he was not at ease. Winter would suddenly look up and find the boy regarding him from the kitchen door with a knife in one hand and a half-peeled potato in the other.

Winter would nod his head in question.

'You staying Rasuka a good time, Mista' Winter?'

'Some time. Yes. End of year, next year perhaps. Why?'

Rachid's English was not good for he had only picked it up incidentally from the previous occupants of the bungalow, and since it was the bungalow reserved by the Company for visiting officials and the like, none of them had remained long enough for Rachid to get used to any one man's idiom. Winter knew but little Arabic, so their conversations were usually carried on in a spirit of emotional sympathy, anticipation and imagination on both sides, so that they often succeeded in saying far more than would have been possible with the clumsy medium of the spoken word.

But after the first week this intelligent sympathy between the two of them seemed to be dying down, at least on Rachid's side. He seemed to be withdrawing into himself, giving Winter less and less of his confidence, and replacing the open grin on his face by an expression of puzzled concern. When he was not actually looking at Winter he would forget to assume this thoughtful frown, but the moment it occurred to him he would go and stare at Winter, his eyebrows meeting crookedly above his nose.

'Why, Rachid?' repeated Winter.

'Nothing, sah—but——' and Rachid looked at the books piled on the floor, the suitcases still unopened lying on top of one another, the great trunk with the lid thrown back, the camp-bed which Winter had brought and not even allowed to be assembled. He preferred to sleep on the divan underneath the open window.

'You mean I don't seem to be settling down?'

'It's not too smart, sah, I mean, if you tell me I can fix O.K.'

'Good man doesn't need to be told.'

Rachid understood this mood at once. The frown disappeared from his face. He knew that Winter was joking, though there was no relaxation in the white man's face.

'I can fix all this O.K. This, this, this.' He indicated camp-bed, books, chest and suitcases.

'Not now though. *Ba'din*. Plenty of time.'

When Winter had first come to the bungalow he had found it cleared out in preparation for his arrival, and the previous occupant had left nothing more behind than an engraving of an Italian mountain scene, some books in a box-wood case, Baedeker's 'Egypt' in French, a dictionary of scientific terms, a technical book on oil 'cracking' and an Arabic phrase book. On top of this bookcase there had been a cherry-wood pipe which Rachid had immediately seized upon as soon as he saw it, claiming it as his own property. There was a certain amount of permanent furniture in the bungalow. There was a cretonne-covered arm-chair in which Winter was, at that moment, sitting, and a long divan under the window which gave out on to the balcony. There was fly-netting at the window and over the door so that they could be kept open all the time for coolness, although Winter soon found that it was a better plan to close them in the early afternoon until the sun had got down somewhat in the sky, for the hot air off the sand would come in like the breath from a furnace. The kitchen had a supply of pots and pans. The divan, on which he slept, the arm-chair in which he would sit doing nothing by the hour save watch the shadows shrink and then grow long across the valley, occasionally flicking at a fly that had penetrated the netting, the unopened books in the little case, all this was quite sufficient for him. He wanted to add nothing of his own. There was an impersonality about the bungalow. It and its contents might have belonged to anyone, but the moment Rachid started to sort out his clothes and take Baedeker and the dictionaries out of the bookcase the place would be his. For some reason Winter shrank from manifesting himself in this way. He was resisting all attempts on the part of Rachid to arrange anything in a way that would suggest permanence. Rachid had even picked up some of the books on one occasion, but Winter had stopped him. 'No, no—leave them. *Bukkra.* I want to look at them.'

For a time Rachid had thought that this indifference was due to thinking arrangements like this were beneath his dignity and that he expected Rachid to get on with the job without any orders. The boy had acted on this thought. Winter had stopped

him. '*Lissa sw'oia*,' he had said. So Rachid had come to the
conclusion that he was not stopping there very long.

Winter's habit of sleeping underneath the open window led
to a curious incident. After six o'clock in the evening, when the
Diesel engine at the well would cease pumping, an intense stillness would lay hold of the valley, a negation of sound in which
the creaking of the woodwork now that the sun was going down
and the air was cooler tingled nervously. An enormous purple
shadow from the western cliff would creep across the derrick
and the compound. There would be one last sighing of distant
voices and the lights would prick out. There would be an un-
earthly crepitus amongst the rocks and the sand now that the
blaze of light had gone; in the cool breeze that sprang up from
the interior with a silken whisper there was no more than a
little officiousness as it hollowed out the night sky and its stars
for the echoless silence. Then the breeze fell and it was a
silence to hold one's breath in.

Sometimes Winter would spend an evening with Ford and
his wife, but he usually managed to be back in his own place by
nine o'clock. He found that the change of air was having a
wearying effect upon him, so would go to bed early. Because the
nights were so warm he could lie on the divan with no more
covering than a single sheet over his pyjamas. Often he would
find it impossible to sleep because of the silence, and then he
would lie and look up into the starlight with the clamour of the
evening spent with Ford still in his ears. Rachid had a small
room of his own at the other end of the veranda, and sometimes
Winter would hear him turning over in his sleep and groaning.
The sound was human in the non-human night and Winter
liked it.

After his first afternoon of real work, when he had helped
Cator supervise the monthly paying of the workmen, he had

spent the evening at Ford's bungalow where at ten o'clock he found himself going to sleep in a basket-chair on the veranda. Ford had walked part of the way with him over the sand. There was a three-quarter moon and the night sparkled like a crystal. Winter felt his eyes powdered with sleep. Rachid was already asleep in his little room, snoring gently for a change. Winter lay down on the divan, fully clothed as he was, with the moonlight full across his face. Immediately he went into an oppressed dream in which he was chained and could not move, was about to be struck and could not avoid the blow, was in great danger and yet paralyzed. He awoke suddenly, aware that he had been snoring, for his mouth was open and abominably dry. The moon had gone, but between him and the stars he was aware of the black shape of a human head. Coming out of his sleep, his spirit naked against this unknown quality, Winter was terrified. It was the cold, unreasoning fear of a nightmare. The head was un-modern, medieval, monkish. Winter cried out and the head vanished as though by magic. As though released from bonds, he sprang from the divan and ran full into the fly-netting that covered the open doorway, tearing the flimsy stuff down by the sheer weight of his body. On the veranda there was no one. The moon was just going down behind the western cliff and the rocks of the wadi bottom were casting large fantastic shadows in which an army could have lurked unseen, but Winter looked round fiercely, wanting to get his hands on something that was flesh and blood so that he could squeeze and hurt it. Aroused by the noise, Rachid came out of his room. He was dazed with sleep, and although Winter knew that he would only understand a half of what he said, he poured into the boy's ear an account of what had happened. For some reason he was shouting at the top of his voice. The echoes came back from the surrounding hills as though they were in a closed room, and

away up in the compound the dogs began to bark. Winter told
Rachid to stay where he was. He himself walked all round the
bungalow, but there was no one to be seen. He had been very
shaken but had now pulled himself together. Nevertheless, he
locked the door and closed the shutters before going to sleep.

He was awake even before Rachid in the morning. He opened
the door just as the dawn was coming up. Against the door he
found three native loaves piled one on top of the other, a square
of cheese wrapped round with fig leaves, and an earthenware
jar containing yoghourt. It was a gift; he knew this immediately. When Rachid awoke, Winter showed the articles to him
but said that he was to tell nobody. The bread, cheese and
yoghourt were to be destroyed.

Rachid had no explanation. It was so inexplicable that he
disbelieved Winter when he said that the articles were found
just outside the door. Probably they had been brought from
Ford's, but nevertheless he did precisely as he was told and
threw the cheese and the bread into the sandpit at the back
of the bungalow that served as a rubbish-dump. But the pot of
sour milk was too great a prize to be thrown away. That afternoon Rachid's cousin, a boy of about twelve years of age,
came up from Rasuka and received the yoghourt together with
the container as a gift. He sat on a rock on the way home and
ate it. He looked at the earthenware pot and saw that it was of
some value and took it home to his mother.

Winter took his revolver out of his trunk and oiled it. From
that night onwards he slept with the weapon under his pillow.
What is more, he gave Rachid permission to assemble the camp-
bed and set it up in the small ante-room that was to serve him as
bedroom. He locked the door personally each night. Rachid
washed out the living-room and afterwards carried the suitcases from the veranda where he had temporarily lodged them

into the bedroom where Winter sat on the camp-bed watching him transfer their contents to the small chest of drawers that the small room boasted. The books were taken up from the floor and packed neatly into the hanging bookcase, side by side with the Baedeker and the dictionaries. Winter gave instructions that if flowers were brought up from Rasuka and placed in the pots on the veranda, then those pots must be filled with water. Rachid was delighted. Then Winter took the photograph of a woman out of his travelling-trunk and set it on a chair at the side of his bed. Although the photo was not coloured it was obvious that she was fair-haired and that her eyes were blue; there was a cheerful English schoolgirl kind of beauty about her. It was an enlargement of a snap, and she was leaning back and laughing as though protesting that she was not really ready for the snap to be taken. There was the shadow of a head on her dress where the photographer had got between her and the sun. It was a photograph of spring-like happiness. It was Winter's dead wife. Winter was settling in. He began to take a pride that everything should be in its precise place. Whenever he thought of the incident of the head and the gifts of bread, cheese and sour milk he felt angry: and as the weeks went by his anger increased. But for the moment he mentioned the incident to no one. Rachid, of course, had told all Rasuka, and in this way it came to the ears of the Sultan, Ford, and all the other Europeans of the settlement.

But no one spoke to him of it and there was no repetition of the incident.

'Come, *sidi*,' said Rachid in the hot afternoon. He had been working quietly at his end of the veranda, but, moved by some sudden impulse, had suddenly presented himself to Winter with a small box in his hand.

'What's the matter, Rachid? What's up, eh?'

'Making present for you.' The boy showed the box. It was rather crudely made out of local soft wood, but a fine geometrical pattern was being worked out on the lid in what appeared to be black wood, conceivably ebony, and a white substance, possibly bone. Rachid had that pleased expression on his face, a dog grin, like some creature that was waiting to be taken for a walk. An invisible tail was being wagged, an invisible tongue lolling.

'For me.' Winter was touched. Yet at the same time he was so comfortably settled in his long chair that he had no inclination to make any further move, even to please Rachid. It was Friday afternoon, and there was no work at the well, so that the Diesel was silent, and the valley plunged into its awful calmness. Winter was already feeling the benefit of the change from the delta.

'Too far, out there!' he said to Rachid, but the boy, as though he could not understand, remained motionless in front of him with the box still gripped in his hand. Then, although Winter had quite made up his mind that he was not going to move for anyone, he suddenly found himself levering himself up out of the chair and stretching casually, throwing his shoulders back, yawning, refreshed. He was mildly shocked, and pleasingly shocked with himself. What am I doing? he thought.

Rachid would not venture to pass through the doorway first, so Winter stepped through and marked lazily that the sun had already left the veranda in shadow. A small lizard flickered over the boards and was gone. Meanwhile Rachid had scampered up to his end of the veranda and had seated himself behind a small work-table which consisted of an upturned butter-box. To the right a pot of glue was steadily bubbling over a subdued primus stove and all around, in confusion, were slim lengths of the black wood and slivers of what Winter could now see to be white bone. Clamped to the side of the butter-box was a small saw which Rachid used to cut the wood and bone into decorative diamonds and arrows. Already he was picking up a black diamond on the end of his dampened little finger.

Winter, willing and unwilling at the same time, went and stood over him. The boy had already divided up the surface of the box into a number of large diamonds, and these he was now in the process of filling up in a chequer-board manner with the wafer-thin minute diamonds that he had patiently cut off with his saw. The wood was first of all given a thin coating of glue so that the pieces would stick in position and then Rachid went to work with breathless deliberation. Now that he had Winter in front of him he was satisfied. Further words were superfluous. Every few seconds his left hand would flick out towards a pile of black diamonds and one of them would adhere to the ball of his little finger as though by magic. It was placed in position. Rachid would give it the merest touch with a metal pointer, first on the left side and then on the right. That was all. Then back again the left hand would flick. To the boy it was obviously a labour of love, but even in watching him Winter felt his brain creaking at the thought of just how many times he would have to stretch out that left hand, just how many left and right taps he would give with that metal pointer before the lid was covered with its dazzling chequer-board.

Now that I have got so far, thought Winter, and come out here quite against my will what else is there I do not wish to do at the moment? His thought raced away ahead of him. In spite of himself he knew he would have to follow. The long chair in the shaded corner under the protection of the fly-netting was calling one way but a thought was worrying him out into the sun and across the brilliant sand to Ford's bungalow, which he could see quivering in the heat haze. He was not putting on his large hat because he wished to and neither was he putting it on out of self-discipline. There was an invisible carrot in front of his nose. At that moment this carrot would have led him into each room of a large mansion, the reception rooms, the retiring rooms, the bedrooms, the kitchens, the servants' quarters, even into mysterious cupboards under the back stairs; it would have led him exhaustively and unwearyingly through any routine. He would have counted the black diamonds on the top of Rachid's box. In the grip of this restlessness he was quite helpless. I will go and see Ford's machine, he thought.

After a quarter of an hour's patient walking with the sun in his eyes he arrived at Ford's bungalow just in time to meet the manager coming down the steps. He looked extremely surprised at the visit.

'Do you know, I was just going to call on Charlie Flynn. Now that's a funny thing, isn't it, for you don't go and call on people at this time in the afternoon and here you are paying me a visit.'

'I thought I'd just step over and see—have another look at your machine.'

To Ford this did not seem in any way surprising. Obviously a walk at two o'clock in the afternoon, even if it was across the sun-bombarded wadi bottom, so long as it was to see the machine, was perfectly rational. 'Why, of course. You're interested, eh? Now that's funny, because the first time I showed you I thought you weren't too taken. However, appearances are not always what they seem. Ha! Ha! Now I should be very grateful if you could suggest anything in the way of an improvement.'

'No—no.' Ford whisked him round the corner to the entrance to the cellar. The Arab boy who had been feeding the spools on the last occasion was asleep across the doorway.

'There! There she is, the beauty!' Ford flung the door back and allowed Winter to pass inside in front of him. 'Although I'm afraid I can't stay long. I was just off to see Charlie Flynn. Tell you what! You come and see Charlie Flynn, too.' He pressed the switch and the machine gave a sudden start as though it were an animal fiercely goaded. For a moment the arms whirled and then it stopped. 'That's funny,' said Ford. He bent down to examine the switch. He pressed it again, and this time the machine was alive, shaking the room. 'Bit of trouble with the switch now and again. Nothing much.'

The two men stood and watched the copper wire receiving its coating of white cotton.

'Yes, I like it,' said Winter. 'I like it very much.'

'Ah! You know I'm so pleased to hear that. See how perfectly the one strand of cotton kisses over the other. It is the perfection of nature itself, almost.'

'I've not got it in me to do anything like this. But tell me, doesn't it mean anything that you can't commercialize it? Don't you feel that it's—labour lost?' He was asking this question almost smiling. He knew the answer already and had only put it to receive a kind of confirmation.

'We need copper wire bound in this way here. We have the raw cotton. Why not do it ourselves?' But this was not the answer and the almost gentle way that Ford had uttered the words, and finally the happy smile he had turned on Winter, showed this clearly.

'You are really doing this because you like doing it, aren't you?'

'Some people believe that when you die and go to Paradise there you will pass the time in doing just what you wish. No matter what it is—making love, eating, writing poetry, anything at all. I shall build machines.'

'I don't think that's all the truth though.'

'Oh, yes. What else is there to say?'

'You would get tired of your machine. In any case I hope there is no such thing as time in Paradise. I'd like to know what's going on.'

'Going on—where?'

'Going on here in Rasuka. Going on in your mind. There's something very strange I feel about this place. You seem almost desperate about your machine.'

Ford looked bewildered. 'I'm sure I don't know what you mean. There's nothing strange about Rasuka. That's just an idea that you've got. Got to remember you're getting over an illness. Mustn't get imagining things.'

'You think I imagined that incident the other night?'

Ford did not say a word. He stood close to the machine, looking small and faded. 'What incident?'

'Somebody looked in at my window in the middle of the night and in the morning I found food on the doorstep.'

Ford stopped the machine. The silence throbbed. 'No, you didn't imagine that. I didn't mean that. That was nothing, I can assure you. I heard about it, of course. Some wandering Arab.'

'Then why the food?'

'Ah, that I—I really can't . . .'

'It's true.'

'Very strange. Very strange. Well, I really must go to see Charlie Flynn. I don't want you to think I'm running off, but really . . .'

'I'll come with you.'

'Good. Excellent. We can walk up together.' Ford was nervous and when he and Winter left the cellar he swore at the Arab boy. 'A lazy rat of a boy, that.'

By now Winter had met all the Europeans working in connection with the well. Charlie Flynn he had known slightly back in the delta, for when Winter had arrived from England twelve months previously Flynn was working on the 'cracking' plant. He had not known him well, but the important thing was that Flynn had seen Joyce, could actually remember her as she was. For this reason Winter felt that he and the tall Irishman were sharing something very rare and precious but at the same time forbidden or unmentionable. There was more in it than the reticence of the European in the face of mourning.

'So there you are,' Winter had said, coming up to him in the drawing-office. He was pleased to find someone to whom he did not have to be introduced.

'I'm so glad,' said the Irishman simply. He got to his feet and thrust out a large hand. 'I'd heard you were here. If there's anything to do, I mean in the way of helping you to settle in, you've only to say the word.'

'No, everything is going very smoothly.' This had been at the time before the head had appeared at the window in the middle of the night.

For a moment Flynn had hesitated. 'I really was most grieved to hear . . .'

'Thank you. That's quite all right.'

In spite of the poverty of the words Winter had looked at him for some moments with an unnatural glow in his eyes, but that was all the mention they made of the bereavement. Flynn had gone on immediately to show him a cross-section of a new type of borer they had been installing in the delta. 'Not too wise, I think. Would've paid 'em better to experiment on a small well like this one. Then nothing would be lost if anything went wrong. It's a beautiful thing on paper, though.'

Every time that Winter met Flynn he was aware of a greater

feeling of intimacy than with any other member of the community. Flynn was tall and scholastic in appearance and as he always wore steel-rimmed glasses there was an effect of the over-grown schoolboy. He spoke with a deliberate slowness, measuring out his words, and then going back on the measure to check whether it had been the right quantity. In his drawing-office he always wore grey flannels and a brown leather jacket with a zipper fastener up the front. But when he had retired to the privacy of his own bungalow he would cast off the constricting European garments, so he had informed Winter, and wear one of the loose flowing native gowns. But this was only possible in privacy, or in the company of Europeans only, for he would never permit himself to be seen by the natives dressed as one of them.

The bungalows of the community were scattered about the sides of the wadi as though deliberately dispersed to minimize damage from bombing. There may, conceivably, have been something of the sort in the mind of the Company's architect when the settlement was planned but for all that Rasuka was remote enough and insignificant enough to make any such precaution as superfluous as the rams' horns on the corners of the Sultan's palace. Flynn lived nearer to the compound area than anyone else and his bungalow was certainly the most attractive of them all. The woodwork was in white picked out here and there in leaf-green, and at this time of the year there was a creeping plant on the east-facing wall with large green leaves and trumpet flowers of heavy purple. The bungalow was heavily shuttered on this side, shuttered always, it seemed, for the jasmine had crawled up over the woodwork and bound roof to earth in flowery tresses.

Winter and Ford approached the bungalow from this east side, walking in silence and kicking up the fine sand so that for some yards behind them the solid ground seemed insubstantial under the cloudy drift. Walking round to the western side, they found half a dozen enormous white butterflies fluttering over a clump of lemon trees.

'Most active and likeable,' Ford was whispering as they walked up the steps. 'All this garden work he has done himself. Almost unheard of for a European to work his own garden in Rasuka. You should have heard what Dr. Plunkett had to say, although you mustn't take everything he says very seriously.' The little oasis that Flynn had contrived in front of his bungalow was a pitiful protest against the desert. A certain area had been demarcated by posts and some coarse cabling wire, but the one or two thick-leaved plants that had taken root were now lying flat on the baked ground. In the course of their walk across the wadi bottom Ford seemed to have lost a great deal of his nervousness but he still had an over-eagerness to say something. He began talking to Flynn before entering the bungalow, not even knowing whether there was indeed anyone there to listen to what he was saying.

'Charlie! It's me, old man. Just come over—where are you? Where are you? Ah—there! It's about the . . .'

To Winter's sun-dazzled eyes the room appeared to be quite dark but as soon as he had crossed the threshold after Ford he came to a sudden stop, feeling that he had stepped not out of the sunlight into the cool dark interior of Flynn's bungalow, but out of the everyday world into an existence lying behind it. At the one end of the dark room the light was pouring in through a skylight. It was a column of crystal thrust down through an earthy atmosphere, and in this column, flesh radiant in the rarefied air, a woman was sitting on a three-legged stool and looking up at the skylight with wide, unblinking eyes. She seemed quite unaware of their presence and made not the

slightest movement. Winter could see her breast rising and falling a little slower than normal. But the angle of her head was
such that the sun had taken away all shadows and any
blemishes there might have been. Not a stir, not a flicker. How
could this be? Winter was wondering and yet never in all his
wondering felt that it was to be answered or satisfied. So many
times he had been on the point of finding this other something,
the otherness that would lie around the corner of the house if
only he could run round there quickly enough, the brightness
of the world one would see if only he could open his eyes
quickly enough on first waking in the morning. It was the high-
bridged nose and dark curve of the brows wide and clear of the
cheek-bone though long and fine and the cheek-bones almost
orientally high, the small mouth that could be humorously
pinched in—all this was as familiar as any sight that has been
part of one for so long that one forgets its physical look and
only realizes it in the loving heart. Age or blemish cannot touch
these faces. Winter had placed the photograph, the one on the
table near his bed, so that he could see it on first waking in the
morning. But the photograph had not the reality of the unseen
image in his heart which was his wife's face graced by his own
love, nor the startling objectivity of this pale woman sitting
at the foot of her column of crystal. For both faces were the
same, the image in his heart and this. The photograph could
say nothing half as effective. 'Then you are not dead,' he was
shouting silently, 'not dead and I knew it all the time. There
is no death.'

Between him and the sitting woman it was as though a wall
of clear water rippled. In one wave of activity she had turned
her head and was looking directly at him, the figure of Flynn
in his long white robe had come out of the darkness of a corner,
and Ford was advancing towards them and stretching out his

hands in greeting, talking rapidly and loudly. 'I simply had to come and see you, Charlie. Of course I wouldn't interrupt you for worlds, but this affair of Hebechi is all very worrying. You know him, after all, and somehow I think that Cator might have been more discreet. It could have been handled better.'

'I don't see how else you can handle robbery.' The woman was still sitting on her stool, now looking towards the little group with an expression of annoyance on her face, but Flynn came forward, rubbing his hands down the front of his gallabieh. Winter could not take his eyes from the woman's face. Flynn noticed the fixity of the look.

'You know Miss Leader, don't you? Miss Leader, this is Mr. Winter. Oh, but of course, you know one another. I was there—how stupid of me! This is my hobby, you know, Winter, modelling. Nellie is my model for the time being.'

Winter was aware that they were all looking at him rather strangely.

'I'm sorry. Yes, of course we've met. A most curious thing, though. Coming in from the glare and seeing you sitting there, you looked entirely different. An effect of the light, I suppose. I can see now. I thought you were someone else here that I would have to meet.'

Nellie Leader smiled, still without moving. 'Well, I hope you're not disappointed. In any case, I suppose the sitting is over for to-day. Yes, Charlie? It's an awful strain just sitting there. Well, disappointed? You are disappointed, aren't you?' As she spoke she got to her feet and removed a large silk shawl which had been covering her shoulders and concealing the lower part of the body. It could now be seen that she was dressed in khaki shorts and a white cotton blouse. 'Well,' she persisted in the silence, 'you are disappointed, aren't you?'

'Come,' Flynn broke in. 'That's a most ungallant question. You just can't ask things like that.'

'And why not? I'm trying to make him say something nice to me. No one else ever does.'

'Nellie—you will never get any greater flattery than my condescending to model your head.'

'Oh, you and your . . .'

She came down to them and looked into Winter's face with a malicious amusement in her eyes. 'Well, no illusions now, eh?'

'Well, what of it?' Now that he had got over the shock he was suddenly angry with her. 'Yes, I am disappointed. But no, the whole thing happened too suddenly. Oh, I don't know.' He was unpleasantly off his balance. 'Didn't know you were interested in this sort of thing, Flynn.' He walked over to the clay head that the Irishman had been modelling.

'May I?'

'Yes, by all means.' When his visitors had arrived Flynn had thrown a damp cloth over his work, but Winter was now gently lifting this up. The work had no farther advanced than a mere modelling of the proportions. The mass of the head was poised on the neck at just the angle Nellie Leader had been holding in her column of light. 'I must come and see this in a month's time. Looks as though it's going to be good.' He went back to the girl immediately. 'I can see that he is going to flatter you.'

'I can see that you have made up your mind to avoid anything of the sort.' He could smile with her now, and the group moved to the other end of the long cool room where they seated themselves in cane basket-chairs.

Ford had not noticed anything strange in the atmosphere,

and was soon plunged into the middle of his story about the thieving cashier, Hebechi. What Ford wished to do was to keep him on, give him another chance under stricter surveillance, for a man of his capabilities was hard to come by in Rasuka. Hebechi was one of the few Rasuka men who held a position of trust in the Company, and Cator had caught him out in the misappropriation of roughly a hundred pounds. Now Ford wanted to know what Flynn thought of the business.

'As far as Hebechi is concerned,' said the Irishman, 'the question will be, what will his own people do? After all, he's a Rasuka man. What do they do for this sort of thing—chop their right hands off, don't they?'

Ford stirred uncomfortably. 'Oh, I don't think it'll come to that. Not if we don't say anything about it. And as we've got the money back . . .'

Winter was sitting in the next chair to Nellie Leader and he knew she was following the conversation no more than he was. She was Cator's secretary, and although she had not been in the office when Winter had first paid Cator a visit, he had seen her many times since, once in Cator's home, where she was the paying guest of Cator and his wife. She was a young woman of about twenty-seven or twenty-eight, and although Winter had been sufficiently interested in her to wonder what on earth she was voluntarily doing in Rasuka over such a long period of time, a thing that never occurred to him in connection with the other members of the European colony, it seemed that only now in coming through Flynn's doorway and seeing the girl bathed in that melodramatic light had he seen her for the first time. Yet when she moved and spoke, the woman in the crystal column faded. Then she was twenty-eight and ordinary once more, a girl with a gap between her two front teeth.

As if sensing what he was thinking about, she turned her head and smiled at him. 'You're a funny fellow. You went quite white just a little while ago.'

'Walking in the hot sun,' said Flynn from out of the middle of his talk with Ford. So even he, it appeared, was not interested in Hebechi.

'You must dismiss him,' said Winter, intervening. 'You can't have a dishonest cashier, no matter what the consequences to the man himself or the inconveniences to the Company. In any case, I'm quite sure that Cator would not work with the man any more.'

'Yes, I know, I know——' Ford's havering made Winter's remarks sound dictatorial and almost brutal. 'I suppose you're right, but it is all most unfortunate. I would give anything for the thing not to have happened.'

'Winter's right,' said Flynn.

'Well, now that's settled,' said Nellie Leader, 'let's talk of something much nicer. For instance, Mr. Winter, I'm quite sure that if you asked Charlie nicely enough he would make a model of your head too.'

'I'm afraid the asking of things nicely comes difficult to me. Perhaps if you would help me in the asking. If you'd tell me what to say, for instance——' The sentence was covered up by her bubble of laughter.

'There, Charlie, I've got another customer for you. And Mr. Winter's got a much more interesting head than mine. See the nice way it sticks out behind, and then the long stretch there is from the forehead to the chin.'

'That's perfectly true. It's a much more interesting head than yours.'

'You are looking after yourself? You must look after yourself, or we shall have to look after you.' Ford could not easily assume a serious manner in the adult way, but behind the light way he uttered these words with lips that were now faintly smiling and then relaxing into their normal line, Winter was aware of serious purpose. There might even be something vaguely threatening in them.

As Winter made no reply or, indeed, even the slightest movement to show that he had heard and understood, Ford looked quickly at Flynn and Nellie Leader, before bantering on. 'You are looking much better, though. Some colour in your cheeks. We are all healthy, every one of us here. Wonderful climate, really. When travel is easy and the Sultan builds an airport you'll see luxury hotels going up . . . people'll come here for their rest cures. We shall be very unimportant people then, eh, Flynn? My wife looks forward to that time, though true enough, I'm due to go home next year. But you do look after yourself, don't you, Winter?'

'What Ford means,' Flynn broke in, 'is this. I wouldn't wander about alone too much. None of my business, I know, but I can't help hearing about the way you go for walks out of the wadi and stay away for hours. I'm sure you'll take this in the spirit it is given. We've been here longer than you. And though the place looks peaceful enough it is not really safe to be alone except in this immediate area.'

'I have been for walks. Yes,' said Winter, conceding the point gently. Flynn's words made him very curious. It was not mere ingenuousness that gave Winter the feeling that he was perfectly safe in the desert. It might be that they were right, of course.

'And then you went down to Rasuka last night,' Flynn went on.

Winter looked up sharply. 'To the town? I didn't leave my bungalow after seven yesterday evening.'

'But it's not safe, you see. The very jacket on your back could be sold and realize enough to keep one of those families for a month.'

'I wasn't in Rasuka last night. Really I must . . .'

'Then it's all a mistake,' Ford hastened in with a propitiatory smile on his face. 'Some stupid misunderstanding. It was just that Ahmed, my boy, said that he saw you. But, of course, these fellows are always imagining things. They say anything they think will please you—yes, or annoy you too, sometimes. I suppose he thought it would make me anxious. For your safety, I mean.'

'Yes, of course. I expect you're right. It's a natural temptation for a man to wander, especially when he feels his strength coming back. I've been in dry dock, so to speak, for so long . . .'

'Look here, Winter, I shall be only too glad to come on any trips with you—in the immediate area, that is. As a matter of fact, it is easy enough to get horses. I want exercise, anyway.'

'Do you think you'd be a good guarantee of my safety?'

'Naturally, we should be armed. There's an interesting stone fort a little way up the coast. We could go out and have a look at it.'

'I'll come. Yes, you must let me come.' Winter had never ceased to be acutely aware of the presence of Nellie Leader. She was sitting on the other side of the wickerwork table, but he could, it seemed to him, almost feel her heart beating. She tossed back her fair hair in excitement and drew it to a bun on the nape of her neck.

'Do you think that my company will be sufficient guarantee of your safety? That's the question.' Winter could not keep out the note of irony.

'When they see a man alone it's a great temptation. But two men on tall horses—well, it looks a little more resolute.'

'Funny, I don't feel that there is any danger. The general feeling I have is one of—well, friendliness. I think Rasuka is a friendly place. But I expect that you are right.'

'In such matters———'

'The curious thing is that you almost convince me that I was in the town last night.'

Flynn opened his eyes the merest fraction wider and Ford leaned forward. The girl did not cease to knot her fingers in her hair so that her breasts were raised and prominent. Winter knew that he was taking this all much more calmly because of the aura of femininity.

He continued. 'Oh, an illusion, of course. One of the after effects of typhoid, I expect. I can almost believe anything now. Almost as though I had gone down there, had forgotten it and was now dimly remembering.'

'But that's a joke, of course.' Ford hastened to assure him of this.

'And when I came into this room just now, for a moment I thought that the miraculous had happened. I think I believe in miracles. It's all very bewildering really. When I saw you sitting in the light, Miss Leader, I don't think—yes, I am almost sure of it—I've ever had such a moment of startled happiness before. It was because you were almost . . . not a woman.'

For all her self-assurance Nellie Leader coloured slightly.

'Well, I don't know that that's a very nice thing to say. That's the last thing I want to be considered as—not a woman. Anyway, it's not at all complimentary. As for happiness! Oh dear, I don't understand this at all.' Her voice took on a plaintive note. She turned to Flynn. 'You tell me, Charlie. What does he mean? Tell me, Charlie, I do look feminine, don't I? Anybody would think that you didn't like women, Mr. Winter.'

'I'm devoted to them. I don't think I could live without them.'

He was looking at her intently, not a flicker in his eyes.

'Oh, Charlie dear! Do explain. I feel all at sea! Just what is happening? You know, Mr. Winter, you say all this nonsense so seriously, and I don't know whether you mean it or not. Anybody else would have winked . . . or—or . . . done something . . . leered even, like Cator does!'

'Cator leer?' said Flynn quickly.

'Oh, dear me, yes!' She had released the bun of hair at the back of her head and it fell in fair tresses down to her shoulders. 'But it's all so flattering really. I rather like it. He's a sort of professional leerer. Sometimes he looks so very funny.'

'He must stop that,' said Flynn righteously. 'He's a married man.'

'Oh, really, Charlie, you are impossible. I didn't tell you that so that you could wax all moral. There's no harm in it. Mr. Cator and I understand each other perfectly. I wish Mr. Winter would leer. No, Mr. Winter, I don't like it when you say . . . not a woman.'

'Not a woman and all women at the same time. I'm a very sentimental person, really. You reminded me of my wife, sitting there. And yet there was just that difference. I should be speaking about all this humorously, I know. I can see you all wriggling away from the direct way I am expressing all this. But I just don't care, quite so much, what people think of me. No, I'll speak seriously. I felt happy just now because for the moment I believed in the illusion. So really it is a tremendous compliment to you, Nellie. I think you're a very delightful person.'

Ford began to giggle and creak in his wickerwork chair. Flynn sat up very stiff and straight. Nellie was quite pink by now, her eyes sparkling. Only Winter was relaxed and the words were falling almost lazily out of his mouth. 'Well, why shouldn't I use your Christian name? Mine's Robert.'

'Bob or Bobbie?' she asked chokingly.

'Robert,' he repeated gently.

She gave herself up to a strange kind of laughing, not really humorous. She searched for and eventually found a large white handkerchief. It was in the pocket of her shorts. 'This is really! You *are* an impossible person. You'll be making love to me next.'

'No, I shall probably never make love to you. Are you married or engaged?'

'No, neither. You see, there's nothing to stop you.'

Only then did Winter lift up his eyes and look at her. The relaxed lines in his figure disappeared. He was as taut as the string of a bow. 'People's inability to talk seriously is just annoying at times. They just take refuge in giggles. I am not a particularly humorous person. Fortunately. It's such a destructive thing. Nothing is sacrosanct.'

Ford looked as though he had been personally rebuked. It was Flynn, who had possibly less humour than any of them, who took it upon himself to defend it. 'Oh, I must disagree with you there. You must see the funny side now and again. Makes life sane. Gives a man a sense of proportion.' All this was very serious. The conversation was upsetting him.

'Well, perhaps so. I can't argue about any of these things any more. I've come to a stage where I can only be dogmatic. I've been reasonable too long. Humour is, too often, just a sop to fear or it is self-flattering or it destroys sincerity or . . .'

'No, no, no, no, no,' protested Ford, laughing gaily. 'You're a bigger joker than any of us. You don't mean a word you're saying. I'll tell you a joke and make you laugh. I defy you not to laugh.'

'Oh, yes, I'll laugh—if it's funny. It's a lot easier to laugh. That's why people do it.'

'You remind me of my wife,' said Ford with tears of laughter in his eyes. 'When she was a girl she used to pray. "Please God send me pain and suffering and distress so that I can be strong. I want to live." That's what my wife used to pray for. She told me.'

'Your wife told you that?' said Winter, and now it was his turn to be startled.

'Oh, yes, just a phase, you know. Of course, she's lost all that now. You wouldn't find a more normal or balanced person than my wife. We all go through these phases.'

This, at least, showed that Ford, if he was speaking sincerely, was not the slightest judge of character. Winter had not forgotten the way she had received him on the day of his arrival.

'It all depends what you mean by the normal.' There was something of the scoutmaster about Flynn. He could not see that the others were prepared to talk any nonsense just now and that his seriousness was a little out of place. Nellie Leader settled to listen to him, smiling over at Winter. Winter had already come to the conclusion that Flynn was in love with her. In many ways it would be surprising if he were not, he reflected. Flynn went on talking with the utmost gravity, pointing the stem of his pipe first at one and then at another of them. He brought out one or two platitudes and then proceeded to give an illustration that Winter thought rather surprising. Of course, there was nothing improper about it. Winter himself would never have hesitated a moment to talk about stool tests, but Flynn's bearing had given the impression that he would have been much more reticent, especially in the presence of Nellie.

'You see, I once had to go and have a stool test. It was for dysentery. You know the sort of thing. In order to be of any value the stool has to be examined as early as possible. So you've got to go to the laboratory and defecate, to order, in a sterilized container which, after emptying, is returned with the request for more. As far as the analyst was concerned, I was of no importance unless I could do this. I wasn't judged as a man. I suppose he did that sort of thing a dozen times a day. For him I was just a creature who had to produce a stool and there is no measuring of achievement until this becomes a reality. He is quite detached. Quite non-committal. Then you settle down with a book to wait for the purge to act. Now the thought that occurred to me was this—if I failed I should feel ashamed and humiliated. What is more, I should feel, in some extraordinary way, guilty. I should feel that I had committed a sin—a sin of omission, so to speak. Well, there you are. It is just that there are different laws inside an analytical labora-tory. It is just a question of the convention. It so happens that we've got other conventions in our world. So, what is the nor-mal, see? What is the normal person? What is the balanced person? Yvonne just gives you the idea of being normal. Other people, the Sultan, for example, would think her very unusual. You see, I don't know. It makes everything so unsettled.'

But he did not look in the slightest bit unsettled. He looked remarkably poised and in control of himself, smoking his pipe now, and obviously enjoying himself.

'Yes, I suppose it's all very true,' said Ford vaguely. 'That's the way to look at it, of course. I don't know what I'd do with-out my wife. She's a wonder.'

'How is she? It seems ages since I've seen her,' said Nellie.

'The point is you have to find some basis——' began Flynn once more, seeing the conversation slipping away and trying to get back to his convention idea. But no one wanted to talk

about it. Ford, of course, had entirely misinterpreted what had
been said, and Winter thought the item that had struck Nellie
was certainly not the theory but the picture of the serious Flynn
going along to the laboratory with a book under his arm, quite
prepared for a wait until the purge began to act. He had caught
her smiling once or twice. She and Ford talked about Mrs.
Ford and how she had found it necessary to take a siesta every
afternoon nowadays.

'You see what I mean,' said Flynn, turning to Winter. He
meant to have at least one person with whom he could continue. 'I think you'd go mad if you saw life through two conventions.'

'Yes, of course. I don't suppose the question would arise
though, would it?'

'Oh, yes, I think so. It might. The Christian religion . . .'

Although Ford was chattering happily and making small
gestures with his hands, it was very much a solo performance.
Nellie was giving her attention but now she was saying little.
Then Winter saw that she was not even listening. He rose to
go.

'Look after yourselves. I felt a bit restless this afternoon.
That's why I came.'

'You're not going?'

'Yes, I'll be on my way back now. Thanks for your . . .'

'I'll be coming your way—at least, for part of the distance,'
said Nellie, getting to her feet. 'Do you mind if I come with
you?'

'Of course not.'

And everything fell out as easily as that. When Nellie and
Winter stepped off the veranda it seemed to both of them that
it could not easily have happened otherwise. Winter felt quietly
pleased. Until they were actually clear of the area that made

up Flynn's garden she was turning and talking and laughing to the two men still sitting on the cane chairs. Beyond the wire fence Winter turned and raised a hand to them. Then he and Nellie set out across the slightly undulating sand.

During the day the landscape had been flat, painted in pale colour washes, but now that the sun was so far down the west that night would come within the half-hour, its long level rays gave each pebble and shrub a three-dimensional solidity. The crags of the eastern side of the wadi, with the setting sun full on them, were as red as roses. Bars of purple were laid across the sand, violet shadows against the bungalows so that now they stood out with stereoscopic clearness. The palms round the Sultan's iced-cake palace were an unnatural green, like trees under lamp-light. And then, of course, wide and free and pale, so that, looking up, Winter felt released and soothed, was the broad band of the sea. Making in towards the harbour were a number of dhows. Their tall sails winked in the setting sun and when they came into the shore current they pecked at the ocean like hens on a barn-yard floor. The evening was already cool, but the hot ground could still heat the air, so that Nellie and Winter, walking amongst the boulders, felt the heat still rising into their faces.

For some time they were silent. But it was not a silence that had nothing to say. Winter felt no need to say a word because their conversation was being made for them by the still, evening air, the quietness that only comes in desert lands. Nellie walked on his right and slightly in advance, something gay and alert in her dancing walk.

'There now! A penny for them,' she said suddenly, stopping and smiling.

'A penny for them? Oh, they're not worth that. No thoughts! Just nothing.'

'I don't believe you. You're laughing at me.'

Winter was genuinely surprised. 'Laughing? No, that's the last thing . . .'

They had an idle, butterfly conversation. They were so much engrossed in it that they forgot what had happened in Flynn's bungalow and even where they were. When Nellie said, 'Well, here I am. Thank you for your company,' Winter looked up in surprise to see that they had already come to Cator's place, where Nellie lived.

'Good night,' he said with a great sense of loss.

'Good heavens, man. Cheer up!' she said with a little burst of laughter, and left him standing there.

The evening closed in around him as he walked slowly up the gentle incline towards the bungalow. The wind had changed and came in from the sea, so that he could hear its murmuring, such a small sound, the breathing almost of a child. When he was younger Winter found so much surplus energy inside him that he would often run, instead of walking, when alone. It was not that he had none of that energy and excitement this mild evening. That was not the reason for his pacing so slowly over the sand and scattered rocks. It was just that the arrival at his destination, the arrival at any destination, now seemed of little importance. He could find his happiness on the way. There was no need to hurry to catch it. There were the rocks and the sea and the air. In that evening moment, when the sun finally went down and the western rim of the wadi had the intense rich blackness of velvet, the rocks and the sea and the air were enough. He went on quietly, smilingly, unthinkingly.

CHAPTER V: *Avatar*

WHATEVER ELSE HE MIGHT THINK about him, Winter soon came to the conclusion that Dr. Plunkett knew his job. He sounded Winter's abdomen searchingly, saying not a word but drawing his old lips in quaveringly. Winter closed his eyes. Plunkett made an attempt to palpitate the spleen. Then he drew back and walked vaguely away to wash his hands in the white porcelain sink under the window.

'I must take some blood. I'd like to take a count.'

After this operation had been successfully performed and he had put the test-tube into his ice-box, the doctor drew on his white linen jacket. He looked very spruce. He was wearing a large spotted bow tie, a green waistcoat and brown flannel trousers which were cut in a very youthful way. His face was red and well scrubbed, so that the flesh looked soft and malleable. Winter, in contrast, felt faded and inelegant.

'Don't take too much exercise. Exercise is a curse. Quite a nonsensical modern fad. Men spend active years in developing muscles—and then they turn to fat in sedentary jobs. And then they carry on exercising and over-strain their systems. If only people would look on their youth as a preparation for middle and old age they'd live longer. Who ever heard of an athlete living to a ripe old age? No, it's the parson, snug in his vicarage with a pipe of tobacco every evening, or the village idiot sitting on a wall all day—those are the people who touch the ninety mark. That is, if you want to touch the ninety mark. Now, you've got a sound enough constitution. In a year's time you'll feel a hundred times better than you do now. In fact, you'll be better than you were before. Hm? What's that? Well, of course, that's my way of looking at it. That's what any doctor would tell you. A stupid profession, really. Keeping people alive. God!'

'I'd like you to keep me alive for a bit.' Winter dressed quickly and knotted a white handkerchief round his throat to give protection against the sun which even at this time of the year was dangerous in the late morning. He had been wearing a very wide-brimmed straw hat which Plunkett had snorted at contemptuously as soon as he saw it. He said that there was nothing that he despised more than going native. 'The best thing is to live normally. No frills like this. Where do you think you are, anyway? On the equator? Ford wanted me to wear a sun hat! Think of it! No, the best thing is to make no concessions to the climate. Sun glasses are another thing, for example. People get so used to wearing them that they feel naked when they get into bed and have to take them off. Now, what'll you have? A good gin, here!'

'I thought you said "no alcohol." '

'Well, well! That's true enough in its way, of course. But how long is it since I said that? A good quarter of an hour. Time enough for me to change me mind, anyway. No, a drop of gin would do you the world of good. Does me good, anyway.' He seemed deliberately careless in his speech, as though to show his great contempt for all rules and regulations. What does it matter if I do say 'me' instead of 'my,' anyway? his look seemed to say.

'If it's doctor's orders.'

Plunkett had not waited for Winter to accept the invitation. He had dragged a little table out from beneath the bench that bore his instruments, and then, in one movement, stretched out his hand, opened a small cupboard and produced a familiarly shaped bottle of gin. It was a practised hand. He found a couple of glasses, filled his own half full, and then told Winter to say 'when.'

'When,' said Winter.

'God,' said Plunkett to himself. He was genuinely shocked by the small amount.

'Any water?'

'You take water with it? God!' Plunkett drank his gin at a gulp before nodding towards the surgery tap. 'That water's pure. Here, let me. Say when. Now gin is a good medical drink. In an emergency you can use it as an antiseptic. I don't think a germ could live two seconds in my stomach. And I learned the value of gin during the last war. Ah, I was young then. God, I was young. In the ranks, too. A medical orderly. It happened this way. The M.O. and me had to examine a bunch of recruits. I did the eyes. He did the rest. Well, before we began he set a bottle of gin on the table between us, just as I might set that bottle—there! you see?—like that. And between each recruit we had a nip. There were twenty recruits. By the time we'd finished 'em we'd finished the bottle. They all passed. A1. It might even be that those twenty men turned the scale somewhere. You can imagine it, can't you? The extra machine-gun post to be manned. And there they are, the whole twenty of 'em. You might almost say that that bottle of gin won the war. Have another? Well, I think I will. Doesn't do the stuff much good when you've opened a bottle to keep it standing about.'

His eyes looked unsmilingly into Winter's. His pink hand trembled slightly as he poured the spirit out and the bottle chuckled against the glass. The baby-like cleanliness of his face and hands, the extreme neatness of his surgery, the sheen on the instruments as they lay in a case on the well-scrubbed table-top, the brilliance of the light in the room, for Plunkett disdained anything in the way of curtains or shutters and the sunlight was streaming in, it was all somehow profoundly satisfactory. Winter felt pleased with every detail of the room and its occupant. Even the wrinkles on his forehead and the small blue vein at the side of his nose.

'As a young man in Rasuka it's your personal relationships that you'll find so—unsatisfactory. There's no blighter here that you can trust. But not only that. There's no blighter here you can get to know. That's what I don't like. I like to know people and be friendly. In my own way, mind you, and on my own terms. Not in Rider's way. God blast me, what a man that was! If he'd not been knocked on the head there'd 'ave been a ruddy revolution.'

'That's his,' said Winter. He nodded over to the door. Against the wall a blue china jug, the kind that goes with a basin in a bedroom, was standing, the same that Ford had seen salvaged from the burning bungalow on the day of the fire.

'What, that? Where'd you get that from?'

'I bought it. Fifty piastres. A native came up to me and offered to sell it. He said it was Rider's. It was just as I was coming along.'

'Well, there you are, you see. You buy it, not because you want it, but because it belonged to Rider. Now that's just . . .'

'On the contrary I wanted a jug like that.'

Plunkett ignored the remark completely. 'And that's just like him. Even when he's dead he can get you to do things you don't want to.'

'Was he so very persuasive?'

'God no! That's just it. He'd never persuade anybody. It was as much as he'd do to talk to you. Very stuck up. No, it was just his way. But he'd never get me to fall in with his ideas. Wanted me to treat the natives. For nothing, you know. Oh, I don't mean the natives employed by the Company. That's my job. But any Tom, Dick or Harry from the town who wanted to pop in. It just wasn't practical. They'd run me out of drugs. Then what's the point of keeping 'em alive? But he—well, he started buying drugs on his own account and giving 'em away. Natural result that one fellow died through taking an overdose.'

'Rider paid for this out of his own pocket?'

'God! He wasted all his money on things like this. And what was the result? A man dies and the Sultan had to come down on him. Took it as a reflection on his own medical services. They're awful, anyway, but . . . No, Rider was a fool. He meant well, but the floor of hell—he used to give a dozen M. and B. tablets to a man suffering from V.D., for example. He'd tell him to take three a day, or something like that. God, what nonsense. As soon as the man got home his wife would say, "Why not take them all at once, and then you'll be cured more quickly?" So that is what happens. Blackmail really, of course, on the part of Rider. He knew it would force my hand. I'd got to do something to protect these fellows against him. Unscrupulous! You see, one man died. It wouldn't work, though. I treated one or two of them. Then the news went round and they began coming in dozens. One morning they woke me up.

The sand was black with 'em. I went out on to the veranda and looked at 'em. They just howled at me, lifting up withered arms, taking off their clothes to show me great running sores you could put your fist in. I felt like God A'mighty. They just howled at me. I'll swear there were five hundred of them. I think they'd 've worshipped me. Course it was an absolutely impossible situation. I had to send over to the palace to get some soldiers to clear them all away. It was done very brutally. They clubbed one man to death. So that was the end of that. I think the Sultan passed some law, but by that time Rider had lost interest in the medical welfare of Rasuka and was going round trying to teach them to read. Mind you, that was damn funny, in its way. Rider couldn't read much Arabic himself—not much more than I could. But then he was always changing. The next thing was that he was trying to persuade the Sultan to put in a drainage system. Then he wanted everyone to have mosquito nets. The cost of a mosquito net would keep one of these families for a month. If you were to issue them free they'd only sell them. Then he would be round the Europeans trying to get them to form a discussion group. Now, if there's anything that I detest it's a discussion group. I don't like arguments.'

By now Winter had a reasonably clear picture of Rider. Like all the other Europeans in Rasuka, he had been employed by the Company, and Winter had discovered that he had been Cator's immediate superior on the administrative side, a post which Cator succeeded to when Rider disappeared into the interior. Obviously he had been a great busybody, probably with a great fund of dull Christian platitudes, and a knack of doing the annoyingly unexpected and unnecessary. Winter felt his interest in the man diminishing considerably, and as a result the mental picture that he had formed of him, that of the tall, spare man with the slight stoop and the persistent beard, began to fade also. A bore and a humbug, he thought.

'Nevertheless,' said Plunkett with a much less pugnacious note in his voice, 'somebody should've gone to look for him. I'd have gone myself only I can't ride a ruddy horse, and as for a camel . . . Besides, why should I when there were others? I tell you, it's all very well for the Sultan to wash his hands of the matter, but he's talking nonsense when he says he'd lose men if he sent them up the valley. Those tribesmen wouldn't dare to attack a band of well-armed soldiers. Half-naked wretches, some with just a spear, faces dabbed over with some blue dye.'

Plunkett was not easy, not at all easy. He had even omitted to fill his glass and was twisting it round between his two hands, glinting his eyes at it to see how it prismatically caught the sun.

'There is no chance of his still being alive, I suppose?'

'Not a ghost. It's four months since he went,' Plunkett replied almost gloomily. 'Poor bastard!'

'Seems the sort of fellow who needs protecting against himself.'

'Eh? Yes, that's it.' For a moment he was lost in thought. 'I'll tell you what he was! He was a man, the sort of man who is as pleased as punch to find some God-awful circumstance out—the fact that half the population of Rasuka has V.D., for example. It would seem to . . . to sort of illuminate him.' Momentarily Plunkett paused in a kind of wonder over the word he had found. 'It would illuminate him. Give him a hell of a kick. Pleased as hell to find anyone miserable. Just give him the chance he wanted. Oh, I don't know.' Finally he shrugged his shoulders and held up the bottle of gin for the pleasure of seeing the spirit swilling backwards and forwards.

Winter had covered about a quarter of the journey back to his bungalow when he remembered that he had forgotten to bring the blue jug that he had bought. He cursed and had turned round, had even started to retrace his steps before he changed his mind once more and decided that Rachid could be sent to fetch it. For Rachid, he thought to himself, it will mean a journey exactly four times as long as the distance I would have to travel to fetch the jug. It is very unfair. I am getting lazy. And why not? What do I pay him for? He's the servant, isn't he? Besides, he will be only too pleased to go.

As he walked over the sand Winter became aware that he was not thinking about the jug, or about Rachid, but that all his hopes were suddenly and illogically pinned on finding Nellie Leader waiting for him in the bungalow. There was not the slightest justification for this hope. He had not seen her since they had walked back together from Flynn's place on the evening of the previous Wednesday, and he could not even say that he had much thought about her. But, for no reason at all, he suddenly wanted to speak to her, something he wanted more than anything else he could think of that was capable of reasonable fulfilment. It was not impossible that she was there waiting for him. She was obviously a person of impulse. Rachid would tell her that he had gone to Plunkett for an examination, but that he would be back shortly. Rachid would pull out the chaise-longue so that she could sit on the veranda in the shadow and when he turned the corner he would see her, wearing some white dress and looking deliciously cool, with her head turned away, for she would be pretending to be asleep. He would go up the veranda steps with the utmost quietness.

The bungalow was still some thirty yards away. The sand had drifted up against this western corner like so much brown sugar. What a poverty-stricken place it looks, he thought, the

paint all peeled off the woodwork. He knew that this could not
be helped in this climate, but he ardently wished that the bungalow should have been, at this very moment, shining in a new
coat of paint, some light colour for preference, with the shutters
picked out in green.

In spite of himself his heart gave a great thump as he came
round the corner and saw that a white-clad figure was occupying a chair on the balcony. But it was not Nellie. Winter was
furious with himself for feeling so intensely disappointed. It was
someone he had never seen before, a young man with a very
dark, almost black colouring, who got to his feet as soon as he
saw the Englishman. The young man was smiling delightedly,
showing perfect teeth.

'Good morning,' said Winter shortly. He was so disappointed
that he did not even permit himself to wonder who the visitor
might be. 'Please sit down.'

'Sir, I wanted to see you. I hope you will forgive . . .' The
young man spoke very good English. He looked as happy as any
man would be on the realization of his dearest ambition. 'Oh,
sir . . .' he went on with soft delight, looking keenly into Winter's face. He was almost overcome with his emotion.

'Do please sit down.'

Then there was a startling transformation. In a moment the
smiling face was overcast. 'Sir, sir . . .' he tried to commence,
jumping up from his seat once more as his strong emotion was
released. 'I have come to you because I want to explain. I have
a wife. We were married but two years. Now there will be a
child. God willing, a man.' He now seemed to be overcome with
grief. The corners of his mouth were heavily turned down and
all the light had faded out of his eyes. He was a stricken man.

Winter clapped his hands for Rachid to prepare some coffee.
Rachid came immediately. He did not look at the visitor.

Winter stormed at him. 'Why did you not make any coffee? When a guest comes always make coffee.' Rachid withdrew, smiling to himself.

'Look,' said Winter, turning to the young man who now seemed on the point of tears. 'Hurry up and tell me what is the matter. I can't stick here all day listening to people weeping. Though why you've come to me I can't imagine. Now, come on! Out with it, and then you must hurry up and go, because I'm busy.'

It was only now that Winter could bear to look closely at his visitor and see that he was rather primly dressed in European-style clothes, probably made in Egypt. He was wearing rather a vivid yellow tie, which matched well with the particular shade of his skin. He was a healthy-looking, handsome young man.

'Sir, I am a finished man. I am a dead man. I am lost,' he wailed.

Rachid brought the coffee in. The young man took his cup with trembling hands, apologizing profusely all the time. Winter remained silent, looking out at the faded sandhills. He could have shaken him.

'Pull yourself together,' he said as brusquely as he could manage.

'Yes, sir. I am indeed sorry.' He had sat down to drink his coffee, but now he stood up once more. 'I come to you, sir, because I know you are wise and good——'

'What's the trouble now? Come on, or I shall have to tell you to go.'

'My name is Hebechi.'

'Hebechi? Where have I heard that name before?'

'Ah, yes? You know my name? Good.'

'You're the man who's been stealing money from the Company. Ah yes, that's right. Well, what do you expect me to do about that?'

'Sir!' He was quite outraged. 'I never steal in my life. This is all wicked lies specially to disgrace me. I am an honest man who work here since a long time.'

'Well?'

'Mr. Cator took the money. He is a very bad, mean man and he took the money and now he's blaming it on me. Of course, everyone believes him, but me—no, they just look at me and immediately they say, "That man is guilty." '

'This is no business of mine. In any case, I won't have you coming here and making accusations against Mr. Cator. What you are saying is absolute nonsense. Mr. Cator would not dream of taking money. How dare you talk like that. Now, go on! Get off with you. I've heard enough.' Winter got to his feet and would have entered the bungalow, but Hebechi, now almost beside himself with despair, sank down on to his knees and caught him by the jacket. He could utter nothing that was coherent, but looked up into Winter's face with eyes that were suddenly brimming with tears.

'I won't have it!' shouted Winter. 'Let me go. Rachid! Where are you?'

'Sir, you don't know what this means. Rasuka is my town. If the Company sends me back there as a thief the local law will punish me as though I'd been found guilty in one of the Sultan's courts. They will cut my hand off!'

'You should have thought of that before you took the money. And how dare you come here accusing Mr. Cator. You're lucky I don't have you beaten.'

Hebechi at once released Winter's coat, almost as though he had indeed been struck. He stood very stiff and upright.

'It is shame on me to come and humble myself before you.

God sees! It was not for me.' Except for a slight uncertainty about his upper lip he was in dignified control of himself now. He would not even look at Winter but gazed at some point above his head.

'What can I do, man? I can't go to Cator and ask him to reconsider the question—and then tell him that you are accusing him of taking the money himself. What you are talking is just slander.'

Hebechi, very stiff and straight, made to speak, but Winter interrupted him. 'Do you know what that word means, "slander"?'

'I am an educated man, sir. I was educated in Egypt.'

'Well, then, what you have been talking is just slander and you ought to know better.'

'What I have said is the truth. I can prove it.'

'I want to hear no more about it. Now I think you had better be going.'

Without another word Hebechi immediately went.

This was hardly what Winter had wanted at all. Really he would have liked Hebechi to have gone on pleading for a little while longer, even though the whine in his voice had been unpleasant. Winter made half a move to the rail of the balcony as though to call him back, but he caught himself in the act and turned back immediately into his cool living-room, swinging the fly-netting to one side as he passed.

'Rachid!' he shouted angrily. Then clapped his hands. He had remembered that the servant had not appeared when summoned some five minutes earlier. 'Where've you been?' he asked testily when the boy came through the bead curtain from the kitchen. He did not wait for an answer. 'Look at the state this place is in! Look, books all over the place, ash on the floor, bed not made. That's your job, you know. I make all this—

this mess and you've to clear it up. That's your job, you understand? That's what you're paid for.' He sank into a cane chair.
'Bring me some lemonade.'

This last was about the only sentence that Rachid had understood. He grinned and disappeared.

The flies came in through the open doorway, no longer covered by the netting, to beat furiously against the light-coloured
ceiling. The vibration of their wings could almost be heard in
the profound silence. Even Rachid in his kitchen was silent,
and Hebechi, pacing away from the bungalow, was walking
with muffled feet through the sand.

Winter could not get Hebechi out of his mind. The walk
back from Plunkett's and the energy taken up by the scene with
Hebechi had been exhausting. Winter stretched out as fully as
the chaise-longue permitted him and as soon as he closed his
eyes his imagination went delving through the complicated recesses of the situation.

Rachid brought the lemonade and placed it on the small table
in front of him. Winter did not open his eyes. He heard the
chink of the ice in the glass and the rustle of the boy's gallabieh,
but already in his own mind he was asking Cator to show him
the books. Of course, this could not be done in so many words.
The financial side was no concern of Winter's and the occasion
when he had helped Cator to pay the men had been exceptional.
He had wanted to see the employees, he had been occupied in
discovering the routine to satisfy his own sense of duty, and in
any case he had had a free half-hour. The only person who
could, in his own right, ask to see the books was Ford. And it
would be more difficult to approach Ford than Cator himself.
No, Winter could see himself going into the administrative
block and making straight for Cator's office. Nellie would be
there, but on this occasion they would be quite formal and busi-

ness-like. Then almost casually, in conversation with Cator, he would inquire about the misappropriation of funds. Out of curiosity he would like to see the books. Cator could not very well refuse. If it were shown that Cator were guilty—but how would the books really show this?—Winter assumed that they would—what then was to be done?

Winter opened his eyes suddenly and looked round. He was startled that he had so far gone in his reflections that he was already assuming Cator guilty. That is as it may be, he thought.

The man would be dismissed. He could imagine the scene so very clearly. Cator would be very stiff, drawing into himself with a kind of gnawing fury, unable to say a word. Poor Ford! He would not know what to do. Only he, Winter, would intervene when Ford went so far as to say that the scandal must be hushed up at once. Ford would do anything to save Cator. He would go to him at night with sufficient money to enable him to adjust the funds. He, Winter, would intervene and stop the crime being smudged over.

Mrs. Cator would be in despair. She might even come and appeal to him personally but it would all be in vain and the Cator family would depart on the first boat. Where would Nellie live then? When the Cators went she would hardly carry on in that large bungalow herself. As he was a bachelor and living alone it would, no doubt, be improper for her to come and share his bungalow. No, she would probably go to the Fords.

Winter pulled himself together with a curse. He had caught himself out. It is hard to nail oneself down in a fantasy-weaving mood. The pictures seem to be painted at just one remove behind the consciousness and it is much more normal to live through a momentary fantasy, come back to awareness and carry on with no awareness of the absurdities the mind has just perpetrated. But this time Winter felt ashamed of himself.

He called loudly for the boy and sipped the ice-cold lemonade.

'Sah!' Rachid was at the bead curtain.

'Here! Come here!'

Rachid came over and stood at Winter's feet.

'That man you saw just now, d'you know him?'

'Hebechi Effendi. Yes, I know him, sah.'

'What sort of a man is he, then?'

Rachid had, of course, listened to the conversation that Winter had had with his visitor. He was quite determined to say nothing that would not meet with approval.

'Oh! Him, sah? Not much good. A Rasuka man.'

'Are all men from Rasuka no good, then?'

Rachid struggled between his contempt for the home-grown variety, even though they were his own countrymen, and his wish to avoid any identification with them in Winter's mind.

'A very bad, proud man, Hebechi Effendi. No wear gallabieh like me. Yet me know his family. Don't trust him in anything. I've seen him house. Very rich man now. Got new umbrella white on top, under green. Nobody like Hebechi Effendi. Very big liar. All that he say lies. He took money all right.'

Winter felt that he would have to discount everything that the boy said about Hebechi. He was so obviously jealous.

'Next time he come here I tell him go away?'

'Certainly not,' said Winter indignantly.

The boy looked at him in some surprise. Judging by the conversation he had just overheard, one would have thought that Hebechi would have been a very unwelcome visitor in the future. Rachid's mind worked rapidly.

'Course, him not always been bad. Might be good really.'

Whatever else happened, the boy wished to please Winter and sensing this at last, realizing that any information thus obtained was therefore quite useless, the white man sent him away. Rachid went into his kitchen with the conviction that however unpredictable the actions of Europeans might be one thing was now certain; and that was Winter's interest in the case of Hebechi Effendi. Something might be gained by warning the ex-employee. In any case Rachid was going to keep his eyes open. There was more than one way of earning money.

As for Winter he was conscious of having treated Hebechi with more brusqueness than was necessary. That face, with its expression of preposterous dignity, had left its image with him. Winter felt guilty and uneasy. He came to a sudden decision.

'Rachid! Rachid!' The boy appeared at the bead curtain. 'I'm going over to Mr. Ford's house. If anyone calls . . .'

He pulled on his wide-brimmed hat and set out. When the servant showed him into the Ford living-room it seemed for the moment that the room was empty. Then, in a dark corner, he was aware of a movement and dimly discerned that Ford was there at his writing desk, now screwing round in his chair to see who the visitor was.

'Hallo! I couldn't see you for the moment. My eyes haven't got adjusted after the glare.'

'This is the coolest corner in the house except for my cellar.' Ford had got to his feet and was coming into the light. What a really tiny man you are, thought Winter. And then—ah! the cellar. The very use of the word conveyed the impression that they were talking intimacies. Ford's sentence had not been so much a sentence as an admission. Winter did not want to talk about the cellar. If possible he was going to avoid ever entering there again.

'Look!' he began brusquely. 'I've just had a visit from Hebechi. I was very short with him because what he had come to say was this. I thought I'd like to let you know. He says that money was taken by Cator and he wants me to intervene. You can guess what I told him, but . . .'

'Oh, really? Oh dear, oh dear!' Ford had his hands lightly clasped across his stomach. He should have been wringing them to be completely in character. 'That is what they always say. If they're caught red-handed, so to speak, they always blame it on to somebody else. They were just carrying it for someone. This is particularly unfortunate because Hebechi has always been such a respectable man. And if he goes spreading this lie around Rasuka it might cause a lot of trouble.'

'My boy says that everyone knows him to be a liar. It seems they think he's the sort of fellow who's getting too big for his boots. I rather thought that they would welcome it. One in the eye for him.'

'Oh, dear no. I don't know why your boy should say that. You see, Hebechi is a man who has got on. He's made a bit of money, bought a house, and so on. Nothing else matters to these people except success. You see, they admire other things . . . You mustn't tell Cator about this. He'd be very upset.' There was a maiden-aunt distress written all over Ford's face.

'The thing to do, it seems to me, is to check up on the books. Then we can show anybody who is interested—I mean, there's the case in black and white.'

'Oh, no, I shouldn't like to do that. I think we've got to take Cator's word in this matter. It wouldn't look very nice to go and ask him to look at the books.'

'Why on earth not? Good Lord, you don't mean you've not seen the books?'

'Naturally Cator's word is good enough for me. I've known him for a long time. Besides Mrs. Cator is a very sweet little woman.'

'This is preposterous. You mean this hundred pounds has

just been written off as dead loss, Hebechi dismissed, and there the matter ends? No, I . . .'

'Oh dear! I can't go questioning Cator.'

'Well, if you don't, I will.'

'No, no. That's out of the question. After all it isn't really anything to do with you. I mean, it isn't your job . . .'

There were no words to go on with. Ford subsided into a chair and looked at his hands. It was not now, as far as Winter was concerned, a question of believing whether Hebechi were guilty or not, or to what extent Cator himself was involved in the affair; it was simply annoyed impatience with Ford for being so cowardly and lazy.

'Now, what's the matter, you two? On such a hot day too.'

Mrs. Ford came into the room looking a little more brisk and alert than usual. She was wearing a riding habit and carrying a whip.

Winter had taken a seat but now he rose. 'Good morning, Mrs. Ford. We were just talking about this unfortunate money business in the administration.'

'Oh, yes! This Hebechi man. He ought to be whipped.' She slapped her crop against her thigh as though she were prepared to administer the punishment herself. 'As a matter of fact I just met him.'

'Where?' asked her husband suddenly.

'Well, I was riding up the wadi and he went striding past. He had a face like thunder. Looked fit to murder somebody. Then when I looked back he was sitting on a rock and looking back up the valley. Naturally I didn't speak to him. I hope the Sultan will take a firm hand with him.'

'Ford, I feel that if this thing is not handled properly, there is going to be trouble. What we'll have to do is to get all the evidence together and present it to the Sultan. Let him decide.'

'No, it's no good. I really don't know what all the fuss is about. The man is dismissed and the money written off. It's very unfortunate, of course. But even if we were to . . . prepare the evidence the crowd will only say that it was all faked. Anything connected with writing and paper is almost supernatural to most of them. Naturally, they'll say, you can prove anything if you do it with papers. Let's leave it. In any case we can't upset Cator. I know he wouldn't like it.'

'I should certainly think not,' said Mrs. Ford. 'Whatever next, I'd like to know?'

What an obstinate pig you are, thought Winter, looking at the manager.

CHAPTER VI: *The Buffalo*

THE VERY FIRST OCCASION THAT FLYNN and Winter went out riding together, the day of the party, they came across a dead buffalo. They returned by the same way that they had gone and as the dead animal had not been there when they first passed by the curious rocks, grey giblety-shaped rocks and some like enormous livers and kidneys, the accident had happened within the previous hour. Winter's horse had taken a wrong turning, pacing out on to an inclined plane of rock that brought him to a position where he could look down and see the dead beast lying in a pool of blood.

'No, not this way,' he shouted back to Flynn, who was some thirty yards behind. 'There!' He waved towards the path that would lead down to the hollow where the buffalo was. But he made no move himself. He continued to look down into the hollow because of the beauty of the dead beast. Someone had crudely tried to cut the animal's throat and from the gash the blood was even now sluggishly trickling. But there was not a tremor in the body. The beast was quite dead. It was an unpleasant sight, he told himself. It would be an unpleasant sight if you told anyone else about it, but, looking down from the height of his horse, he could see nothing but beauty in the colour of the tarnished silver skin and the rich red of ox-blood. One or two sharp-edged flints had taken the blood like opaque enamel. The beast was lying on its side, its legs drawn together, the tail lying clear behind, the head raised above the line of the spine. He might have been wildly galloping for it was the very poise. The exquisitely sensitive line from the point of the horn, along the muscular neck, then up over the shoulder, the length of the spine, the modelled falling away over the buttock to the thick tail, might have been caught in some Chinese print. The eyes were unstained and translucent. A little froth was held in the half-open mouth. The colour! thought Winter, looking at the skin once more. Like rare pewter. Then even as he looked the tail writhed and turned over. It had been caught and constricted when the animal fell.

Winter twitched his horse's head round and the creature delicately picked its way to the main track before turning to the right. They trotted quickly past the buffalo and Winter felt his stomach tensing even though he looked down on it no longer. Flynn was already well ahead, not having given the buffalo more than a glance.

Perhaps in all they had not covered more than eight or nine miles on their journey northwards along the coastal strip. They had passed behind the palace and made down to the sea at a point a little north of the town and then trotted along the firm sand. The plan had been to reach the stone fort that Flynn had spoken about some weeks previously but when they had been riding for some three-quarters of an hour without any sight of it they decided to leave it until another day. Nowhere had they galloped, but now, seeing Flynn some two or three hundred yards ahead of him, a stiff figure that rose and fell on the cream-coloured Arab mare, Winter kicked his heels into the tall horse he was riding and the restless, spirited creature bounded like a dancer. Flynn turned in his saddle to see where his companion had got to. 'I'm coming, I'm coming, I'm coming,' said the drumming hooves on the sand. The sere landscape whirled back towards him, rocks, small shrubs, all fusing to a finely granulated surface that flowed dizzily. The desert thundered like a drum. Winter was standing up in his stirrups, gliding through the air, hatless, happy with speed. In no time he had caught the Irishman up and together they spurred towards the bungalows and the compound which had now come into sight.

Winter was slightly in front and of this he was glad for there was no possibility of Flynn's seeing his face; the Irishman could not turn in his saddle and see the queer exaltation written there. In a moment of speed, when his blood had been flowing a little faster than normal, Winter had learned something. It was a moment like the bursting of a tight-skinned grape within the mouth when, after the tension, there comes sweetness. Oh, it was so easy to forget and be happy! That was the truth of the matter. There was no real remembrance and regret. Even the dead buffalo lying there had not, at first, seemed anything else but a thing of beauty, silver-skinned on the red sand. Winter was excited. Queerly, his dead wife's face flashed upon his sight, even as he rode up to the veranda of his bungalow, and now it brought no chill of pain and bewilderment as before, but a warm comfort like a hot rock to clasp in the hands on a freezing night. There was a creamy lather on the flanks of his horse. Rachid came running out on to the veranda at the sound of the drumming hooves.

'Did you see that dead buffalo?' Winter asked as Flynn came up.

'Couldn't miss it,' said the Irishman shortly.

His mare was much fresher than Winter's mount and pawed

up the ground, backing and turning. 'Shows that somebody's got an enemy.'

'Yes, yes,' said Winter. He did not want to hear about feuds and enemies.

'Those animals cost a lot of money. A creature like that would be—let me see now—well, last year you wouldn't have got one like that for thirty pounds. Yes, I should think that a beast like that would cost fifty pounds nowadays.' Flynn pursued the matter gravely.

Winter dismounted and felt, for the first time, just how sore he was. It was the first riding that he had done for a long time. His legs felt weak. Yes, yes, he was thinking. Who cares whether it is fifty or a hundred pounds? A stupid thing to talk about. But he smiled up at Flynn cheerily, for he was happy.

'You see, it is a good way of getting your revenge. That is what happened back there.' Flynn jerked his head back. 'When things are not sufficiently serious to justify your killing your enemy, just set upon him, drive him off and then kill his buffalo. Means ruin for some of these fellows.'

Winter did not think it a suitable occasion to mention how beautiful he had found the beast. Flynn would not dismount and come in though Winter did his best to persuade him. But he would come early for the party that evening and then they would be able to talk. His steel-rimmed spectacles glinted in the morning sun and he even smiled. Then he was gone, trotting steadily over the sand like an illustration out of a book on equitation. Rachid took charge of the horse: after a clean-up he would ride it quietly down to Rasuka and say that the owner could bring it up at eight o'clock every morning as his master had decided to ride regularly.

For some moments Winter stood on the veranda with his

hands plunged deep into the pockets of his riding breeches. That dead buffalo, he was thinking, and the red sand. How hard it is to know the real things about oneself, and now in inviting everyone to come to his place for a party, Mr. and Mrs. Ford, the Cators, Nellie Leader, Flynn, Plunkett, he was becoming a little more aware of himself. So hard though. It was like, when he had been a boy, lying in the long grass on the bank of a stream, trying to catch minnows with his hands. And now he knew, it seemed that he knew suddenly in spurring past the blood-stained hollow, what a longing in him there was for human contacts. Nellie was already calling him by his Christian name and he had called her Nellie from the first, nothing seeming more natural. But it had been a different kind of pleasure when Ford and then Flynn had, almost accidentally it seemed in the course of their conversation, called him Robert. He had been pleased at the time but now it seemed that he knew why.

Standing on the balcony with the morning sun dazzling on his white breeches although the upper part of his body remained in shadow, he began humming to himself, turning over in his mind the anticipations of the evening to come. He was a bad hand at a party, even as a guest, so that as a host he knew that he did not count. But he was not worried. He was making no plans. There would be food to eat and drinks, and then people would talk, and he would pass from one to the other, talking. Conversation would come easily. He was just bringing people together. And, of course, there would be nothing else for it but one of those semi-serious, semi-jesting conversations with Nellie. That was how they always seemed to talk now, a light conversation that would suddenly, with the expression in her eyes, or the stiffening of his own jaw, take on a double meaning; then they would look into each other's eyes.

He could see now why he had been so pleased when Flynn and Ford had called him by his Christian name. At the time it had given him a small thrill, of which he had been almost ashamed so that he had not confessed the pleasure even to himself. But something had been lit up inside him. Now this thrill was more clearly understood. They were words that crossed the gulfs between human beings. There he was living on a dried-up plateau land, and all other humans on their own plateaux, tragically cut off one from the other. Words like this were bridges thrown across; they were planks, ropes thrown over, and eventually one could pass over completely from one plateau to another and there embrace on the other side of the gulf.

Rachid had rubbed the horse down with a cloth and now he brought him pacing gracefully in front of the veranda so that Winter could see the warm chestnut glowing like fire in the sun. There was a richness of colour that almost turned to purple when the muscle produced long shadows down the flank.

Although two extra boys had been got in to give a hand with the preparations for the evening, and Rachid was very much in charge of them, he was not going to allow that circumstance to cheat him out of the ride on horseback down to the town. The two assistants were elderly men who normally worked in the canteen for the workers inside the compound area. They were slim, dignified men, one with a cluster of white curls on his chin, for all his denial that he was no more than forty years of age, thinking that Winter would refuse to accept him if he were any older; for all that, Rachid bullied them unmercifully, sitting on a stool in the middle of the floor and quietly watching them walk about until one of them made a mistake. Then Rachid would be on him like a flash, calling upon those within hearing distance to wonder at the stupidity of this curly-chinned one who wanted to put hot water into a glass tumbler. His criticisms were accepted meekly for it was recognized that he had superior knowledge in this matter: that justified all the bullying in the world. To these two Rachid gave full instructions before departing on the back of the hired horse, his flowing gown tucked up around his waist so that his loose white drawers were to be seen reaching right down to his ankles.

Winter had given him instructions not to gallop the horse, but as soon as the boy was on the far side of the rocks and out of sight of the bungalow, where at the last moment he had caught a glimpse of Winter's white breeches on the balcony, he kicked his heels into the side of the horse and galloped wildly down the slopes towards the white buildings of the town. He loved riding and did it as naturally as he could swim, with the grace of animal beings. As he rode he held the reins high above the horse's neck with his left hand and rhythmically smacked the horse's flank with his right. He roared with laughter, now sitting bolt upright and then bending low over the horse's neck as though to whisper something in his ears.

With a swerve so sudden that Rachid almost pitched out of the saddle the horse attempted to leave the path as a white-robed figure seemed to rise up out of the very ground in front of them. Rachid cursed and drew the reins back firmly in his hand.

'O fool! May your house be——' As he tried to calm the excited beast he hurled the picturesque Arabic curses at the man who had stopped them, who now that he had succeeded in his object was waiting quietly by. Rachid was so busy patting the horse on his great, curving neck and whispering soothing things in the quivering ears that he had no eyes for the stranger.

'Is there no . . . ?' he began once more. The horse slipped

and staggered on the stones, biting furiously for a foothold. At length Rachid slid from the saddle and took the soft muzzle between his two hands. 'Oh, my dear, my uncle,' he murmured to the frightened horse, and then kissed it gently with his lips.

Then he turned to the stranger and saw that it was Hebechi. But it was no longer the conscientious accountant dressed in an Egyptian-made cotton suit who stood there. He was wearing the loose white robe of the country and around his temples a protecting length of striped cloth. His feet were bare.

'May your wealth increase,' he said to Rachid.

For the moment Rachid was so startled at the apparition that he forgot to rave. He could only pat the horse's muzzle and stare.

'O Hebechi, may you prosper!' Looking into the ex-clerk's twisted face, Rachid could see how much he had been humiliated.

'I wanted to speak to you. I saw you coming on the white man's horse. I've been watching him all the morning. I would have stopped him but there was that other with him.'

Rachid watched the blaze in the eyes. He knew that the other was furious at having to appear dressed as a native when for so long he had prided himself on being the European. Undoubtedly he would still have his European clothes at home for it was unlikely that already he had been forced to sell them for food. Rachid had heard that apart from being dismissed from the Company there was going to be no further action against him.

'O Hebechi, where is your fine suit and your white umbrella that is green underneath? Where is that now, eh?' he mocked him. And then suddenly turning to rage: 'What do you mean by jumping out like that? You might have broken the horse's leg. Or my neck for that matter! It would have been a good thing if I had run you down.' Rachid was quite merciless in his mockery and in his anger. He shouted at the now silent man at the top of his voice.

Hebechi was controlling himself with some difficulty. He was five years older than this boy who was, after all, only a common servant. Besides he hated the way those white teeth flashed in the sun.

'O boy, I stopped you to give a message to your master. Tell him that I ask his permission to speak with him once more. I shall be waiting in these rocks'—he waved his hand back to the rocks that looked down on the bungalow—'at sunset, and if your master comes out on to the balcony and waves at that time then I shall know that I am to come.'

'That is impossible,' said Rachid with contempt. 'Dost thou think that my master would come out on to the balcony and wave to thee when there are friends in his house? He is receiving friends to-night and will not be waving at any rocks.'

But Rachid was not quite sure in his mind what Winter thought of this Hebechi business. He had made one mistake already in talking to Winter about the ex-clerk and did not wish to do anything now that would cause his master any displeasure.

'I am not offering you a bribe, O boy. I am telling you to do it,' said Hebechi abruptly. The party made no difference to him. He had so prepared himself for this meeting at sunset that it was inconceivable that anything should now stand in the way. And he made off without another word, striking up amongst the sun-glittering rocks at right-angles to the path that Rachid would have to follow down to the town.

Meanwhile Winter was feeling very pleased with himself. He walked into the living-room and peopled the chairs with the guests that he was expecting. He could even smile at himself in

thinking that in two adjacent chairs, those immediately opposite the bead-curtained door that led into the kitchen, he
would be having that anticipated conversation with Nellie. He
hoped that they all came early. The room was fragrant with the
perfume of roses that he had had sent up from the town early
that morning. It was no good leaving such arrangements to the
last minute in Rasuka. He went into his room to change and
make preparations for the walk up to the office where he would
put in a couple of hours' work that morning. At least a couple
of hours, he promised himself.

Sitting on the edge of his bed in order to lever his boots off,
he found himself looking straight at the portrait of his wife. The
effort of removing his riding boots had contorted his face up
into a grin and even when he had safely tucked them away
under the bed his face still wore the grin. He was grinning at the
portrait. Then he put out a hand and patted it, amazing himself all the while. How pleasant it was to ride out early in the
morning, even in the company of such a man as Flynn. Between
himself and Flynn there had been a growing coldness during
the past few weeks and he, himself, was at a loss to explain it.
The genuine sympathy that Flynn had extended on his arrival
was mainly because of the death of Joyce; and once that
sympathy had been expressed, once the firm handshake had
been given, once Flynn had looked at him in his own peculiar
way there had seemed little further contact of spirit between
the two men. Indeed he was aware of a reaction away. That's
because he knows that Joyce is dead, Winter thought, and he
wants to say something consoling. And I don't want to be consoled. There is nothing to be consoled over. When they met,
therefore, their conversation was always on the surface. He
thinks I'm closing a door in his face, thought Winter. And
then, he's so rigid and—ceremonial.

Plunkett was the first of the guests to arrive. Winter knew to the minute what time it was when the doctor crossed the threshold, for the invitations had been for six o'clock and from time to time Winter had been looking irritably at the clock as soon as that time had passed. Plunkett arrived at quarter past six and looked round the room cheerfully.

'Hm! First here, eh? Well, what d'you expect? Yes, don't mind if I do.'

Winter gave him a whisky, poured one out for himself and the two of them went out on to the balcony. 'Sorry I'm late, but I'm getting old and stiff. Had to sit down on a rock and rest twice. About time the Company made some decent roads so that we could have cars. God! Now where did you get this whisky?'

They were looking out on to a deserted landscape. Now that the sun had so much declined there was a warmth of colour in the rocks and sand; even the Sultan's white fantastic palace looked mellow among the black palm trees. Salt crystals in the sand of the wadi bottom glittered like water. Against the edge of the eastern escarpment the sky was as hard and blue as enamel. Sunset would not be for another hour yet. Even if the other guests were already well on their way nothing would be seen of them from this side of the house and although Winter was impatient he did not wish to show his impatience by going to the back of the bungalow and looking through a window. He and Plunkett remained standing.

'But you didn't expect 'em all to turn up, did you?' said Plunkett as though reading his thoughts. 'Have you ever seen 'em all gathered together?'

The walk over the sand had made him sweat profusely but the whisky put him in a good mood. 'Negative magnetism— all pulling different ways. Me, for example, I don't want to see

'em! Got to hate the very sight of 'em, but thought it wouldn't
be very—how d'ye say? wouldn't be very neighbourly not to
come. But you'll not expect much from me. Understand me
pretty well, I suppose. Give the old chap a glass of whisky and
he'll be happy. Well, it's true enough in its way, too. And
what's the harm in that, I'd like to know? Does nobody except
me any harm. Which is better than some people. And nobody
really wants to see anybody else here.'

'You're not very encouraging.'

'But, God, it's true, man. Don't mean to tell me you've not
noticed the way everybody seems to avoid everybody else.'

'No, I've certainly not noticed it. You're imagining it.'

'All right, all right! But anyway, the reason why you're so
popular, for the time being, is that nobody minds meeting you.
You're new, you see.'

'Oh, I understand what you mean. You mean that everyone
has got rather tired of everyone else, being shut up with them
for so long. Like people living on a desert island.'

Plunkett put his now empty glass down on the wicker table
and looked at him with as much shrewdness as his aged ponder-
ousness would permit. 'Call it that if you like. I shall be surprised if they turn up, anyway. If they do come it'll only be out
of curiosity to see how you've fitted your place up.'

Winter, it is true, had noticed a certain lack of enthusiasm for
his party. People had accepted his invitation a little off-hand-
edly. 'When is it—next Wednesday? Six? Yes, of course.' And
there had been other things to talk about almost immediately.
Even Nellie had not been very enthusiastic. But she would
come. They would all come. He was sure of that. Even as
Plunkett was wiping his face with a red handkerchief and grunting to himself as though his body had become a burden to
him and was taking control in spite of his best endeavours, the

Fords came round the corner of the bungalow. Winter could not resist grinning at Plunkett. Ford waved his hand as soon as he saw Winter. There was a spring-lamb-like jollity about him.

When Winter had pushed Plunkett gently into the living-room once more and ushered the Fords to follow he noticed that Ford seemed over-excited. He was talking too much for example, rather as though he were anxious to make a good impression. When Winter offered him a drink he picked up an empty glass and did a sort of dance, chuckling in what Winter thought was rather an idiotic way. 'The grape, the grape, I press the grape,' he chanted.

Plunkett immediately spoke up from his chair. 'Any man who thinks that whisky is made with grapes has had a damn bad education. God!' Plunkett had taken his glass away to one of the chairs opposite the bead curtain as though to avoid conversation. Winter noticed where he was sitting and wondered how, diplomatically, he could move him. Those places were reserved.

'Purely figurative, old chap,' said Ford gaily. 'And indeed who cares? It's the grape to me.' He put half an inch of whisky into a tumbler and proceeded to fill up with water. All this Plunkett watched with disgust.

'It seems that we're the first to arrive,' said Mrs. Ford.

'No, me!' said Plunkett. 'Can't you see me?'

'You don't count.' This might have been light-hearted banter, of course, but somehow Winter thought that it was not. Mrs. Ford's attitude seemed tinged with contempt and her own husband was not immune from her attacks. It was obvious that his frivolity annoyed her. But she was not going to allow anyone else to comment on it.

She took a gin and lime and fell into a gloomy silence, sipping

at it. It was the first time that she had been in Winter's bungalow and he could feel her taking everything in, the quality of
the curtains, the design on the carpet, the bare walls. After this
bold appraisement her eyes rose and happened to meet Winter's. She coloured slightly, and made to speak but prevented
herself at the last moment. He knew immediately that she was
going to say the bungalow lacked the feminine touch and had
realized, at the last moment, what an indelicate remark that
would be to make.

'How do you like my tie?' he asked her jestingly. He was
quite annoyed really at the way people had taken the six
o'clock appointment to mean six-thirty, or seven, and was not
a little pleased to find that he was able to banter and cover
it all up.

'In very good taste. Everything in very good taste——' her
husband interrupted, but what he said afterwards was covered
by a sudden hoot of laughter from Plunkett.

'See, he's tipsy already. Tipsy on that stuff. The smell's
enough for some people.'

'At least with the practice that you've had you'll be pretty
well inoculated against anything of the sort,' snapped Mrs.
Ford. But Plunkett continued to roar with laughter and slap his
thigh, closing his eyes with joy. Ford looked across at him with
a bewildered and slightly pained expression on his face, rather
like an innocent old lady who has been accused of a crime she
has never heard of.

Then all Winter's impatience, and Ford's embarrassment,
disappeared when Flynn, together with Nellie Leader and Mrs.
Cator, were shown into the room by a widely grinning Rachid.
Only Plunkett continued to laugh to himself, oblivious of the
new arrivals who seemed more used to his idiosyncrasies for
they only gave him a glance.

'I'm sorry we're late,' Flynn began awkwardly, 'especially since I said I'd come early . . .'

'My husband will be along shortly,' Mrs. Cator put in vehemently. She was a little woman, considerably older than her husband, judging by appearances. She had a Jewish cast of features, large nose, rather high cheek-bones, and hair that had some touches of grey over the ears. As she spoke she made violent muscular movements with the whole length of her arm; but Winter was not looking at her, and indeed, hardly listening.

'Good evening,' he said to Nellie. 'How are you?'

'Thank you.' But there was not complete confidence in that smile. She looked tired and the smile trembled on her lips rather out of duty, it seemed to him, than real gladness.

'Anything the matter?' he asked. 'But please sit down.'

'No, what could be the matter? Thank you.'

'I like the——' He made a gesture with his hand. She had gathered her fair hair back with a length of green ribbon.

'Thank you.' She didn't seem very interested in the compliment and Winter had the feeling that she was trying to disassociate herself from any particular success her personal appearance might be scoring. This is me, but as for me, I don't think very much of it, she seemed to be saying.

'There, what did I tell you, Winter?' Plunkett interrupted from his chair. He had his glass balanced on his knee, and was watching it with the greatest concentration. 'He didn't want to come! He was afraid to come. Just what I told you, you see. Really I must congratulate you, though, in having succeeded so far. There are—let me see,' he raised his eyes and counted everyone solemnly, 'counting yourself there are two, three—five—seven. That's more than I'd thought possible.'

Mrs. Cator immediately snapped at him with Hebraic violence. Her face went scarlet and she rose from her chair to

make her gesticulations almost in Plunkett's face, which seemed
to register nothing but delighted joy.

'How dare you talk like that! My husband will be coming
immediately to face you and face all of them. He's not a coward
—nor a whisky-swiller.'

'Be a lot better for 'im if he was.'

'You're just a low, sneering good-for-nothing. You wouldn't
dare to talk like this if he was really here. You can only talk
behind his back. I will not have it—everyone is against us!' Her
voice rose to a wail and she seemed on the point of striking
Plunkett when Nellie caught her two elbows from behind and
coaxed her back to her seat. Any other woman would have
stormed out of the house but Mrs. Cator apparently allowed
herself more violent displays of emotion than most people and
did not take even herself too seriously.

'If you would only listen to what I was saying instead of flying off the handle it'd be better for you. Nobody wanted to
come to this party and I wasn't meaning your husband in particular. However, if the cap fits . . .'

'No, really, Plunkett'—it was Ford who had tried to interrupt, for Winter himself could not take all this fierceness to
heart except in so far as it seemed to involve Nellie. Hers was
the only presence of which he was really aware. About her
there was a kind of sombreness as though she was depressed
by the quarrel. Now that Mrs. Cator had consented to sit
quietly down Nellie was content to sit at her side not apparently listening to what was being said. Although Winter looked
at her repeatedly there was never any answering regard. About
her eyes there was a darkness, almost as though some little
while before she had been crying.

'He is coming. He will come, and then we shall see,' insisted
Mrs. Cator. 'He said that he would come, didn't he, Nellie?

It was just that he was tired after his work and wanted to take a cold bath. He wanted to arrive fresh. That was what he said, wasn't it, Nellie?' The question was urgent and pleading.

Nellie lifted her eyes and looked directly at Winter.

'Yes, of course he is coming. He will be here any moment now.'

As if there had never been any argument a dead calm descended on the room. Winter was oppressed by the thought that the evening was foredoomed to failure. Even Ford, who had found nonsense in plenty to chatter, was silently fingering his glass. By accident, it seemed, all the guests were grouped at one end of the room and Winter, in going to the bead curtain to see where Rachid and the sandwiches had got to, found them all regarding him when he turned to face them once more. Simultaneously their eyes were raised, it seemed, some looking coldness, none warmth, and only in the red weary eyes of Plunkett the gleam of humour. It was a wry humour. Winter's own look faltered. He was confused by the sense of distance between him and them. In the eyes of Mrs. Cator there was even a hate; surely that is meant for Plunkett and it happens that she is now looking at me!

'Well, what about some sandwiches,' he said, coming forward cheerfully into the room. He had eyes for nobody else but Nellie now. Light up! cheer up! happiness! he wanted to say. I've not done anything.

'Look at the sunset,' he went on. Through the open window they could see not the sunset but the sand and the rocks lit up vividly from within as though they were bloody membranes over a bright light. 'Well, not the sunlight—I mean the reflection.' The heads of the guests turned to look out of the window and caught some tinge of the warm colour on their noses and cheek-bones. The window was a panel pouring radiance into the room.

'Sah!' It was Rachid's soft voice breaking the silence.

'Come on, everybody. Have some sandwiches,' for that is what Rachid was bearing on the tray, 'sandwiches for everybody's taste. Let me see now, what are there—fish, cheese, tomato, beef. Oh, and let's have a bit of light on the subject.' He snapped the electric light on and everything in the room blazed yellow and only the panel of the window was a sombre jewel. A wave of cheerfulness ran through the guests in spite of what Winter felt to be an underlying hostility.

Rachid alone stood uncertainly in the middle of the floor, after setting the tray of sandwiches down on a low table.

'Come on, lad. Pass them round. *Igri,*' said Winter cheerfully. But Rachid had been reminded by the sunset. 'Sah, I met one man.'

'Eh! What's the matter?'

'I met Hebechi Effendi, sah.'

Everyone stiffened. Winter himself stiffened. In a flash he thought he understood.

'You met Hebechi? What did he want, the rogue!'

Rachid smiled now as though it was a joke. *'Macnoon,* him. Said he wanted to see you. At sunset he among them big bricks there. Said you were to wave and him come. Just wanted you to go on the veranda and make like this. Then he come speak. Looked very funny in gallabieh.'

'You mean he's out there now. The man must be a fool. Why should he want to see me, of all people? He's been very lucky to get off as lightly as he has done.' As he was talking Winter was looking round cheerfully from one to the other of his guests, addressing them rather than the servant. As soon as Rachid had mentioned the forbidden name there had been a tension and even Winter's words had done little to relieve it. Mrs. Cator had a sandwich poised in her hand. Plunkett alone looked at his ease, and that was because he seemed on the point of dropping off to sleep. It was as though a string had been drawn unbearably taut across the room and even the slightest breathing caused vibrations.

'Let him go to the devil,' said Winter. 'Why should he want to see me, that's what I'd like to know? Come along, you're not eating anything. I'm a rotten host, I know, but at least you can eat my sandwiches.' He had resolved to be especially nice to Mrs. Cator. By a flow of words and moving from one to the other of them Winter was suppressing the image of Hebechi sitting out there among the rocks, waiting for the signal from the balcony. Never since his arrival in Rasuka had he been able to talk so easily and irresponsibly. Even Plunkett pulled himself together and looked surprised. It was a new and more genial Winter that they were seeing.

'Come, you're quite deserting me,' said Ford's wife. 'Look, come and sit here.'

'I should imagine that you're the only cook in Rasuka who knows how to make decent bread.'

'Oh, but he spoils his servants. It would be no good trying to entice them away.'

At last, things were going. There were smiles. And Winter felt suddenly tired and passed a hand across his brow. Why in the name of hell should he want to please these people anyway? Aware now that he was doing all the pulling and they all the resisting, it would have been nothing if they collected their belongings together and suddenly decided to go. All, that is, except Nellie. It was true what Plunkett had said. There were gulfs between them and no willingness to bridge them save on his part. The thought of having to make conversation to amuse them was not stimulating. He thought that he would escape, even for a few moments, and went out on to the veranda where it was already night. It was already night and already too late. There were no stars, nothing beyond the wooden balustrade to give relief to the eyes and he stared out into the velvety blackness.

There were footsteps and Nellie was pressing up against the balustrade at his side.

'You were going to call him, weren't you?' she said.

So far from this being true he knew now that he had only come out on to the veranda in the hope that Nellie would join him. The unbelievable fact was that she was wearing the same perfume that his wife used to wear—a perfume that he could never put a name to, but redolent of summer ripeness and warm, moth-like evenings.

'You've upset everyone terribly, you know.'

'Is that why Cator hasn't come?'

'You know what people are like here. They have to hang together or they're lost——'

'But I've never said that I thought Cator was to blame——'

'No, but you shouldn't have listened to Hebechi or even shown him anything but—well, you should have been angry. That's what you should have done to please these people.'

'And please you?'

They were standing very close together. Behind them, in the bungalow there were low voices and Winter wondered what they were thinking of his remissness as a host. For the life of him he couldn't see how it mattered anyway. The night was warm and the perfume that meant, more than any other imaginable thing, the aura of love was stealing into his being.

The moment was poised on the crest of the breaking wave. He put out his hand and took hers in his: so far from making any objection, she turned her hand over and laced her fingers with his. Yet it was not a moment of love. There was expectancy. In it there was not even much pleasure for him. The room behind them was silent now and the guests might even have been listening, but the thought did not trouble him.

'You know this is only because you remind me of my wife.'

'What a hateful thing to say.'

'What was that?' He started and shot the question out, drawing his hand suddenly away. She recovered it.

'Nothing. A dog barking.'

Yes, perhaps after all that is what it had been. There had been a sound that had been experienced rather than heard, as though the tender fabric of the night had been tinily but coarsely scratched with the point of a needle. He drew even closer to her.

'Or a rock falling,' she suggested.

The silence in the room behind them was at an end. Voices were raised and they could hear Plunkett laughing wheezily. Winter and Nellie drew apart as a step sounded at the doorway. Until they heard her voice they did not realize that it was Mrs. Cator. Quite dazzled by the darkness, she could not see a thing. The 'Oh dear,' that she allowed to escape from her lips was a private expression of anxiety, not meant for anyone's ears.

'Here we are,' said Nellie brightly to her.

'Who is it?—Oh, it's you, Nellie, is it? What an awful party this is! I'm so worried about my husband. He did say that he would come, didn't he?'

'I'm sure there's nothing to be worried about, Mrs. Cator.' Even though she had been dissatisfied with his entertainment, Winter still thought that such comfort was required of him by his duties as a host.

Then Mrs. Cator did a strange thing. She shouted her husband's name into the night as though this were some means of reaching out for him. 'Willie! Willie!' She was in great mental distress, and reached out over the balustrade. 'He isn't there. I don't think he is coming. I want to go home.'

The darkness made no reply to her call. One could fancy that it replied. One could fancy the granite crying, rocks falling in the darkness. Winter thought of the dead beast out there among the rocks, the dead buffalo, silver in its pool of blood. A dog barking, Nellie had said, but the buffalo could stagger to its feet and stretch his neck, and bellow once more among the hills.

'Well, we'll go home then,' said Nellie to the frightened woman.

It was as though the guests had been drawn out on to the veranda by the magnetism of the night. Winter recognized them by their voices. Plunkett was still jocular and, apparently, still eating, for the sound of his jaw working in the intervals between actually talking was unpleasantly noisy.

'What's this? Cooler out here?' laughed Ford gaily as though it had been the most daring of witticisms.

Then they were aware that someone was running. Bare feet were racing over the sand towards them and the small crowd of people tensed themselves up to meet the news. They leaned over the balustrade, searching the darkness with their eyes.

'Someone running,' said Ford.

'He's coming! He's coming!' It was he they had all been waiting for. Mrs. Cator began weeping quietly. Winter switched on the veranda light and the area of sand in front of the bungalow was flooded with yellow light.

'It's a man. He's hurt,' said Flynn and hopped down the steps to meet the staggering figure.

'Where is he?' shouted Mrs. Cator hysterically. She had recognized one of the servants, a youth of eighteen or so, who now stood in the light rolling enormous eyes and clutching his shoulder, which was black with blood. He was so exhausted and his breathing came so painfully that he could do nothing but stand there and look at them.

'What's that?' said Flynn, shaking him by the uninjured shoulder.

'Misser Cator——' he said, and then a jumble of Arabic. Flynn made him repeat it. Then they all understood. Cator and this boy had been making their way across the sand when they had been attacked by a man with a dagger. Cator had been stabbed in the back immediately. The boy had been wounded in the shoulder but had managed to get away.

'Damn his eyes! Now I've got to go and look at him,' grumbled Plunkett. 'Fool of a man to get himself stabbed.'

'Bloody well stay here if you want to,' Winter flashed at him.

'I'll come. I'll come,' he grumbled. 'Go and get a revolver. And some torches. I'm not going out there without a gun.'

The three men, Winter, Flynn and Plunkett, travelled at the pace set by the slower of the three. The old doctor grumbled all the way across the sand as though the attack had taken place specially to drag him out when he preferred to be drinking whisky. Winter was sweating with anxiety.

CHAPTER VII: *Ruler and Ruled*

Bᴜᴛ ᴄᴀᴛᴏʀ ᴡᴀꜱ ɴᴏᴛ ᴅᴇᴀᴅ. ᴀꜰᴛᴇʀ ᴄᴜᴛ-
ting away his coat and looking at the wound Plunkett went so
far as to say that it might not even be very serious, although it
was always difficult to tell in a stab wound. There was no
knowing quite how deep the penetration had been and, in con-
sequence, just what organs had been affected. But, as Plunkett
said afterwards, he could see immediately that the wound was
too high up under the scapula for the lung to be involved. The
assailant had not made a good job of it at all—just this one
wild plunge downwards and a little outwards—it was this
which saved Cator—and then he must have run away. 'Not an
expert murderer,' said Plunkett with a note of something like
regret in his voice. Cator had lost a great deal of blood.

'Probably the worst thing that can happen to him now is
that he'll catch pneumonia,' said Plunkett.

The others stood round shining their torches down while
Plunkett carried out his examination.

'Hm! He'll do! Remind me to tell you something in the
morning, Winter.'

They removed their coats to wrap round Cator. Winter
realized how cold the night air was and shivered.

'We'll take him to your surgery?'

'Must clean that wound and probe it. No knowing what's walked in there.'

As they carried him Cator began to groan.

'That's a good lad! That's a good lad! You're all right now, if I don't saw your leg off absent-mindedly.'

'Hadn't somebody better go and tell Mrs. Cator?' asked Ford.

'Yes, but don't bring her up to the surgery for at least a couple of hours. You can tell her that the wound itself is not very dangerous. I think he's fainted out of sheer fright. That and the loss of blood. Ah, yes, he'll be on the club for a bit with this.' It amused Plunkett to talk like a panel doctor.

As soon as they reached the surgery Cator came round completely and could lie on his stomach drinking a cup of hot tea while Plunkett ran a wide bandage around his torso. He was almost contemptuous of the wound now. 'Done with a pen-knife, anyone would say.' Of course he was exaggerating but in his experience patients liked their disabilities to be scornfully minimized.

'Someone attacked me,' he said at last.

'So it seems,' remarked Plunkett dryly.

'But somebody stabbed me!'

'Who was it, d'you know? Catch any glimpse?'

Winter had never seen Cator in a milder mood. Still lying on his belly, he clasped the mug of hot tea between his hands like a man on a picnic.

'Stabbed,' he said once more, very gently. 'Of course, it was Hebechi.'

'You sure o' that? I mean, if you didn't see him . . .'

'No, I didn't see him. It was Hebechi.' But there was no bitterness, no anger in anything that Cator said. There was even a slight smile on his face. Winter and the doctor stood and looked at him. Ford had already gone back to reassure Mrs. Cator.

'This'll be a serious thing for Hebechi.' Winter, it seemed, was more upset and angry by the affair than anyone else. Ford had been subdued and a little absent, the doctor was sustained by a professional jocularity, but Winter felt as guilty as though he had struck the blow himself. 'Thank God it's not serious, anyway,' he said.

Cator drank some more tea and then smiled up at him. 'Oh, I don't know,' he said in a stupid, weakly way, like a schoolgirl who has taken too many gins. For some reason or other he was as self-satisfied as a cat. He made no inquiries about his wife and when she burst in on him was quite undemonstrative. He even told her that she must go because he wanted to sleep and the doctor was going to allow him to sleep there that evening.

Standing in the next room with Winter while this conversation was going on, the doctor found a bottle of gin in the cupboard and withdrew the cork with a squeak. 'I'll tell you something, Winter. Sure you won't have a drop? Well . . . It isn't that I don't like Cator. I'm quite indifferent to him. But it would have happened if it had been you who'd got yourself stabbed, anybody I mean. When we got there and found that it wasn't as serious as all that—you know it's not that I'm callous or anything like that—but, well, I was disappointed. And all doctors are like that. Doctors like people to be badly hurt— oh, yes, they do at bottom. Especially in the street. Then they can show everyone just how important they are. The first time—' the doctor said, quite earnest and quite sober in spite of the amount of liquor he had put away that evening—'the first time I realized that was when I saw an accident for the

first time in me life. I mean actually see it with me own eyes—
that doesn't happen as often as you might think. It was just
after I qualified. Well, I was walking along a road, latish at
night, but there was a good moon. A bit farther along the road
there was a level crossing leading out of a what-d'you-call-it—
a—?'

Winter couldn't imagine.

'A place where they shunt—a marshalling yard! And for
some reason or other there was a goods train parked right
across the road. There was a man with a red lamp in case of
traffic. Well, just as I was walking along I heard something or
other overtaking me at a hell of a bat. I turned. It was a damn
big truck, big as a house, tearing along that road at God knows
what speed.'

The doctor's face was very close up against Winter's, breathing the fumes of gin into it, but Winter's thoughts were in the
next room. He could not understand why Cator was so quiet
and passive about it all. Still less could he understand why
Cator could smile and give the impression that it was all something of a joke. Of course, it had been a shock. Shock would
affect a man's mind in strange ways.

'I knew that truck couldn't stop. I knew that the driver—
blast his eyes—must have been tight—because he couldn't see
the train, nor the man waving the red light, nor nothing. Anyway, the truck went into the train with a wallop. It hit it at an
angle so there wasn't so much damage done as all that. I can
tell you I legged it up that road just bubbling over with enthusiasm. I was the first one there. I lugged open the door of the
cab and, my God, I shall never forget my disappointment when
that idiot of a driver just leered at me from his driving-wheel
and said—oh, what the hell did he say?—"What-ho, mate!"

and then went fast asleep. I could've punched his jaw for him, the bastard. His windscreen was lying in splinters round him, the bonnet was folded up like an opera hat—and this lout hadn't got a scratch. Ah, I was young in those days. I tell you, Winter, I could've wept. The least I expected when I opened that door was to find the driving-wheel through his abdomen. Well, since those days I've had no illusions. And Cator has been a great disappointment to me. A great disappointment.'

Since her arrival it seemed that Mrs. Cator had hardly ceased screaming and protesting for longer than was absolutely necessary for the taking of breath. She supplied the background noise for everything that Plunkett had been saying.

'She's had about enough of that. Must pack her off now.' And he went through into the reception room where Cator was lying.

'That's enough now. I can't have you upsetting me like that. I've got a delicate constitution. Puts me all on edge. Drives me to drink. There, there, now. Off with you. He's all right. Probably do him good in the long run.'

Winter had followed Plunkett. Nellie was standing at the foot of the operation couch on which Cator was lying, but as soon as she heard Winter's step she looked up and smiled. He was delighted to see that the smile was replaced almost immediately by an expression of harassed tiredness. It had been a smile all for him. Her eyes had seemed the largest things in the room.

'Has nothing been done about catching Hebechi?' he demanded.

'You're sure it's Hebechi?' Ford asked. He looked like a sparrow dressed up as a man in a children's comic strip.

'Obvious, isn't it?'

Cator seemed to be taking not the slightest interest in the proceedings. He had finished his mug of tea and was blinking his eyes lazily now at one, now at the other of them. Plunkett tried once more to get rid of the visitors, but even as he was pointing out that it was his bed-time they heard hooves clattering on the shards in the sand in front of the dispensary. A horse shudderingly neighed.

'Wouldn't surprise me if somebody else had been attacked,' said Plunkett. 'You'll have to get off that couch in that case. The third time he'll just about have got his hand in. This'll be a nice, nasty one.'

But it was the Bash-Shawish from the barracks to say that a man had just given himself up to them for murder. It was, of course, Hebechi. Guessing that the result of the crime would probably be lying in the doctor's surgery, the Guard commander had come over immediately. He stood in the middle of the floor, with the door wide open behind him, legs apart, smiling broadly. He was wearing a khaki peaked cap, with a silver lion as badge. The rest of his uniform only went down to his waist, the sort of jacket that a private soldier would wear in the British Army, and beneath that was the flowing skirt of his white robe. He was a handsome fellow and knew it. He wanted to see the corpse or, more hopefully, the corpses. When he understood that there were no corpses, not even one corpse, his smile disappeared immediately. He looked at Cator respectfully enough, but conveyed the impression that he would have preferred seeing him under sadder circumstances. But he cheered up a little at the thought that Hebechi would be hanged, or shot, or something, in any case. A serious view could be taken of this sort of thing.

'God blast it!' Plunkett suddenly shouted. 'Where's the other man?'

'What other man? Oh . . .'

'You see what I mean,' the doctor went on indignantly.

They all looked at each other, a little bit ashamed.

'Well, really, I am sure that it has all come as such a terrible shock to all of us . . .' said Ford.

'Look,' said Plunkett, seemingly possessed of a devil, and rushing round his surgery, putting first one thing and then another into a leather case. Then he was out through the door and they could hear him pacing over the sand in the direction of Ford's bungalow.

'I think he's making too much fuss, don't you?' said Ford.

'Wanted to impress us,' Winter mumbled, looking at Nellie, who was trying to persuade Mrs. Cator to go and allow her husband to sleep. The Bash-Shawish, seeing that no one had the slightest interest in him any longer, sat in a chair and amused himself by filling a hypodermic syringe with water and squirting it into the air. He was resolved to make up for the disappointment over the murder in some way or other.

'You two can't go by yourselves. If you'll wait until Plunkett comes back I'll see you home.' Winter found these words coming so curtly to his lips that they sounded like an order. He turned to the soldier and spoke to him in Arabic. What had Hebechi said, he wanted to know, and why had he given himself up, anyway? Why hadn't he tried to escape?

The Bash-Shawish put the syringe back into the sterilizing tray and found a spare piece of elastoplast which he stuck on the back of his hand with evident pleasure. Winter's questions surprised him very much, but he would not have shown this for anything.

Actually he had only seen Hebechi for a few moments. The orderly had come to him, the captain of the Guard, and reported that a man had given himself up for murder. How many

murders? the Shawish had asked, implying that the information as just given was almost unworthy of notice. The orderly
had said that Hebechi had confessed to killing a Frangi and a
Rasuka man, so the Bash-Shawish, now grunting his approval,
had gone to the cell and stirred Hebechi with his foot. 'How
many murders?' he had asked again. Hebechi was lying flat on
his face like a man in a fit. He made no answer. 'You see,' said
the Bash-Shawish authoritatively to the man on guard. 'This
man has murdered and now he will not talk. I would not wonder but that it is a serious matter.' Then immediately he had
come over to the doctor's bungalow.

That had been the truth of the matter, but in telling the story
to Winter, the Bash-Shawish thought it could be made more
worth the telling. Hebechi, in his insolence, had even threatened
to strike the Bash-Shawish himself. He had come into the office
and insolently boasted of the two murders that he had committed. He had insisted on a chair being given to him so that
he could take his rest while telling the story, and it was only
when this was refused him that he became violent. 'Myself, I
had to disarm him,' the Bash-Shawish said, giving a yelp of
pain as he tried to remove the piece of elastoplast from the
back of his hand.

Winter thought that it would have been much more con-
venient if Hebechi had not surrendered himself but had made
off into the interior. He, Winter, would have followed him unmercifully and would himself bring back the guilty man to
Rasuka. He would be killing two birds with one stone. More
than anything else he would have liked to be the person to
catch Hebechi: and he would have made that journey into the
interior which he knew that he must make some day, anyway.
They would not have hurried back. They would have spent
nights among the rocks with a hot fire in their faces and the

cold starlight on their backs. But eventually they would have come back to Rasuka and, yes, Hebechi would be hanged or whatever they did to them in this part of the world. But he wasn't concerned about Hebechi. Winter was thinking of himself.

'Perhaps the Shawish could see us home. I think Mrs. Cator should have some rest,' said Nellie.

'I don't want to go. I want to stay. How could I leave my chick?' Mrs. Cator at once threw herself on her husband's neck, but he, still lying on his stomach and looking straight ahead, only frowned and told her not to make so much fuss.

'You must mind his back,' said Nellie, trying to draw the excited woman away.

For some reason this seemed to put Mrs. Cator into a temper. She drew herself up to her full height, looked straight in front of her—this meant that she was now looking at the point of Nellie's chin—and began demanding on what right she was attempting to keep husband and wife apart. If anyone knew how to look after her husband it was she herself. She knew what was best for him and she had not the slightest intention of leaving him.

The only person who was pleased by all this was the Bash-Shawish, who sat watching her with his legs apart and the sort of sympathetic smile on his face with which one awaits the end of a poem that a child has learnt by heart. Winter was so angry that he went to the door to see what sort of a night it was. The moon had come up but it was old. The sky and its stars were clear. The valley was in obscurity and there would be need of torches for the return journey. If Mrs. Cator would not return now Winter had made up his mind to take Nellie home.

Even as he had come to this decision and turned to rejoin

the rest he heard a footstep on the steps leading up to the veranda.

'Who's there?' asked Winter. It could hardly be Plunkett returned so quickly.

'It's me.' Flynn came into the shaft of light shining from the doorway and kicked the sand from his boots.

'Where've you been?' Winter had forgotten all about him. Come to think of it, he couldn't remember having seen Flynn since the arrival at the scene of the attack. Winter stood in the doorway so that Flynn had to push him politely in order to pass.

'Where've you been to?' Winter insisted, following him into the room.

Before answering, Flynn smiled all round and then went over to Cator. 'I met Plunkett on the way up. He told me that everything was all right. Hallo, Mrs. Cator! Nothing to worry about. Hallo, Nellie, my dear. What a shock this has been for all of us.' He was so pleased with himself that he couldn't keep still. First of all he patted Cator lightly on the shoulder, then took steps, first towards Mrs. Cator and then towards Nellie as he spoke to them. His face was damp with perspiration.

'Where've you been?' asked Winter once more, quite irritated by him.

'Dear me! You are curious, aren't you? But, you see, I am so glad to see that everything has turned out so well. Rather spoiled your party, Winter, that's one thing. Where've I been?'

'Would you like a drink? I'm sure that Plunkett wouldn't mind my giving you some of his gin. You look just about all in.'

'Me—all in?' Flynn was quite genuinely astonished. 'I can assure you that I'm fine. That walk over the sand just toned me up.'

'What . . . ?'

'Yes, I know! Dear me, you are impatient, aren't you?' He smiled at all of them merrily. He was a little puzzled why Winter had said that he was all in when it was quite obvious that he was absolutely fine. 'Well, I followed the tracks.'

'What tracks?' Winter asked nervously, almost before the word was out of Flynn's mouth.

'The tracks of the would-be murderer. When you fellows went off I realized that there would be no time to lose. The wind would have blown them over by the morning. Wouldn't they, sergeant?' he asked the Shawish, who didn't understand a word of English. 'But it was very difficult. I know a little about this sort of thing, but he went straight up into the rocks. I hunted around for quite a long time, but I'm afraid that it was useless.' It was obvious that he was pleased not so much by the success of his tracking as by showing that he was a man of the moment in thinking of the vital necessity of following up the tracks when they were fresh.

'Well, I'm sure this is all very nice. Hebechi has given himself up, anyway,' said Winter, getting a bitter sort of pleasure in watching the way that Flynn raised his eyebrows. 'He must have gone straight to the police post. The Bash-Shawish here brought the news.'

Winter felt that he had had the last word.

'Well—if you're ready, you and Mrs. Cator,' he said, turning to Nellie. He took the pair of them home across the sand. Occasionally Mrs. Cator would stop to groan and say that she wouldn't stay in the place a moment longer than was necessary.

The following morning Ford and Winter were sent for by the Sultan. Winter was surprised by this. Ford, as manager of the well and officially the most important European in Rasuka, would naturally be summoned over a question like this. He remembered what Cator had said just after the last visit they had paid to the Sultan. 'He's taken to you all right.' So in all probability there was nothing more in this than a personal preference on the Sultan's part. Uncomfortably, Winter felt that Flynn was the person to be accompanying Ford on a mission like this.

Since his last visit the palace seemed to have had a tidy-up. The doors leading off the reception hall had been newly painted a custard-yellow and, although the door of the room in which he had seen such confusion on the previous occasion was now closed, Winter was sure that the cardboard boxes, the ball of yellow wool and the blue cloth had all been tidied away into some cupboard. Ford and Winter were made to wait in this hall for a minute or so and then the servant, a long-legged Negro, came back to say that His Excellency was now ready to receive them.

His Excellency was sitting behind his glass-topped desk.

'Mr. Ford. Mr. Winter. I send for you on a sad occasion. Please be so kind . . .' He waved his hand towards two chairs. Coffee was brought in immediately.

'Your Excellency is referring to the attack on Mr. Cator?' asked Ford, supping up his coffee in the noisy oriental manner.

Instead of answering the question in so many words the Sultan leaned forward over his desk and to Winter it seemed that he succeeded in inflating his face in anger, like the mask of a lion. The muscles of his neck stood out and the pupils of his eyes showed white all round them.

'This man will be executed immediately, I am in a position to assure you. Mr. Ford knows and I want you to understand, Mr. Winter, the extreme rarity of incidents like this. We here, in Rasuka, are peaceful people. If necessary I will institute torture to keep people in order. This man Hebechi. Would you like to have him tortured before he is executed, Mr. Ford?'

'Good heavens, no! That would be too terrible for words. What I would really like to say is that the death sentence—after all, there *wasn't* a murder, was there?'

'As you know, Mr. Ford, as you know and there is no need for me to tell you, we have few punishments in Rasuka. We don't weigh people's crimes up in weeks and months and years. This man Hebechi must be executed and I think, too, as a sort of example . . .'

'No, Your Excellency, I beg you no. The whole business is terrible enough as it is.' He went on hopefully, 'After all, Hebechi came and confessed. Otherwise perhaps we should not have known who did it.'

Even in the middle of his anger the Sultan allowed himself to smile. 'Yes, we should have known.'

Winter thought fit to ask whether Hebechi would have a trial. It was an unfortunate question.

'Really, Mr. Winter, I am not an *ingénu*. It shocks you that I seem to have decided already that the man will be executed. You think I am going to say something funny, something out of a comic opera—yes, he will have a fair trial and then be shot. You think I am going to say something like that, I suppose? Now, I ask you, what kind of a country do you think Rasuka is? This is most disturbing to me. I am not used to this violence, killings, savagery. Rasuka is a great deal more civilized than certain European countries I could mention, Mr. Winter.'

'I'm sorry, Your Excellency, that was not the sort of impression that I wanted to give.'

There was something grandmotherly about the Sultan's rise of passion. His fat body was shaking and Winter expected him

to put his hand under the desk and pull out a bottle of smell-
ing salts. He wanted to take one of those plump white hands,
so white in contrast to the darkness of his face, and pat it
gently.

'Mr. Ford,' said the Sultan a little more weakly but with
sufficient authority for Ford to give a distinct start.

'Your Excellency.'

'I am to understand that you are reporting this to your Company?'

'Er—yes, Your Excellency. Dr. Plunkett will have to make
a medical report, I suppose. The employees of the Company
have certain medical benefits, and a lot depends on whether or
not they sustained injuries in the course of duty or not.'

'And you, yourself?'

Ford was a little confused. 'Oh, yes, I have the same medical benefits as——'

'You are to make a report, yes? And this report goes to your
Company, yes?'

The Sultan pondered for a moment. The room was filled
with creaking noises as though bare-footed people were pacing
the room overhead, and in the adjacent rooms pressing their
bodies against the flimsy walls. There was a sensation of being
under observation. There was nothing of the sovereign about
the Sultan this morning. His palace, in spite of the smartening-
up, still had the atmosphere of a council-house. This morning
the Sultan was just a cunning man who had been led into a difficult situation through no fault of his own. There were several
things that he could not understand. One of them was his failure to make a good impression by his offer to have Hebechi
tortured before execution.

'Mr. Ford . . . er . . .'

'Your Excellency?'

'Would you like some more coffee? You, Mr. Winter?'

'No thank you, Your Excellency. It was very nice though,' said Ford.

The Sultan was telling himself that after all he was the head of the state. 'This report, Mr. Ford. Would you allow me to see it before it goes?'

There, now it was out! The Sultan continued to lean forward, his fungoid moustache well advanced, to watch Ford's reactions closely. Ford was distinctly embarrassed. His sense of duty told him that he must refuse to allow the Sultan to see his report. It was going to be a delicate matter explaining this to the Sultan for in matter of fact Ford was terrified of him. Actually there was not the slightest reason why the Sultan should not see the report. There was no rule about it and if, for example, Cator or Flynn had suggested that out of courtesy the report should be shown to the Sultan, Ford would have been extremely pleased. But the Sultan had built up an atmosphere. He had sent for them with just this one question to ask —this was quite obvious now—he had looked at Ford with the greatest fierceness, the very way that he had put the question implied that he was conniving at a breach of trust.

'It's a——' began Ford.

'Of course it will be all right,' said Winter.

The Sultan looked at him with no expression on his face at all but in that moment Winter knew that he had been invited to this meeting expressly to say those few words. The Sultan, it seemed, had thought that nobody else would have been so impulsive. Then the Sultan smiled. It was not true that this was the only reason for Winter's presence at the meeting.

A lot of things were now understood. 'You must permit me, Mr. Ford, to make a donation to the funds of your medical services.'

'Your Excellency is very kind.'

Winter thought of Plunkett drinking gin. Funds. Resources.

'On my own behalf I would like to address a communication to your Company. The thing is that I want to *évite*' (he couldn't think of the English word) 'that people think this not to be an orderly, civilized country.'

Winter thought of Rider. The Sultan didn't want official investigations into his territory. He certainly didn't want to see a troopship off the Rasuka landing-stage. And if this could be avoided by torturing Hebechi and hounding his family into the street then these things would be done.

'I think an impression could be made by leniency,' he remarked.

'Yes?' The Sultan cocked a flat ear.

'I think that the . . .' In the middle of the sentence Winter realized that what he was saying was not true. At that moment he had been moved by an impulse to make things easier for Hebechi. If the Sultan sensed this his next remark was small comfort.

'For this attack—and he's been pinching, hasn't he?' The slang expression coming from the Sultan was quaint. 'I should have to give'm fifteen years. You can give three years to a Rasuka man—perhaps he'll live through it. More than that— well, they never live. So it's either a quick death or a slow one. By the way, Mr. Winter, he wants to see you.'

'Who? Hebechi? Wants to see me?'

'Yes, Mr. Winter.' The Sultan had passed round cigarettes and was puffing away contentedly himself, screwing up his eyes and looking blandly into the air. 'Says that if it hadn't been for you there would've been no attacks. Yes? Silly boy, of course. Silly boy. He'll learn.'

He sounded like an old-time schoolmaster.

Well, he would go. He knew that he had no choice in the
matter really. By refusing to go he had an idea that the Sultan
would be amused. But he allowed himself the luxury of coming
to a decision because he didn't quite know how the rest of the
European community would take it. He insisted to himself that
he didn't care. In order to show this he did not refer the question to Ford. The Sultan said that he could have free access to
the prisoner for the whole of the morning. The trial would be
that afternoon and the execution the following morning. A soldier was provided to conduct Winter to the prison and, having
bade good-bye to the Sultan who, now that he had gained his
point, was in an excellent mood, the three of them, Ford, Winter and the soldier, followed the same track through the sand
for some little distance. They passed out under the isolated
gateway, watched curiously by the dirty-looking soldier sitting on guard there.

'I'll come and see you when it's all over,' said Winter and,
not waiting for Ford's reply, marched abruptly off after the
soldier who was already making his way down the slope
towards the town. There was no proper road here. They were
taking a short cut down through the rocks, keeping close to
the mud brick wall of the palace gardens, looking up occasionally with sweat in their eyes because it was hot, to see the cool
swing of the sea in front of them above the white houses and
the mosque of Rasuka.

The wall came suddenly to an end. The prison—Winter
knew it as soon as he saw it—was one of the few buildings in
Rasuka that was built exclusively of stone. The square limestone blocks had been crudely hewn and held together by sheer
weight for there was no mortar. The natural cleanness of the
stone gave the building a military neatness. The men on guard,

one imagined, would have their equipment beautifully clean,
and there would be a tap for them to wash their hands and
feet before carrying out their daily devotions. But when the
soldier had led the way round the angle of the building, Winter saw that the prison was quite in character. The door was
not actually off its hinges but it was sagging awkwardly, probably because the wood had warped. To the right of the entrance was a small room in which a soldier, having removed
his jacket and boots, was fast asleep on a trestle table. A second soldier was in the cell itself, squatting on the floor and
talking to Hebechi. They both looked up when Winter walked
in, hearing the European clatter of his boots. The soldier immediately sprang to his feet and made off. Winter looked
round the cell curiously. Apart from the small ante-room in
which the soldier had been asleep it was the only room in the
prison. In contrast with the heat outside it was astonishingly
cool in here. The two small windows were barred, but in both
cases sufficient bars had been removed to allow a normally
built person to make his escape with ease. This, and the fact
that the door was gaping open and one of the guards asleep
seemed to indicate that all the government of Rasuka wished
was that its prisoners should make their escapes as soon as possible. Then Winter realized that he had been looking all round
him and thinking these irrelevant thoughts because he had not
wished to look at Hebechi and think his thoughts.

'Why don't you escape?' Winter asked bluntly.

Hebechi was sitting on the floor with his back against the
wall, dressed in what looked like a pair of blue pyjamas but
which were obviously the regulation dress for the prison.

You don't look like a man who is going to be executed in
the morning, thought Winter. He wondered why the man did
not stand up when he had entered. Obviously Hebechi seemed

a little surprised by the tone that Winter had taken. Perhaps
he had been expecting a storm of abuse. It was this slight astonishment that gave animation to a face of stone. The ex-clerk
had all the dignity now that he had carried away with him
from Winter's bungalow on the one and only occasion on
which he had visited him.

'Sir,' said Hebechi, and moved slightly. As he did so there
was a slight chink and Winter realized immediately that he
was chained to the wall. That explained the missing bars and
the broken door. The warders had complete confidence in these
manacles.

'Let me see.' Winter bent down and examined the chain
and bolt. Hebechi's wrists were fastened to his ankles and his
ankles to a large ring in the wall. 'Fancy that! Made in Doncaster. See that on the bolt there?'

'Sir?' Hebechi was bewildered. Was Winter going to help
him to escape?

'These chains. It's a funny thing, I say. Just fancy their being
made in Doncaster.'

'Doncaster is in England?'

'Yes. In Yorkshire.'

Winter tugged at the ring in the wall, Hebechi moving over
slightly to give him more room. 'You see, it's in quite firm.
Well made, these chains and things.' He stood up once more
and looked at Hebechi thoughtfully. 'Well, they tell me you
wanted to see me. What's it all about?'

If there had been some inner strength sustaining Hebechi it
deserted him now. He seemed to sag like a sawdust doll, and
found such a weight in his head that he could not raise it and
look at Winter.

'I hope that your God curses you,' said Hebechi as quietly
as though he were crooning over a kitten.

'Eh? What's that?' He had feared that Hebechi would cry, would be in hysterics, would plead his intercession with the Sultan. He had expected anything but this deep, cold anger. But he was pleased. 'What are you talking about, man?'

'May God curse you, that's all.' Hebechi would not look up into Winter's face, but there was nothing of weakness in this. It gave his words an imperious coldness, as though they were spoken beyond all passion and personal rancour. Winter felt that he had been judged.

'You must be crazy.' Winter looked down on him. There was no response. 'Is there anything that I can do for you? Is there anything you would like? Your family, for example.' Winter had mentioned his family deliberately, but there was no response. He was aware that one of the soldiers had lounged into the cell and had slumped into one of the corners to see what was going on.

'God sees,' said Hebechi at last. 'He will judge that you and me—He will judge that all this—all this your fault.'

'You'll be telling me next that I tried to murder Cator and not you.'

'You did,' said Hebechi coolly. 'I struck the blow but you were the force behind it. You knew me. You knew what risks you run when you ignore me. Why should you ignore me? I am a man. And an honest man. I am a thief, am I? I am to be beaten. I am to be dismissed. What else is there for me to do but—yet you could have made everything all right. Why did you not come to me in the rocks, or wave your hand, or stand on the veranda? Rachid told you?'

'But why me,' asked Winter, exasperated, 'any more than any of the others? Why should you pick on me to solve your problems when there's Mr. Ford—and Mr. Flynn . . .'

.   'Because——' said Hebechi.

'What do you mean, "because"? You mean because the others knew you and I didn't, wouldn't know so much about you . . . But look here, I didn't come here to snarl at you, heaven knows. If that's really all you've got to say I'll be going.' He had not wanted to sound so callous, but Hebechi's vehement resentment did not dispose him to much sympathy. 'You'll be pleased to know that Mr. Cator is doing very well, and the other fellow, the boy, well—it was very slight really.'

Hebechi looked up at him with a sort of dazed blankness on his face that arrested Winter in the middle of what he was saying. He thought that the ex-clerk was on the point of saying something, accordingly stopped, and then went on to finish what he was saying.

'What's the matter?' he insisted, rather brusquely.

'Mr. Cator—all right. What does that mean?' Although Hebechi looked at Winter with wide, frightened eyes, it was to himself that he was talking. He ran his eyes round the room and ran the tip of his tongue over his lips.

'Didn't you know that Mr. Cator was not severely injured? He fainted. This is a really good thing for you because he is going to make an appeal for you—or so he tells me. You've been very lucky.'

'He was lying on his face. I know it. I put my foot on his head. I would have struck him again.' The tide of his emotion was suddenly so strong for Hebechi that it could not seep out through the narrow channels of his English and he began wailing in Arabic, rocking himself backwards and forwards, as though this last revelation that his enemy was not in fact dead was too hard to bear. Winter looked down on him in perplexity. Any compassion that he felt he was trying to swamp. As clear-cut a case of attempted murder as you'd see anywhere.

The guard who had been watching this scene with the greatest interest now thought that it was time to intervene. He came and stood by Winter with a conciliatory grin on his face and then bent down to tear Hebechi's fingers from his face. Before Winter had realized what was happening the guard had administered two backhanded slaps across the prisoner's face that brought blood to the lips. Hebechi trembled, his hands on his knees. The guard looked into Winter's face, gave a clumsy sort of salute and went to the back of the cell. This was something that Winter felt that he could not interfere in. The guard would not understand what he meant if he remonstrated with him over his treatment of the prisoner. Besides that, in some obscure way Winter felt that it had been the right thing to do. The prisoner was now in control of himself. There were not even any tears in his eyes.

'See what a dog I am. I am ashamed of myself. That'—he used an explosive noun in Arabic—'hits me across my face and it makes me quiet. It makes me feel that it is all right. I am a dog. I am not even angry with him. If I could stand on his head I would not even kick it.'

Seeing that the Frangi was not going immediately, the guard brought a chair. Impulsively Winter told him that if ever he struck the prisoner again, he, Winter, would personally see to it that he was punished. The guard grinned and retired.

'You go,' said Hebechi, with hostility in his eyes.

'You want me to go? Now look here, Hebechi. You sent for me. I'm perfectly willing to help you. If you want me to help state your case this afternoon—or if there's anything, anything . . . your family, for example.'

'You keep saying my family, my family, just for the pleasure it gives you to see me suffer.' Obviously it was useless to attempt to reason with the man. He was mad with bitterness. 'I would rather that man'—and he nodded towards the guard—

'who comes and hits me across my face than you who comes and laughs at me.' Self-pity now so seized hold of him that for the first time he began to weep, looking up into Winter's face and allowing the great tears to well up from his swimming orbits and go coursing down his cheeks.

Winter got off his chair and sat on the ground just in front of Hebechi. 'Now look here,' he said, genuinely moved. 'I'm not laughing at you. You imagine too many things. You're so sensitive. Let me tell you at once that Cator himself, and Ford and me—we're all going to make an appeal. We find there is no one who can do your job.' All this was untrue, but Winter was beginning to realize that Hebechi had had an unimaginable pride in his work.

'You don't give anything in the right way—none of you. It's always given like something dropped out of your pocket on to the sand. And we've got to run and pick it up. And if we don't pick it up you just leave it lying there. Like the food you give to a dog. Once it's been sniffed it's no good for anyone else. You come and talk about my family so that I cry and am ashamed. I would not cry, you say to yourself. But these natives cry. They do other things than us. We don't have to notice them, not mind.'

This man is going to die to-morrow morning, thought Winter. Mainly because he's so proud.

'There was only one man,' Hebechi went on. 'He was the one man for all of us. You could laugh and cry with him and you wouldn't be ashamed because he'd laugh and cry with you. Once he made a box for a rabbit. He hit his hand with the hammer. He cried. I just came round the corner and saw him throw the hammer to the ground—and he cried—well, like me. He saw me and just said, "Hallo, Hebechi," and went on with his crying. He said, "Hallo, Hebechi, I've hit myself with a hammer," and went on crying.' He stopped and looked at Winter.

'Rider?' There was no doubt in Winter's mind that this was the man to whom Hebechi was referring. If this was the sort of man that he had been, probably giving money away at the same time, no wonder Hebechi would feel more drawn to him than any of the other Europeans. In Winter's experience the man who had allowed undue familiarities from the natives had ended by being despised by them. This, it seems, had happened in the case of Rider, witness the general amusement when his bungalow had been burned down. Indeed, the damage, anyway, had probably been done by one of these natives. That was what you got for being sentimental.

'Yes—he cried! Just imagine that. How could you help loving a man like that? He got you on his side always. Go into his house, use it like your own, read his books. You forgot that he was English. He was a man. He was a man. That was why they were all jealous of him—coming, going, laughing, weeping, giving, taking—that was a good thing, he would take from you as well as give—always starting things and never finishing them. Everyone knew that this was what they should be doing too. They were too proud and lazy.' Hebechi drew back his teeth in bitterness and scorn. The enthusiasm with which he had been talking of Rider had almost caused him to forget his own position. 'He was a god, and that is why he is not dead. If you want to know why he is not dead it is because he is a god and gods can't die, can they?'

Winter feared any talk of death. He could not presume to take the subject up with Hebechi. Especially now that his distress was driving him into this hysteria. It was not an impassioned hysteria. The very thought of Rider gave Hebechi calmness and a fixed point in the air on which he could rest his eyes. It was a more or less neutral subject, Winter thought, and it was what he wanted to talk about. . . .

'What sort of a fellow was he to look at, this Rider?' He had been on the point of saying 'Mr. Rider,' and realized that such formality would have sounded ludicrous to Hebechi with this idealized scoutmaster in mind. That is what Rider must have been—a scoutmaster, a prefect.

'Cool-looking, and he had white teeth.'

'What d'you mean—"cool-looking"?'

'He always looked cool, that's all. He's hard to describe. Always seemed to have cool air blowing round him, blowing between his shirt and his body.'

This gave a picture of a thin man, his clothes hanging on him.

'Laugh very high in the air—like this!' Hebechi gave out an amazing cachinnation, the shrill laughing of an old, old man, and yet with something coarse and bird-like in it. Winter thought of the rooks in an elm before evening.

'He used to laugh like that.'

Hebechi drew his lips in tightly. 'I would like to sleep.'

Winter felt that he had been dismissed. 'I shall see you this afternoon. I don't want you to persist in this idea that you are being persecuted. So far as we can we want to help you. You're a very good clerk.'

Hebechi's eyes were closed, but there was a scornful smile on his lips. Listen to the Frangi talking, he seemed to be saying.

Winter felt a wild spasm of anger take hold of him, but he restrained himself from speaking. You're a difficult, stubborn-headed, proud blighter, you are. Well, you'll see. That's all. . . . The desire to utter these words was so strong inside him that he could barely trust himself to say good-bye. He walked

quickly out of the prison, climbed the hill in the blinding sunshine and the heat, walked straight into the palace where he
asked to see the Sultan. The Sultan was not there, but Winter
was received by a man who claimed to be the Sultan's secretary, a quick-moving little man in a green turban who talked
out of the side of his mouth.

The merest touch, the merest indication, the merest word
will be enough for me to understand your business. The secretary seemed to be saying this by deliciously wriggling his
thin body. It was as if he seized a piece of the atmosphere
which became palpable under his hands and he rounded it into
a waxy convolution. Winter hesitated about telling him his
business. When he did so, he regretted it immediately.

'Oh, no, sir. His Excellency has quite made up his mind.
This man will be executed. There is no possibility, I assure
you—not the——' A flutter of the hands and a trembling of
the eyelids.

Winter left the palace in a greater rage than he had left the
prison.

He would go to see Ford immediately. He was in such a
hurry to cover the ground that, occasionally, in spite of the
heat, he broke into a trot: then, as though realizing the pointlessness of it all, slowed down and kicked unnecessary pebbles out of his path. Once or twice he stopped to get his toe
well and truly under a particularly large one. To-day there
was a difference in the substance of the morning. The sunlight
burned down as clearly, the more distant rocks rippled in
haze, there were as few people in sight as usual at this time of
the day. But somewhere a pulse was not beating. For a while
he stopped to adjust himself to the new omission.

Mrs. Ford came out to meet him. She had seen him coming
across the sand. 'I'm not a one to worry, believe me,' she said

with exaggerated laziness. She rested one hand on the wooden balustrade and Winter stopped with one foot on the step to look up at her. Although it was possibly as late as eleven she was still dressed in a wrap. Her fair hair was loosely tied behind.

'Worried about what? Is your husband here?'

Mrs. Ford was obviously setting out to give the impression that casual amusement became her. Her eyes were half closed, and she spoke with a controlled drawl. Yet Winter was well aware that she had not come out on to the veranda, had not been watching for the approach of anyone, because this morning she saw herself as an amusing sophisticate.

'What are you frightened of, Mrs. Ford?' He endeavoured to speak as gently as possible, but he hated the falsity of it. He felt like spitting in her face.

'Haven't you noticed that the Diesel isn't working? They're not working at the well this morning. Perhaps there's a strike, I dunno. Perhaps they're going to attack us and massacre us all. Take your pick.'

It was the pulse that was not beating.

'Where is your husband?'

'He went up there about an hour ago. But——'

'It's absurd to worry about a thing like this. The Sultan is much too anxious to keep foreign control out of his country to allow anything like this. He thinks in terms of gun-boats and English troops being landed.'

'Don't tell me that that old fox takes you in too. That line of talk is all right for my husband, but you . . . Well, I'm frightened, anyway.' She said this as positively and with as little outward sign of emotion as though she were saying that she was thirsty and could do with a cup of tea.

'And I tell you there's no need to be frightened. Your hus-

band and I only saw the Sultan an hour or so ago. Didn't he tell
you?'

'That old fox!'

'I'll go on up to the well.'

'You're as easy to take in as anybody. Should have thought
you had more common sense.'

It was obvious that she did not wish him to go. Although she
made no movement, he at once understood that she was wearing
nothing under her wrap. It was the expression in her eyes.

'You're not frightened.' He himself was a little bit amused.

'All right, then. I'm not frightened. Have it your own way.
You're always right, I suppose. You never make any mistakes.'

'Well, I'll be going to the well now.'

'Yes, I expect you'll find Nellie there. Unless Mr. Flynn has
given her the morning off. She's quite a favourite, isn't she?'

Although to begin with he had been a little amused, for it was
after all quite flattering, that she should have made such advances to him, he began to get out of temper once more as he
realized that her action had been due not so much to any desire
for him; no, quite honestly he did not think that the woman
wanted him; it was because she was frightened. Yes, that was
genuine enough, that fear. She wanted to be comforted and
soothed.

He found Ford in his office talking with Flynn.

'Why isn't the Diesel working?'

'It'll be going in half an hour. Just a routine check-over.'
Flynn answered for Ford.

'Saw your wife. She was quite worried. Thought there was
going to be a riot.'

'A riot? Because the Diesel isn't working?'

'She thought everyone was on strike.'

'Oh, no! It's not anything like that. She should know better than that. A strike here is quite impossible.' Ford went over to the window and looked out at one corner of the derrick. Everything stank of oil.

'I think we've all been upset by this unfortunate affair of Cator. We're liable to think that anything can happen. I suppose that is what it is. However, she will hear the engine in about ten minutes' time and then she will know that everything is all right. Everything will be all right then, won't it, Flynn, old chap?' He was reassuring himself. He might not have believed a word that he was saying for all the conviction that he succeeded in getting behind each word. 'I think we've all been upset. Hebechi? I suppose he wanted you to appeal for him. Did you tell him that there was no hope?'

'No, he didn't ask me to appeal. He was very strange. It's very hard to understand these people.'

Suddenly the Diesel began working again. First it coughed uncertainly, failed, picked up once more, and then set out on its regular palpitation of the morning air.

Afternoon in Rasuka did not begin until six o'clock. As the morning ended at noon, nobody quite knew what to call the hours between twelve and six. But as there were comparatively few people awake during these hours it did not bother them very much. So the trial began at six o'clock and lasted for ten minutes. It was attended by the prisoner, two guards, Winter and Ford. The Sultan himself sat behind a high desk. The proceedings took place in the court-room of Rasuka, which was a room in the palace got up to look rather like a schoolroom. The prisoner sat in the front desk. Winter and Ford sat in the desks behind him and a guard stood on either side. The proceedings were, of course, entirely in Arabic. The Sultan was judge, jury, counsel for the prosecution, counsel for the defence, and chief witness. Indeed, no witnesses were called. Hebechi's confession was held to justify, it seemed, a dispensation of trial.

The Sultan gave the impression that he was putting on a performance entirely for the benefit of Ford and Winter. He spoke slowly so that they could follow, and not allowing himself to get out of temper, indulged in a terrible irony. 'You thought it would be a good plan to kill, yes? So you took a knife, yes? And you thought that you would kill, like you would kill a hen? Then later on, well, you ran away! Oh, brave murderer! You didn't even wait to see if you had been successful. What a murderer! But nevertheless a murderer.'

Winter could only see the back of Hebechi's head. The Sultan, who could, of course, see Hebechi's face, displayed so little interest in it that he addressed all his remarks to Winter and Ford, even the 'you's.' Now and again he would glance at Hebechi's face rather as a conductor will glance at a score to reassure himself about a familiar piece of music the orchestra is playing. Then his eyes would go away to the spectators, to the two Europeans, to the guards. The Sultan was enjoying himself immensely. He was the cat playing with the mouse. He was the schoolmaster teasing an unfortunate boy for the benefit of the rest of the class.

Eventually he clapped his hands and the guards bustled Hebechi out of his place. The Sultan had not even pronounced sentence, thinking this to be superfluous. When the prisoner turned round it could be seen that his eyes were puffed with weeping. He caught sight of Winter.

'When I was a man I was not like this,' he said.

During the night he escaped from the prison. All along he must have known that this was going to happen. The manacles were too large for his slim wrists because they were still intact in the morning: the only way that Hebechi could have rid himself of them was by careful wriggling and manipulation. Escape through the window was easy. The soldiers went searching through Rasuka and consoled themselves by arresting Hebechi's wife and bringing her together with the children to the prison. A crowd accompanied them, jeering and mocking at the soldiers. Perhaps it was because of that, or it may be that the Sultan was not everything that he seemed, that they were treated reasonably well. In any case they were released three days later. But Hebechi was not to be found anywhere. The guards had their right hands struck off.

CHAPTER VIII: *Dragon and Field*

NEVER HAD WINTER FELT THE STRANGE-
ness of Rasuka so much as during those few days immediately
after the escape of Hebechi. Ford, for example, had seemingly
lost all interest in the affair. During the events leading up to the
trial he had been as tense as a bow string, but now the bow had
been slackened. The characteristic thing was that when Winter
went to call on him, the manager was scribbling on a piece of
paper in the corner of his living-room and smiling at the odd
fantasies he was creating. He turned the paper round and
round, pointing out that, seen from one direction, the drawing
might be a group of people sitting round a fire; turn it on its
side and there was an old man with a beard.

It was as though Hebechi in his going had drawn the poison
out of the air. Mrs. Ford no longer talked of strikes and demon-
strations and even when it so happened that Winter called on
her when she was quite alone there was never any attempt to
make advances to him. She was always quite respectably
dressed now—respectably dressed and callous and slightly
contemptuous as before. 'You don't look much better for the
change of air,' she said to Winter as though it gave her some

satisfaction. Between them, this rather coarse woman and himself, Winter felt that almost anything was possible. Ford himself was too much of a fool to be angry with. But his wife had sensuality and a wish to disgust herself. Winter, like all men, had this wish. He felt that he could love this woman with the greatest brutality. The situation between them was electric. When he was in a room with her the only thing of which he was aware was sex. Hebechi and that business was quite forgotten.

'In the hills,' Flynn said, not opening his mouth too wide—otherwise his pipe would have fallen out—'You'll never find him. Made a clean getaway. Scrounge a bit of food somewhere. The mistake is to think that the hinterland is not populated. There's a bandit behind each stone. A man like Hebechi will soon find friends. Become prosperous. A sort of leader. I can see him, in a few years' time, in complete control of the interior. That's how sultans are made, anyway.' To Flynn everything was fitting into a pattern. He was not surprised. Nothing could surprise him.

To Nellie, when she consented to talk about it, there was even a little romance in it. If you could forget, just for one moment, that Hebechi's original crime had been thieving, and could look upon the attack on Cator as a noble gesture so natural in a country where revenge was the recognized method of preserving one's dignity; if you could twist the circumstances just a little so that you could think of Hebechi as a man wrongfully accused, then this escape at the last moment was surely a very delightful thing. She never got to the point of telling Winter that she was glad that Hebechi had escaped, for that would imply some belief in his innocence—not so much of the attack on Cator as of the embezzlement; and that would mean that she was on Hebechi's side against Cator, and, so it seemed, Winter himself. She was in excellent spirits. She took a walk over to the prison and talked to the new guard. This man showed her the manacles from which Hebechi had escaped and the window through which he had climbed. He told her, very fiercely, that an escape from the prison was absolutely impossible now that he was the guard. Even if a man were aided by the djinns he would be hard put to it to get out of this jail. There had never been such a jailer for vigilance as he. If need be, he would watch the prisoner with his own eyes continuously all the time that he was detained there. He would not sleep. Just watch.

Nellie was delighted by this and went off to tell Winter all about it.

'It's not over yet. It's not finished,' he said darkly.

'Oh, come. You're trying to give me the impression that you know something. And you don't know anything—no more than I do.' He was delighted by her freshness and sudden smiles. What had happened, he asked himself wonderingly, that all the gloom and strain he had felt on the night of his ill-starred party should clear away like this? Hebechi had unsuccessfully attacked Cator, been tried, sentenced to death and escaped. Everyone gave the impression of being very pleased about it. Perhaps it was because so little happened at Rasuka that they were all so heartily glad of anything to break the monotony. But he did not think that this was the real explanation.

He went with Flynn to see how Cator was getting on. The wound was superficial, but even simple wounds like this had a habit of turning septic in this sandy climate and causing the most disgusting desert sores. So the various Europeans took it in turns to go to the Cator bungalow and ask how the wound was healing. The two men strode silently over the sand. Flynn put his large boots down squarely and firmly, looking neither to right nor left, coughing deep in his throat when he thought of it, and inclining his head carefully in Winter's direction when Winter at last found something to say.

'When do we change over to summer hours?'

'Well—let me see now! I suppose Ford will be telling us. Last year I think it was on May 15th. But we shall know.'

That is just what is so impossible, thought Winter savagely. We don't know and can't know anything. You are walking over this sand as steady as an elephant because you know so little and are sensitive to so little. You assume everything, that the sand is bearing you, that the sun will come up to-morrow, that Cator will be all right, that there will be no more attacks, that everything is now peaceful and quiet in Rasuka, that eventually we shall all go home to England and sit in a green field—you think you know all these things! That's why you can bend your head towards me in that peculiarly annoying way of yours. But I don't know anything. I have to understand much more completely than I do at this moment in order to feel at ease. So many qualities and characters here in Rasuka are as unknown to me as x in an algebraic equation, a part of which is missing. More than anyone else in Rasuka the Sultan gave the impression of understanding his environment. But as for the rest, they were like children looking at an accident in the street, not at all excited or alarmed, for it was not an accident to them. It was simply that two cars had run into one another and someone was being lifted out through the windscreen because he was very tired.

Anyway, that was how Winter put it to himself. He tried to say that Flynn, for example, was unaware that an accident had happened. Flynn was the child staring curiously from the pavement. Never for one moment would Winter confess to himself that what he feared was the thought that Flynn understood the accident much more completely than he did—and was unmoved and resolute. 'Get the job done! Carry on! Don't say a word!'

Winter felt that the most extraordinary things were still possible and yet everyone had sighed with relief, it seemed, and gone back to where they were before. One day, the Sultan is going to send for me, Winter thought. For there was one circumstance that Winter knew and nobody else knew. Had Cator indeed been killed by that stab in the back, Winter was convinced that Hebechi would have made no attempt to escape. He would have felt the justice and the need for punishment. But he would not die with nothing accomplished. Winter remembered that change that had come over the ex-clerk in the cell when he had learned that Cator still lived.

'It would be a funny thing if he linked up with Rider in the hills,' said Winter.

'They won't link up in this world, that's definite, anyway,' answered Flynn.

'Almost worshipped the man. Called him a sort of god.'

'Rider was despised by these people.'

'I don't think so, somehow.'

They found Cator sitting in a deck-chair on his own veranda, looking extremely well and very pleased with himself. After all, it is not everyone who has an attempt made on his life. That sort of thing is usually reserved for the politically important and the amorous importunate. He had, as a result, a great deal to say for himself, and a great fuss to make to ensure that his guests should be as comfortable in their deck-chairs as possible. He called into the bungalow for his wife to come, but there was no sign of her. All the time Winter was waiting for Nellie to appear too, but she, it seemed, was not there either. Cator was in an excellent mood and he went on talking his nonsense until Winter wanted to ask him what precautions he was taking to protect himself in case of future attacks. The only thing that made him pause was the feeling that both Cator and Flynn would regard a question like this as in somewhat bad taste. He was bringing up an unmentionable subject. There was a conspiracy to keep it constantly submerged.

'You're a lucky man, having a holiday like this.'

'That's what you say,' laughed Cator. He drew his lips back over his yellow teeth. At that moment Winter was perfectly ready to believe that Cator had embezzled the money. Indeed, it was hard to think otherwise. The very fact that Hebechi had attacked Cator, obviously an act of revenge, seemed to indicate that Hebechi was innocent. That was the extraordinary thing. There had been a gross assumption that Hebechi was guilty, but there were at least a couple of questions that demanded satisfactory answers. Why did Hebechi attempt to murder Cator if not as revenge for having been victimized? And why was Cator so pleased that the ex-clerk was now out of the way, executed or hiding in the interior, it did not matter which? The soldiers of the Sultan would soon find him. Cator grinned confidently from one to the other of his guests.

There was probably something quite admirable in the way Flynn was able to pour out his small-talk. To a certain degree Winter felt it in him to respect the Irishman for persisting in being so matter-of-fact. It was the sensible thing to do—whether due to lack of imagination or not. But Cator's matter-of-factness was detestable. He was purring like a fat, sleek cat, and dimly perhaps, Winter thought that he understood it. Cator, he felt, could not find it in him to be bitter about the attack made upon him. He had no recriminations. Winter could even imagine Cator speaking up for the murderous ex-clerk in a smug, self-satisfied way. Quite definitely, if it had been possible for Cator to stop the trial by refusing to give evidence or withdrawing the charge, that would have been done. Because at heart Cator felt that he had deserved all he had got. When a dog has done something wrong—and it is whipped—it will come back wagging its tail. Cator was wagging his tail now. Winter was so disgusted that he could find nothing to say and sat in a brooding silence listening to the light ball of conversation that Flynn and Cator were tossing between them. Winter consoled himself with the thought that things were not over by a long chalk. He owed it to Cator to warn him that, judging by what he had seen of Hebechi in the prison on the eve of his trial, he would be a very dangerous man once free and roaming about. For reasons best known to himself Winter gave no such warning and soon found an excuse for wandering back over the sand in the direction of his own bungalow.

Nellie was waiting for him in his cool living-room.

'To what—?' began Winter. Then—'But no. I won't ask you. It would be a most ungallant question.'

She had not made the slightest move. She was smiling, of course, that rather odd smile of hers in which the corners of her mouth turned up so abruptly, but she did not withdraw her hands from behind her head. He took everything in a little greedily and she was perfectly content to lie there and look up into his face.

'You look very smart,' he remarked. She was wearing a linen shirt and jodhpurs. He did not want to spoil any of this by sitting down and breaking the intimate little atmosphere that had suddenly sprung up. There was nothing else to look at but her eyes.

'I'm sorry,' she said abruptly, and got to her feet. 'I don't know how to smile properly. I don't smile at the right times. I smile out of nervousness—anything.' She stood squarely in front of him with an absurd gravity, the gravity of a child. He wanted to jest, talk lightly, touch her ears, ruffle her hair.

'And what are you nervous about now, may I ask?'

'You!'

'Me?'

'You want to know things, the whys and the wherefores. You see—the first thing that you were on the point of asking was what am I doing here.'

Even as he wanted to pull her towards him, enclosing her tightly in his arms, he found himself frowning; it was as though he was trying to remember something of extreme importance— not so much for him perhaps as somebody else—sufficient, nevertheless, to trouble the quiet minute.

They both waited. Oh, not so serious, he wanted to say. Those large, round dark eyes, as though you were trying to engulf me in them. She smiled once more.

'Why don't you make love to me?' she asked. On neither of their faces was there any change of expression. He was aware of two things only—her two eyes and the fact that he was listening intently for any sound that there might be. From outside there was nothing. The rhythmical thumping of the Diesel was always to be counted as nothing. You became so familiar with it that you only noticed it when it stopped. There was not a breath of wind stirring the sand, but the woodwork of the house was creaking and straining with the sun upon it. Flies flicked about the room. The only human sound was the low crooning of Rachid in his little bunk at the other end of the veranda. All these sounds he listened to intently, tabulating them, so to speak, and then his eyes which had never left hers flickered slightly.

'What are you thinking of?' she asked. 'Why don't you answer me? Why don't you make love to me? It's rather expected of you, you know.'

'By whom?'

She left the question unanswered for a moment. She might
even have been gravely considering it. 'By me, perhaps.' It was
not her answer that she had been considering so much as the
possible effect it might have upon him. 'You must think that I'm
a very scandalous person. Girls just don't talk like this,
do they?'

'It would be much nicer if they did.'

But no, they were not going to escape from the subject like
that. It just wouldn't be good enough to allow her to expose
herself by such a question without giving her decent cover afterwards. To be flippant would be the greatest insult: yet, to save
his life, he did not know what else he could do. There were even
some stirrings of anger that she should have cornered him in this
way.

'Because you don't appeal to me in that way. That's all!' he
eventually said, a little coldly, but fearing each word as he
spoke it.

'Oh! I see! I didn't know. I thought that perhaps you wanted
to and didn't have the courage. I just wanted to help you if you
were nervous. That's all!'

'Well, you may think it's very funny, but . . . you're just
laughing at me, aren't you?'

'Perhaps!'

'What I say is the truth though. You just don't appeal to me
in that way. Besides . . .'

'Besides what?'

'It's so easy.'

There was dead silence now—for a moment.

'Oh, I see.'

He saw then that for the first time he had hurt her. She
looked away from him hastily as though there were too much

brightness in his face. Her mouth was wry, and whereas a moment before there had been a steady calmness, she was now uncertain, looking here and there, one hand flickering up to her lips. She even glanced at him once more. Your neat, trim figure, he thought. And now he wanted to put out a hand towards her, wanted to draw her down to the chair. As if sensing something of the sort, she moved slightly away and looked wonderingly at him from the other side of a small coffee table.

'You don't know that you are alive, do you?' she sneered.

'I don't know who you are. Who are you? Where do you come from? Who are your other lovers?'

'Other?'

'Well, it's perfectly obvious that you're in love with me.'

'You flatter yourself.'

'Then why do you come here laughing at me—when ten minutes later you'll be telling God-knows-who all about it, what I said, what I looked like, what I wanted to do. That's true, isn't it?'

'You must be mad. One minute you say I'm in love with you and then you say I come here to laugh at you. One or the other, you know. Is it that . . . ?'

He had been talking rapidly and angrily, looking now at the floor, now at the tables, even at her hands, but now he raised his eyes and looked at her face—'Is it that what?'

'Well——' She considered even now whether it was wise to put it to him. 'Is it that you've such a poor opinion of yourself that you think people are ready to laugh at you?'

'I don't care what people think of me.'

'That's not true. You care very much.' And then she went on, 'You're so awkward and clumsy. So gauche!'

'At least, I'd rather have you angry than loving.' That, at any rate, was true. It amused him to see her lose her temper. His own had come and gone rapidly. 'Well, at least sit down and have some coffee.'

'No, I never drink coffee at this time of day.'

'Do sit down—please!'

'You really want me to?'

'I wouldn't ask you if I didn't.'

'Then I think I'll go.' She said this with the greatest satisfaction; obviously she thought she had scored one there. One more shot was to be hazarded. 'I suppose you want to be faithful to the memory of your wife?'

The words themselves were scornful, but the wide-eyed way she looked at him robbed the words of all malice. It was a genuine sympathetic inquiry.

'I don't talk of my wife and memories. They are not memories. Do you understand that? I wonder! I don't have to drag things out of the past—that is a memory, isn't it? She's so living. It isn't that I loved her. I love her!'

This didn't seem to make much sense to Nellie. She looked at him a little calculatingly. That morning she had come to his bungalow feeling amorous. She had come there for amusement and excitement. When she found that Winter was not there she was as disappointed as a child who has been robbed of an ice cream. But by sitting, with her hands up to the back of her neck, lying back in one of his deck-chairs, she had fallen into a kind of feline contentment by the time he walked into the room, his face shining with perspiration. He had looked so much off his guard, so startled to find her there, that like a kitten she had wanted to play with him. Nothing much had been meant by her question. Certainly she would have liked him to make love to her—not just at that moment, for she was so comfortably settled into the deck-chair—but later on, after they had had coffee, for example. She had lied when she said she didn't take coffee at that time of day. She drank it at all times, at any time. She found it agreeable to consider the pleasure of lying close up against his body. But the warmth of the morning gave a certain distance to her vision, and for the moment it was enough for her that she wanted to tease him. So she had asked him why he did not make love to her. It was quite evident that he would make love to her some time or other. She knew it and Winter knew it. For all that they might put into words, no matter how they insulted one another, they both knew that they would finish up in each other's arms. To Nellie this was very desirable—so as a general rule she was in the better humour when they were together. Winter tried to throw up barriers—no matter how poor and flimsy. Everything was a great strain. When he told her that it was all too easy, he also had been lying. Making love was really much too hard.

'Do I really look like your wife?' she asked. For answer he went into his bedroom and fetched the photograph.

'In profile there is a great likeness. In colouring too. I don't mean that you look anything like the photo. Certain expressions that you have remind me of her very much.'

'I see.' She smiled her nervous smile once more and handed the photo back to him.

'I cannot believe that she is dead. It isn't possible. I feel her so close to me.' It would have done to place the photo on the coffee table for the time being, but he went to the trouble of going back to his bedroom. Then, when he came out, he closed the door quietly behind him—as though in the freshly made bed behind him there were someone lightly sleeping who had not to be awakened before evening. When he spoke there was a hush in his voice. 'It has never become real for me, her death.'

He was a small, bewildered boy to her. 'I hope that nothing

ever hurts you,' she breathed, looking up at him intently, and
the mood of the moment was such that the extraordinary
change in her attitude during the past few minutes was accepted
as nothing surprising. She would like to explain all these things
to him. Sit down, she would like to say, and I would tell you
what death means. I would show you that your wife is dead.
Oh, I know that you have heard the hard, cold words of the
explanation before. You could play a part and repeat them
yourself like a child with his lesson. But I can also see that you
have passed beyond the words and your poor, raw soul is being chafed against the coarse stars. Let me protect you and put
a pad of words between you and your inexplicable feelings.

This is what Nellie honestly felt. If she had spoken Winter
would have been even more amazed than he was to hear the
soft words that had just passed her lips. She wanted to mother
him and yet at the same time say—'See, she's really dead and
gone, and you will never see her again. On the other hand, you
can look at me and even hold me in your arms.' Winter would
have understood the invitation to take her in his arms and he
might have done it with no consciousness of unfaithfulness to
his wife. Nellie had been wrong when she thought that it was
an allegiance to a dead wife that was holding him back. He had
grieved so little. Sometimes he thought that it was not so much
that she was dead to him as he was dead to her. The dead, flat
slap on the wall of his mind, echoless, vibrationless! This was
sound! sound! sound! he could say, walking round and beating
on his prison wall. These things I have done in the past and
they are healthily solid. Then comes the moment when the concealed hollow is reached and his raised fist sounds an unfeeling
thump, the dead beat on the empty coffin. The coffin in which
Joyce was laid. He could not find it in him to grieve for her.
There were no vibrations. He was numbed. Even now the

anæsthetic had not left him, and his body could still be lacerated without so much as calling out a groan from him.

He could, of course, pretend to groan and laugh. He could pretend to be alive and make love. Hebechi had interested him. There had been no false assumption of feelings in connection with Hebechi, so perhaps he was not entirely lost. Yet, at the moment, for all the inviting way that she was looking at him, he had no desire to take Nellie in his arms.

He was aware that they had been looking at each other for some time without saying anything. She had no idea of what was passing through his mind, and to him she was no more than a moist-lipped girl, quietly breathing, breasts rising and falling —certainly he was unaware that she wanted to put him into her maternal pocket and at the same time sting him by saying— 'Dead, dead, dead, she's dead.' He would have told her how impossible it was to hurt him with words like those.

But he was under compulsion, just as he had been under compulsion when he had got up from his chair on that hot afternoon and watched Rachid playing with bits of bone and ivory at the end of the veranda. He did it all rather mechanically, and Nellie, for her part, was glad enough of it. He had already removed his jacket and she ran her womanish hands up his arms until he seized her by her elbows. Then he ran a hand round to the nape of her neck where her soft hair hung down and covered it. She parted her lips as he kissed her. What a practised kisser you are, he thought, forcing her head back, drawing her body to his. She could do nothing to surprise him —not even the sudden break away and the flushing, sad, angry face that she turned up at him could touch him where he was sensitive. She had broken vigorously away. There was bitter humiliation in her eyes.

'How hateful you are,' she whispered. 'Cold and hateful.

What sort of a person do you think I am, anyway? It isn't that you kissed me. I wanted you to kiss me! But that you should kiss me like that. Am I nothing to you?'

'I don't know,' he answered simply and quite honestly.

'Never touch me again—if you touch me like that.' And she went immediately into the golden air, leaving moisture on Winter's lips that he was reluctant to wipe away. He had thought too much about kissing her. She had sensed the mockery that it was. He was neither elated nor depressed. He felt that he had done what was expected of him—and perhaps, but he was not quite sure of this, because it had been expected of him. Anyway, who wouldn't kiss a pretty girl like Nellie? For she was pretty, wasn't she? And she had character. She would come back, or he would go to her.

He went out on to the veranda to see how far she had got, having a mind to call her back, but her rapid, angry steps had already carried her a considerable way. She did not look back. Then the heat haze rippled over her.

There was not very much of this that he could take seriously. Her annoyance and sudden departure stirred him pleasantly— it was like having the back of one's neck tickled with a feather, but he got little more out of it than that for he had never felt any vital part of himself drawn out on to the stage. All the time he had been lurking in the wings, watching himself acting out there and taking a vicarious enjoyment of the touch of her body and the moisture of her lips. Never for one moment did he attempt to put himself into Nellie's position. He wasn't going to worry about her for he was quite sure that she had enjoyed every minute of it. What is more, it was the sort of situation, he thought, in which she often found herself. She must have been comparing him with other men, other situations—but he did not mind this very much. For the moment he was stimulated.

He had no wish to sit down. He thrust his hands deep into his trouser pockets and sauntered up and down between the chairs. There was the tiniest bit of life in his body that he had not put there. A small nerve of excitement, that grew in potency as the minutes passed, brought him first of all a mild sense of gallantry and then a desire to mumble words to himself. 'Dragon, dragon and the green field,' were words that emerged quite clearly, and he brought the flat of his hand down on the top of the table. The bang startled him. He felt like a knight-errant. What audacious piece of bravery had he carried out now? He had been flattered, very flattered, by Nellie, and it had left him in a mood where he could talk half-ironically to himself, not wishing to sit down, not finding enough to do in order to express the sensation of having rediscovered his body.

It was no surprise to him that Nellie easily and naturally took the initiative in bringing about their meetings. He was content that it should be so. That one kiss had been the sign of a tremendous undertaking between them, and it did not matter in the slightest what Nellie had said at that late morning hour when they should have been taking coffee. And it did not even matter what Winter felt. His detachment was not of the slightest importance for the bridge had been crossed and there was never a failure of the assumption, when they met, that they would now go on and on. Possibly Nellie knew where they would land up, though that was doubtful, but to Winter there was never any illumination beyond the immediate minute. In the course of the next few days nothing remarkable was done. He did not find himself alone with her until more than a week had passed, but the awareness of the rest of the Europeans during this time had been aroused. To Winter's mind they presented themselves as clumsy cattle stumbling to their feet—

they were white-faced cattle because for some reason or other
white-faced cattle always look more stupid than the others—
and gazing at the pair of them, Winter and Nellie, with a stolid
disregard for privacy. This was really rather mysterious. Surely
Nellie and he had not been seen together sufficiently to cause
the rest of the community to gossip? To them it would surely
appear that she spent more of her time with Flynn than with
him and yet he could feel by the way Flynn looked at him, by
the over-warm smile on Ford's face when he came suddenly
upon him, and the slightly hysterical bearing of Mrs. Ford that
the small European society of Rasuka could sense that a new
relationship had been set up inside itself.

Or perhaps they don't notice anything at all! Perhaps it's
all my imagination. More likely than not. Then that indicates a
lot of things. A fellow with a hole in his sock thinks that everyone is looking at it. I must be very—sensitive—feeling more
about Nellie than I had thought. He had to admit that it gave
him pleasure to think that others might be associating Nellie's
name with him. But just who was she?

When the two of them met and there were others present
Nellie was perfectly natural and charming.

There was no denying the pleasure that Mrs. Ford suddenly
took in life. It would not be too much to say that she was almost
wild with joy and excitement. She made opportunities to see
Winter. She could not have enough of him. She loved seeing
him. About a week afterwards she even made a journey up to the
administrative block where, as though by chance, she found herself in conversation with Winter. It doesn't matter what they
were talking about for their words and thoughts hadn't the
slightest relationship with one another. The words that were
uttered were like beads that a woman will finger as she talks—
the real conversation was carried on at a higher level, without

words. All the time she regarded him with a kind of mocking amusement. If I could only scratch you, scald you, she seemed to be saying.

'You do find that the place is doing you good though?' she asked finally.

'In what way?' he asked.

'In this way, that way—in all ways. Ways that you know best.'

Selfishly enough Winter never tried to imagine himself in Nellie's position, no more, that is, than would give him a brief glimpse of what he imagined himself to be in her eyes. Just how did he appear to her? Not unhandsome—but that was not the quality. It was the assured way he did everything, the mastery over circumstances, his confident masculine character coming in contrast with the pulpy femininity of Ford, the adolescent seriousness of Flynn, the furtiveness of Cator. Plunkett didn't count; his teeth had been drawn. In comparison with all these Winter thought that it was very natural that Nellie should fall in love with him. Any intelligent girl would have done the same under the circumstances and he was inclined to give her very little credit for it. He was a romantic figure. A man who has just lost his wife is always a romantic figure, in the debased modern sense, if he is still young. Winter was young and knew himself to be personable.

But it never occurred to him to think how she was standing up to the gazing herd. How did she find it on the little island on which she now found herself marooned with him? Did she like it? Was she embarrassed—was she humiliated? What would Mrs. Ford find to say to her? No, all these questions never arose, for Nellie had chosen her path with such apparent confidence and light-heartedness that Winter could never have the pleasure of feeling protective. He was the sort of man who is quite unimaginative as far as women are concerned unless the instinct to protect them is aroused. A self-sufficient woman usually deters them. Winter was in no way deterred but he could build no rosy fantasy about her—only about himself. He didn't think that she cared what other people thought.

Mrs. Ford could in no way be regarded as an enemy. She was malicious but she was enjoying herself like a small boy at a dog fight. There was someone who now revealed malice and who, quite definitely, was not enjoying himself—and that was Flynn.

But what could Flynn say? Certainly nothing so much as he was expressing by his silences. The two of them, Flynn and Winter, had never given up taking their rides together, though for some reason they never succeeded in getting as far as the stone fort along the coast that Flynn had spoken about. Winter had even come to disbelieve in its existence but Flynn had such stolidity of temperament that each time they set out he could remark, 'Well, I wonder whether we shall make it to-day.' It never struck him that it was rather absurd that they should go out morning after morning with the intention of reaching the fort and never doing so.

But now Flynn gave up making any remarks at all and Winter, after attempts at conversation, withdrew to a contemptuous distance. One morning they returned by the gully and here, as before, Winter was in the lead and came on the skeleton of the buffalo, the dead beast that had made such an impression on him a few weeks before. The skeleton had been picked perfectly clean, was as decent as an exhibit in a museum. The sand was beginning to engulf it: it was as though the skeleton had made a running, sideways dive into the sea of sand, was on the point of disappearing, caught by the eye for the merest moment like a still out of a movie film. There was yet life in the bones. The socketed, enormous skull was burrowing wilfully out of the sunlight.

Flynn reined up at Winter's side.

There was an uneasy pause and then at last Winter found something to say. 'What a hard flinty country. Just as though the desert itself had sucked the flesh from the bones.'

'It's the birds—and the jackals.' They were almost the first words that Flynn had spoken that morning. His common-sense mind could not resist correcting Winter's fancy.

'I know . . .' Then the silence of the desert once more.

For his resentment and silences Winter felt that he liked the Irishman more. It was the sort of thing that was expected of a man under circumstances like this; on the whole Flynn was behaving very decently. Winter was not warming towards Flynn because it was the thing to do—the generosity of the victor towards the vanquished. No, there was nothing of that in it. For there had been no battle, or nothing more than a vague battle in the clouds between misty horsemen who were always changing their ragged outlines and merging sepias into purples. There might have been a conflict on such a vast scale that it lay outside their apprehensions.

Looking down at the skeleton of the buffalo, Flynn seemed to come more warmly alive for Winter than he had ever been. Never had his silences said more, nor had he conveyed more by an averted face. Winter looked round, enjoying the scenery and the morning air. From the saddle they could see a slice of the sea and the blue-tinted, enormous clouds that laboured along the horizon. He wanted to turn to the Irishman and say: 'It all doesn't matter. Just get on with your modelling. Tell you what, you can model my head. You said you would—or was it someone else who suggested that? Anyway, talk, man! Nothing matters as much as that.'

But the words did not come. Nothing broke the silence. The ears of Winter's horse twitched forward; the long polished neck gleamed in the sun.

'Well——' said Winter. All his unspoken words, comforts and assurances had never meant that he would have given up one small part of his part in Nellie. And they rode back to the settlement not uttering a word all the way.

For two such people as Nellie and Winter meetings were never hard to arrange—in fact they seemed to arrange themselves. There seemed to be very little of the premeditated about them. Yet, if Winter should go out of an evening after dinner— the warm evening, in which the heat still rose from the sand in waves, and there was a sweetness from heaven knows how far distant jasmine, cicadas shrilling like tortured nerves—she would suddenly appear out of the darkness. His first desire was to laugh—a laugh partly of gratified desire as when a man gets his heart's wish, but one also of genuine amusement that she should be so bold. She's making all the running, anyway, he thought, and this in itself brought pleasure. She wanted him more than he wanted her. Any moment he could cut loose. He could tell her to be off—and it wouldn't worry him at all, would it?

'Don't you know that it's dangerous for you to be out alone like this? Don't you know it's dangerous, eh? Eh?' He had drawn her to him and was talking with his lips close up to her ear, so that the words came to her in a rich murmur, intimate and teasing.

'The only danger comes from you. And what else can I do, anyway?'

Quite deliberately she had employed her normal speaking tone.

'Don't shout,' he said.

'Frightened someone will hear us?'

'Why are you so bitter?'

They walked back through the darkness to the steps of Winter's bungalow and sat there not wishing to go on to the veranda for fear of waking Rachid, who was snoring gently in his small den. Winter had little wish to talk. He said as little as possible but Nellie was restless and always whispering some observation about the dark shapes in the night before them. She had plenty of gossip too. And the only way to quiet her, Winter found, was by stopping her lips with his when she would relax and go into a profound reverie. This was the silence that he wanted, his arm round her waist and his right hand rounding on her breast. 'No, don't speak,' he would murmur as now and again she stirred, so she made her stirring an excuse merely to bring her lips up to his cheek. This unknown, impossible woman, he thought, as she lay in his arms! Suddenly he would be aware that her hair was damp with dew. It seemed to bring all the perfume, the sweet perfume of her hair and body, out into the night. She would be startled by his spasmodic warmth and respond a little hesitantly as though it were perhaps, after all, some game that he was playing.

By covering her lips he could stop the words that he feared. He could not trust her to speak. Any moment she would be liable to say something clumsy, make some reference to a former lover, tell him why she chose to remain in Rasuka, exactly why she had chosen to throw herself at him, just what it was she wanted—and all of these things Winter feared to hear. That part of them that wanted to explain and account for circumstances was damped down like a fire in a country cottage at eleven o'clock at night. But there was the red hidden heart that would burn through by morning. Words were enemies. Silence then—silence and love! Never before had he trusted himself so much to his senses. He was above the gulf but unafraid because his eyes were bandaged—no, he would not look down!

Words, questions, ideas came bubbling up from the depths but he never paid them less attention than now and, like the thinnest, airiest water, they arose in immediate evaporation into insubstantiality, while Winter and Nellie passionately gave themselves over to their loving.

CHAPTER IX: *Guardian of the Well*

THERE WAS A SCENE IN THE OFFICE THE following morning and, of all people, it was Ford who caused it. Winter was alone when Ford came through the frosted glass doors and looked all round the room not so much as though in search of someone else but rather as though he were looking for some means of escape. He spoke without looking at Winter. He had been worked up to such a pitch that he had to speak but he was frightened of each word as it came out.

'This is impossible! Really, you know it is! But perhaps it's not true—it is the very last thing that you should do. Leave it to the Sultan. That's his job, surely? By going into the interior now you might be causing—oh, all sorts of trouble. . . .'

'Who said I was going into the interior?'

'Well, aren't you? Dear me! The whole place is full of it. I think it was Flynn who actually——'

'Flynn told you that I was going up country? Why?'

'Naturally, as after all I am the manager of the well he could see—he could realize—that it was the sort of thing that I should know immediately.' Ford said this with tremendous dignity but he was very apprehensive of what was going to happen. He was the sort of man who would suddenly find that he had set the seat of his trousers on fire by standing too close to the flames and try to put it out surreptitiously, keeping up an uneasy conversation and anxious to preserve his dignity at all costs.

'No, I don't mean that. I mean, why does Flynn say that I am going?'

Ford gathered himself together. 'I really can't allow it. Just this minute I heard—no sooner had I sat down at my desk when Flynn came in. Really, it is too much. Why not let the whole thing blow over?'

'Is Flynn there now?' Winter was on the point of going to find the Irishman when he realized that the interest of the situation lay not so much in this false rumour and its propagators as in the nervous state that was agitating Ford. Instead he repeated his first question. 'Why am I supposed to be going on this trip?'

'To get Hebechi, of course, and to look for Rider,' said Ford naïvely.

Winter looked at him incredulously. 'Nothing has been farther from my mind.' It was only now that he was beginning to feel angry. Ford's hesitancy and diffidence only served to increase this anger for on top of what Winter considered to be an insulting attitude there was this clumsiness that seemed to be saying all the time: 'This annoyance of mine is very real and you deserve it. You see that I am not even conveying it adequately. I am not a man to get worked up easily.' So that Ford's oblique approach was an expression of a deeper annoyance than would have looked out through his eyes in a more direct attack on Winter.

When Ford had received his assurance that Winter had no intention of making the journey he began mumbling to himself. He was trying to get rid of his annoyance and querulousness as quickly as possible. There was such a conflict now between the backwash of his annoyance and the present desire to placate

Winter that he looked more foolish than ever. He even tried to change the subject but this was such an obvious stratagem that he caught himself up.

'What I mean is, I've not quite decided,' said Winter. He regretted now that he had hastened to deny that he was making the journey to the interior. He had no intention of going but for the moment it would please him to pretend to Ford that there was still a possibility. 'I can't imagine how the news got round. I've told no one.'

'Then it is true!' cried Ford excitedly, daring to look at the other's face. Winter was now aware of the same sense of conflict of emotions and purpose in the well manager as he had been conscious of the first day he had spent in Rasuka, when Rider's bungalow had been burned down and Ford had been the only one to walk across the sand to the smouldering debris. On that occasion, Plunkett by his positive attitude had seemed to understand Ford completely. Winter decided that he must go and have another talk with the doctor.

'Why, why make—I mean, why should you look for all this trouble? After all, it doesn't concern you. Besides, I'm not sure that I could give the time off. After all, I am more or less responsible for your safety . . .' His voice trailed off when he saw that Winter was smiling at him. The manager was completely disarmed, completely overcome. He sighed wearily and sank into the swivel chair which he did so awkwardly that the seat revolved smartly and he had to put out his hand to stop himself. 'You mean that I'm not capable of looking after you,' he said uncertainly, as though seeking approval for this diagnosis of the situation. He was making a mental comparison between his own soft, smooth, hairless body and the firm masculinity of Winter.

'Tell me, just what is the matter? Why get worked up like

this? What is it that you are afraid of? You seem like someone haunted.' Winter sat on the edge of the desk and looked immediately down on to the crown of the manager's head. He could see that the hair was thinning rapidly and this fact, somehow, seemed infinitely pathetic. All Ford's fussiness and petulance seemed unimportant when he looked at the growing bald patch.

'I don't know,' said Ford a little uncertainly after having given the appearance of thinking for a little while. 'It's so hard to put into words. I think that he is still alive up there—waiting for anyone who may come up. Not to kill them, but to . . . waiting for them to give new strength. He was a revolutionary.' He spoke like a man who had just received news of some great sorrow.

'What on earth are you maundering about?' Ford looked short-sightedly about the room and Winter wanted to pat the bald spot in his bewilderment. 'What are you frightened of?'

'Me! Frightened? How dare you talk to me like that! I am not alarmed in any way, for there is nothing to be alarmed about, is there? It is just that I like things to be—well—safe! That's important.'

It was only then that Winter began to suspect that the well manager was out of his mind. He looked down at the unfortunate man incredulously, all the brilliant little pictures of the previous occasions he had seen and spoken with Ford running into a moving, fluid panorama which might be just comprehensible if one realized the thread of insanity running through it all. For three-quarters of the time Ford was probably as sane as anyone else in Rasuka, but at that particular moment Winter was convinced that he was having a mental incompetency. Who but a madman would build an entirely useless machine merely for the beauty of it?

'Tell me,' he said gently, 'why should I not go? What is it that has to be kept safe?'

Ford burst into such a strong, forcible, masculine strain of invective that Winter stood back, startled. Here was a different man! This was the original demon working out through the flesh, the authentic Ford, the visionary, the poet, for in a moment Winter was convinced by the vehemence of the manager's language of the rightness of the machine and its sufficiency in that it was beautiful. Nearly everything that he had disliked in the man's character had been due to his hesitations and uncertainties. He had to fall back in admiration of this forthrightness, wild and mad as it was.

'What is it that has to be kept safe? Oh, how can you pretend to me? I should have thought that now you could have been honest. As soon as you came I knew that I could not really trust you for you were so much like the other.'

'What other?' Winter was so fascinated that he could not resist putting these questions even though all the time he was making mental reservations about the validity of the replies.

'I always knew that there would, one day, be an attack upon the well. It is an idea that I keep to myself for fear of alarming people. Above all I keep it from my wife but she is such a dear, sweet creature that she is able to guess so many things. She guessed this. You came and told me one day that she feared a strike because the Diesel had stopped—well, even I, who knew why the Diesel was not running, even I felt that same fear. There are so few people that one can trust.'

'But who should attack the well? The natives? The Sultan would shoot them down in no time. He doesn't want any trouble with the English.'

'But the Sultan is very clever. He is at least twice, three times as clever as anybody else I have met, and who knows what the

Sultan knows? He has his own ways of going to work. Why did Hebechi escape, and so easily, and the family of Hebechi —do you know they are better off now than they were before?'

There was a vein of distorted, improbable truth in all this. Ford had greater strength of mind than he had ever had under normal circumstances, but it was a mind working under the stress of great emotion, ungoverned imagination, taking stones for lizards and bushes for goblins. He was a man who had seen a terrible vision and found it constantly coming between his eyes and the normal sunlit world. Winter felt that he could not talk reason to him. For the moment he was interested to see what could be found in this strange sediment at the bottom of Ford's mind. There was no knowing what odd treasure could be found. Ford was sitting comfortably in his chair. To any third person looking in over the patch of frosted glass everything would have appeared quite normal. A quiet conversation like this might be the best way of leading Ford back into more everyday channels.

'Rider was mad,' said the manager coldly and incisively. It was a scientific diagnosis. 'Not a balanced man and I fear that the monotony and solitude of our life here might have played on his nerves. I used to feel sorry for him because of that. Who knows, I might even have got to like him—but everyone was against Rider. So what could I do? I had to be against him too. I can't—I'm not the sort of man—it isn't in me, to stand out against the rest. You see that, don't you? I have to give way.'

Through the window Winter could see the polished blue obesity of a storage tank and a wide pipe that, strangled near the ground by a collar of steel, finished up peering like a blind snake in mid-air. To the right of the storage tank there was a slight brush of the cliff that backed the valley at this

point but otherwise there was only the painful blue of the sky.
As he watched he saw Arvanitaki, the foreman, cross the small
yard in front of the storage tank and make for the office.
Winter did not wish to be disturbed just now. He went to the
door and stopped the Greek before he could enter, telling him
that for the time being he and Mr. Ford were busy and that
he'd better come back in an hour's time. Arvanitaki glanced
past Winter's shoulder and saw the manager sitting in the
swivel chair still talking and gesticulating.

'It's nothing important,' he said, and went away. When
Winter returned to Ford he could see by the look in his eyes
that the manager was not pleased by this temporary desertion.
He explained who had come and what he had done.

'Now tell me—if you suspect anyone this is very important.
Who do you think would want to destroy the well?' He was
not thinking, for one moment, to get any information out of
Ford. He wanted to explore the extraordinary complications
of this newly exposed mind. The destruction of the well was
obviously an obsession that up to now had been very successfully hidden.

'There are many, but first of all there was Rider.' Here
Winter felt himself sailing into the fantastic once more. Would
he never escape from this wretched man Rider?

Ford spoke lazily. He knew this so well that he could hardly
take an interest in what he was saying. 'He was a revolutionary.
He didn't care for us and what was right or wrong. He had his
own ways of measuring right and wrong. They were not our
ways. He stood away from us. You just had to admire him. He
was like Christ. Christ and the money-changers, and I thought
that he would lead a crowd up to the well—and that'd be the
temple. He would destroy . . .'

Winter looked at him incredulously. Of course, each man

understood other people as best he could. It is hard to see another man's character steadily and entire, easy to read one's own character into it, putting there what one hopes and fears, raising a god or a demon, gratifying one's own desires. Ever since Winter had arrived in Rasuka there had been a great deal of odd talk about this man Rider, talk that did not tally from one person to another, the details did not tally, and Winter was only confident in his general impression that the unknown man must have been an eccentric busybody who got people's backs up because he was a little unorthodox, a circumstance that could be considerably more aggravating here in this closed-in society of Rasuka than in the outside world. It was to be remembered that the first time he had heard Rider's name Ford had confessed that in some ways he was 'a good man.' Little had Winter guessed at the time of what a tissue of fear and adulation those words were symbol. It would be quite out of place now to reason with Ford, and point out that it was absurd to regard the missing Rider as the object of reverence and the object of fear that Ford took him to be. Winter did not want to knock down Aunt Sallies. Poor unbalanced Ford had decided about Rider and it would be beyond Winter's power to replace his extraordinary conception with something more rational.

It was the rational that was being overthrown.

Then Winter became aware of an extraordinary thing. It was so surprising that for the moment it took his breath away and he looked at the manager with new surmise. At the moment Ford was no weakling and could meet his gaze steadily. He was more confident of himself. But the interesting thing to Winter's mind was the fact that the well and all that it stood for was in some way evil! How else could one interpret this talk about Christ and the destruction of the temple? Obviously the agent of destruction was the agent of good. Then why should Ford take up a position that led him to fight against his own conscience? To be consistent, and in insanity people are fearfully consistent, Ford would have to destroy the well himself. But this, and Winter could see this clearly, he would never do for the weakness and the lack of decision he knew he suffered from. At the last moment he could be deflected by anything, a casual word by his wife, a look from Flynn which he would misinterpret. No, Winter thought that there was never any danger of Ford doing any damage to the well. The interesting thing was that the guardian of the well was also its enemy.

Poor, dear mad Ford! What a mess you've got yourself into. There's only one thing to be done, of course. You'll have to leave Rasuka. Back in the delta—but they'll send you to England for leave—you'll forget all your phobias. They will drop off like old clothes. Winter did not utter any of these thoughts. He was considering how best to put them into operation. He would have a talk with Plunkett. They would work out some specious medical reason for Ford's leaving Rasuka without compromising his future with any talk of mental instability, for Winter was convinced that it was purely a temporary disability.

'And that's why you're not to go to the interior,' Ford said suddenly.

'No, no, I'll not go to the interior. I was just joking.'

'I'm not joking. I'm very serious. You're not to go, I say. I'll not have it.'

'Don't worry. I'll not go. You can be easy in your mind.'

'For I think you'd find Rider if you went and then there would be trouble. We don't want him back here.'

'Oh, but Rider is dead, surely.' As he spoke Winter thought of that time he had visited Hebechi in his cell and the con-

demned man had declared with pride and confidence that Rider
was not dead because gods could not die.

'And you would take over where Rider left off.' Ford looked
at him with eyes that seemed to darken, as the sea will mysteriously darken in full daylight, sometimes when there is not a
cloud in the sky. As each word came out Winter experienced
a kind of paralysis, an atrophying of thought, and he could not
protest against the extravagant things that were being uttered.
He was bound under a solemn spell.

'Don't you see how people identified you with Rider? Oh,
don't you see?' What wild pleading for vision to be granted
was this? 'There was the gift of food—bread left on your doorstep. Didn't you guess? Hebechi came to you when he wanted
advice. He did not think of going to anyone else. That was
why we do not want you to see too much of the natives. We
don't want you to know them and we don't want them to know
you! Say, why not go back to the delta? You are well now.
Why not go back?'

Winter shook himself free. 'No, I will not go back. But I'll
see to it that you go back. Don't you know that you're a sick
man? You're mad.' He uttered these words with considerable
satisfaction and Ford fell back in his chair in consternation.

'I—you must excuse me,' he said, fumbling in his pockets
for something that Winter knew was not there. If he had been
asked what he was looking for Ford would not have known. He
was trembling with nervousness and by this it could be seen
that the fit was passing. When he glanced at Winter his eyes
were seen to be slightly flecked with blood.

'Is this what you want?' Winter offered him a box of
matches but Ford hardly glanced at them, jumped suddenly to
his feet and went out through the door into the sand yard.
Winter was immediately relieved for they had arrived at an

impasse and if Ford had not decided on action himself Winter would not have known what to do. He had the feeling that these temporary aberrations of the manager's were no uncommon thing. The instability in his character was fundamental and it was only at such moments as those that had just passed that the ordinariness, the suburbanism, the domesticity of Ford sank below those moving sands. Winter had been with the real mad animal. Now he knew Ford as his wife knew him—possibly as the other Europeans of Rasuka knew him. Why had they never given a hint? Or had Winter been shown more than had been revealed to anyone else? To begin with Winter had felt shocked. Now he felt ruthless. He hurried after the manager and tried to catch up with him.

Ford was just passing out through the gate of the compound, walking very fast so that in order to catch him Winter would have had to run. The Sudanese gate-keeper, the chief of the group of three Sudanese who were the official time-keepers, rose to his feet and raised a hand deferentially to his forehead as Ford passed. But there was no acknowledgment. With a quick, awkward, wriggling motion as though the gateway were narrow and there was no other way of passing it than by this particular kind of negotiation, Ford passed through to the sand road beyond where the wind was raising the surface dust so that his feet appeared to be passing through a watery instability into which, at any moment, he was liable to sink. He was some fifty yards away when Winter reached the gate. 'Ford!' he shouted. 'Ford!' But if the manager heard he made no sign. He hurried on like a man going to safety.

Winter had no fears about his safety. His excuse in following had not been that the manager might do some harm to himself for he was going directly to his wife, so much was obvious,

and there was no better thing for him to do. Even as he thought
of her Winter found his admiration for the woman increasing.
As one realized the greater weakness of her husband one realized what a corresponding reserve of strength she must have to
make their life together possible. He could see Ford as a carefully groomed, jacket-dusted, well-instructed figure—like some
child rigged out for Sunday School—but no more than a
dummy, animated from behind by this wife who now took on
awful proportions. If the sudden revelation of Ford's insanity
had transformed him into a mystery, moving him back several
steps from the footlights into the darknesses of upstage, how
much more of a mystery had it made his wife! As Winter hurried over the sand in a vain attempt to catch up with the manager he found himself thinking more and more of Mrs. Ford,
until the blood began throbbing in his temple and he realized
that he was not yet strong enough to hurry like this in the middle of the day. It was no good! He would have to stop. An iron
hand had seemingly clutched at his lungs, his mouth burned,
the saliva sharp and acid like sour wine. He saw his small
shadow twisting at his feet. He bent down to rest his hands on
his knees, allowing his head to fall forward, finding some relief
in this position. There was nothing but the bare sand of the
wadi bottom at that place moving like smoke over his boots
and Winter did not care to lie down on it for in no time he
knew that he would become stiff with grit.

Ford had already gained his own veranda. He climbed the
steps jerkily and disappeared into the cool interior. After resting for a few moments Winter was able to follow more slowly,
still gasping for breath and reflecting on the fact that he was
still weaker than he had thought. Thinking about his own
health so much put Ford's problem into the background that
when he eventually did come up to the bungalow he had half

a mind to turn away again. But Mrs. Ford had seen him coming over the sand, and watched his unsteady progress with interest, from the moment she had seen him bending almost double. She knew that he had been trying to catch up with her husband whom she had told to lie down.

'Is your husband all right?' Winter asked, seeing the woman come out on to the veranda.

'Yes. Why shouldn't he be? He's resting now, that's all.'

She did not invite Winter up the steps on to the veranda.

'How's Nellie?' she asked maliciously, but with a sparkle in her eyes.

So that's how it is, thought Winter. She wasn't taking her husband's attack very seriously but yet did not wish to discuss it. 'I'd like to see your husband a moment.' He had not been chasing Ford all the way from the compound merely to ensure that he arrived home safely. He had wanted to continue the conversation even though he knew it was a mad one. The little that Ford had told him was enough to give him the feeling that he could learn more essential truth about Rasuka—this community which had now become such an inexplicable mystery to him—from this genuine, mad Ford than from all the considered talk of a man like Flynn or Ford himself in more rational moods. Winter wanted to sit in his company and let what words come that would but, looking up at the uncompromising woman on the balcony, he realized that this was impossible.

'I fear your husband is unwell.'

'Yes, he is often unwell.'

'Mentally unwell.'

'You don't think that a sane man would build a machine like that'—she nodded in the direction of the cellar door—'do you?'

'Yes, quite easily. There's nothing insane about that. I can understand that perfectly.'

She made no comment on this but looked at him with her characteristic smile, a certain wildness in it, an abandoned smile which was forgetful of her sick husband in its sensuality and yet terribly aware of him by its brilliant fixity—unchangeableness, everlastingness. It was no smile of revolt. She accepted the situation. Why? Why didn't she pack up with her husband and go off to England? For she had no love for Rasuka —as Winter well remembered her saying. The reason, the pitiful reason, might be money. If so it was a tragedy. Only a woman of great hardness of character or great love for her husband was capable of acting in this way—and whether it was one or the other or both Winter at the present stage could not say. Her smile arrested him as having implications too sad for words. As she stood there in the half-shadow of the balcony he felt suddenly most deeply sorry for her and even forgave her the remark about Nellie. She had meant no harm. Her amusement was harmless. And now, at this moment, she was standing watch over her husband.

'I just wanted to see him safe home,' he muttered.

She made no reply. And he walked away with no further word, aware that she was watching him go. She was as still as a statue and he was sure that she had lost her smile.

After he had been to his own place to have a lie-down and a cold shower he went to call on Plunkett but could get very little out of him. It occurred to Winter that the doctor was being reticent out of a sense of his professional responsibility and with this possibility in mind Winter refrained from pressing his question too much. But Plunkett was not the man to be nice about the proprieties and Winter felt that the restraint might be of another kind—it might even arise out of complete ignorance and, indeed, Plunkett did say after some hesitation that sanity was only a comparative thing; in the case of a man who did his job efficiently and harmed no one a medical man was running a grave risk in interfering.

'You should send him back to the delta on some other count then.'

'Look here, young man! Will you mind your own blasted business? How does this concern you, I'd like to know?'

'In a very obvious way, I should have thought . . .'

'How does this concern you, I'd like to know? This is a medical matter, isn't it? You get back to your paraffin, or whatever you call it, and leave me to manage my own affairs, coming over here poking your nose into my business. You're a sight too cocky!'

Winter took none of this seriously. 'That's as may be, but I think that he's queer in the head. If you'd heard the things he was saying to me this morning—identified me with this man who's missing, identified me with Rider and said that I planned to follow him and Hebechi into the interior. And then, in addition to that . . .'

The doctor was making clucking noises with his tongue, fidgeting round his surgery, and Winter interrupted himself to suggest that he take a drink to calm himself down. This only served to cause the old fellow to flare up once more and say that he would not be insulted in his own surgery just because he took a nip now and again.

'Interesting to find that he's obsessed by the idea that someone is going to blow up his well.'

'And why is it extraordinary?' demanded Plunkett explosively. 'There is nothing in the world so natural. Bless me! What do you think, eh? He's in charge of the place—and wells have been destroyed before now! Wouldn't you have the same

idea if you was in charge? Enough to give anybody an obsession. No, perfectly natural. Don't know what your game is, but
he's not so barmy as that.'

'I have the feeling,' said Winter, 'that he is so obsessed with
the idea that if nobody does destroy the well he will do it himself.'

'Fiddlesticks!' And Plunkett could not be persuaded to continue the discussion. He had been too agitated even to take a
drink.

With Plunkett he had come up against a brick wall. There
was nothing to be learned and no sympathy given—yes, Winter would even allow himself now to consider sympathy as a
legitimate demand. Ford's insane bout had brought to a crisis
a number of the feelings that Winter was having about himself
—nothing was more characteristic than his dismay at realizing
that he was feeling sorry for Ford. And he had pitied that sad,
strong woman, his wife, too, as she had smiled at him on her
balcony—treasonable pity that availed nothing and only
brought sorrow to the person experiencing it. Even in so clear-
cut a case as that of Hebechi's he had not been consistent. To
begin with he had acted in accordance with his wishes. There
was no real love of justice for the sake of justice in his own
nature. He was not going to allow compassion for an ill-treated
clerk to cause him any internal stirrings—why should he
bother? And yet he had followed Hebechi out on to the veranda the first time the clerk had called, almost telling him to
come back. And that night, when Hebechi had hidden himself
in the rocks to await a signal, had he really gone out on to the
balcony in the hope that Nellie would follow him, or was it
really a gesture, the slight concession made to his hidden desire? He thought of the weeping woman on the ship, the woman

whose husband had died and been thrown overboard, and how
he had hated her sorrow to the point where he could even con-
template causing her some physical injury—and then had himself moved up on to the deck and slept under the stars. No, he
was not consistent. He had the wish to protect himself, the desire to avoid allowing any grief or loneliness of spirit, but always, at the dangerous moment, the bone of his resolve gave
way, he wished for Hebechi's escape, grieved over Ford's wildness, and saw visions of his dead wife walking through the
wedding-cake palace of the Sultan. He knew what he wanted
to be! He wanted hardness, resolve, self-interest. But there was
that within him that prevented all this.

That is why I am fool enough to fall in love with Nellie.
That is why we meet at night, why she comes to my room and
there is the oblivion of caressing her nude body, annihilating
all time else but that one rapturous moment.

He tried to tell Nellie about the scene with Ford for the
memory of it was an oppression to the spirit. She had come
over from the office where, exceptionally, she had been working late and the sun was already touching the western escarpment. Rachid made tea and brought it out to them on the balcony and she sipped it noisily, for she was very thirsty, and
looking out on to the purpling wadi, she listened to the low
tones of Winter's voice. How does this concern me and us, she
was thinking, and why does he take it all with such deadly
seriousness? What does it matter if Ford is a bit cracked? But
she made no spoken comment and Winter was grateful for the
sympathetic interest she was showing.

'But surely it's something that you were all aware of?' he
asked at last.

In spite of herself a little twinge of interest was felt. There

was the chance that Ford might become dangerous or do something really eccentric in which chance she was always prepared
to watch events closely.

'What's that, darling?' She had been thinking of other
things.

'I said, surely it's not news to you, this about Ford.'

'Well, of course, he had made his machine. . . .'

'That's nothing. I can understand that. That shows a lot of
sanity—and a lot of ability, what's more.' As far as he could
remember it was the first time that she had called him darling
and he was glowing pleasantly as a result of it. She peeped at
him over the top of her cup to observe the result of her sudden
expression of endearment. She knew what she was doing.

'I always used to think that Plunkett was mad. But Ford—no,
normal people never talked about it. It was just too impossible
for the manager to be mad. And—well, you know how it is—
when you get it into your head that something is impossible,
well, it is impossible. It's like somebody telling you that he's
going to blow up a town—and you laugh at him! Then he goes
and does it!'

'What he was very worried over was that somebody was
going to destroy the well. Has an obsession about it. What to
do with him, that's the problem. Plunkett refuses to believe
that there's anything really the matter. I suppose he thinks that
he's harmless. You know, it was just an idea I had—Ford never
put it into words—that he thought I might attempt to destroy
the well.'

'Oh, but how impossible.' She laughed at this amusing suggestion.

'Well, when a lunatic gets a fixed idea . . .'

'Oh, I'm sure that you're exaggerating. I'm sure that he's as
sane as you or me. Come, let's be sensible, darling. Don't

worry so much about it! After all, what does it matter? I don't doubt for a moment that it was all a lot of nerves, that scene in the office. If you went to call on him now, I'm sure you would find him very apologetic for being so silly. You don't know—or do you know, for I mustn't forget to flatter you— that things just play on your nerves. Put yourself in his position. He's been here—let me see, how long? If he could have a holiday . . .'

'That's precisely what I mean.'

The large night moths had come in like spirits to the lighted area of the veranda. A soft, humid night, such as came before rain in this part of the world. Perspiration lay cold on their throats and foreheads although they had been doing nothing more active than talking. The cracked woodwork of the veranda was sucking up the moisture like blotting paper and there was even a faint phosphorescence down at Rachid's end of the veranda. One or two of the upright posts were glimmering faintly. Large beetles scuffled out of the sand and ran over the veranda, creaking as though they were running over brown paper. There were few snakes so that this night life was quite innocuous. In England it would have been the sort of weather to presage a thunderstorm. Here it might last for days and then fade out into the normal brilliant dryness. But there might be rain. This would be very unusual and the natives, who for all that they were Moslem had streaks of the pagan underneath, would say that God was angry and go to the mosque to ask, not that the rain might cease, for that would be too great a presumption, but that it might go to another district.

'No, it was more than an attack of nerves,' Winter decided. He had been glowering at the night. The girl could feel the intensity with which he was grappling with the problem. 'Otherwise he would not have said I was like Rider—identified me

with him, that is. Said he thought I'd carry on where Rider had
left off. Just the sort of thing that a man with an obsession
might say.'

'He said you were—Rider?'

'Said we were—well, I suppose it boils down to saying that
we were the same kind of people. Because we'd got designs on
the well. Though heaven preserve me . . .'

'Well, it's true in one respect. Rider used to make love to me!'

'What?' Winter sat up with a jerk. This was unthinkable.

'But he was very unsuccessful. So there's a point of similarity
and a point of contrast, you see.'

'Rider used to make love to you!' He could not believe it!
Rider, the irresponsible, the man who washed rarely, the man
who tried to get Plunkett to treat the diseases of Rasuka, the
man who tried to teach the natives how to read, the eccentric,
the well-intentioned, the man who cried when he hit his hand
with a hammer, the man whom Hebechi compared with the
gods, and Ford in his wildness mentioned in the same breath
with Christ—he turned to her quickly.

'You're joking with me! Aren't you? You're joking with me!'

'Of course I'm not. He used to hang about between the
offices and the bungalow so that he could walk home with me.
He used to ask me to sleep with him.'

Winter was scandalized and yet could not quite see why.
Why should he be shocked? Apparently Rider had been unsuccessful or Nellie would not have been telling him all about it
with such coldness.

'But it's impossible. I can't believe it.'

'Why?' There was a plaintive note of amusement in her
interrogation. Why? Yes, why could he not believe it? He
could not imagine Rider hanging about in the desert waiting
for Nellie to go by, like some Cockney street lounger. It was

easier to imagine Rider going up to her in a crowded room and saying, 'My dear Nellie, what a long time since I saw you. Where have you been? When are you coming to sleep with me? It will be so nice.' Winter could imagine that but he could not imagine the furtiveness of the wait in the sand.

Nellie was laughing to herself. She would have stopped immediately if she had known how much she scandalized him.

'But you don't know anything about him.'

'I just can't believe it.'

'He tried to seduce Mrs. Ford.'

'What d'you mean, tried to? How do you know he didn't succeed?' There was an ugly note creeping into his voice.

'She told me about it.'

He laughed a little bitterly. 'That's something I don't believe. I don't believe that story as it's told. Either Rider never tried to do anything of the sort . . .'

'Oh, but he did . . .'

'Either he never tried to do anything of the sort or it's the story of Potiphar's wife all over again.'

'Meaning?'

'That it's more likely she tried to seduce him than the other way round. I may not know Rider but I do know Mrs. Ford.'

'Are you hinting that the same might be true of me, by any chance?'

Oh, you schoolgirl, he wanted to say. You silly little schoolgirl, with your painted finger-nails and the cigarette drooping from the corner of your mouth.

'Don't be absurd,' he said shortly. The news had shocked him profoundly. Was it that, like the others, like Hebechi and like Ford, he had been building up a legend of Rider all of his own? Under the influence of Hebechi's last words, and perhaps under the influence of Ford's also, had he been sentimentalizing the character of this unknown man of whom he had heard so much? It was unthinkable! He had not imagined that his mind was capable of playing such tricks. He had thought he knew his opinion about Rider, the prefect, the scoutmaster, the insufferable, but there was this shock to show him that all was not as it seemed.

He should have been rather pleased at having a hypocrite unmasked. But he was distressed to think that there was this inconsistency in Rider's character. He had wanted him to be the man that Hebechi had thought him. Possibly from the moment that Cator had shown himself to be so bitterly preju-diced against him Winter had taken a favourable interest— and had not been aware of it. It all came back to the same thing.

'I just can't believe it.' He was angry with Nellie for having told him. 'Why didn't he succeed with Mrs. Ford? She's al-ways given me to understand that she's very much in need of that sort of thing.' He spoke viciously, not caring whom he was hurting. What did it matter to him that under the circum-stances Ford was probably no husband to her, that she was a normal woman and in the presence of personable men acted as God would have her act? Yet, in spite of all this there was this wonderful service to her husband. He could not forget her fixed smile as she stood on the balcony the day he had followed Ford across the sand, the smile that must have disappeared as soon as he turned his back. It did not matter to him that he was being coarse at the expense of somebody's tragedy. He just wanted to hit out and hurt somebody.

What was all this talk anyway? Why talk on a warm evening with the shadow of his wife at his elbow? Nellie's words could hurt him, therefore why waste time in talking? He could never rid himself of the idea that he could tear aside some curtain from Nellie's being and find Joyce hidden there. There was always that ambiguity, always that uncertainty—only Joyce could never have spoken like this. She would never have taken adultery so lightly. Dear Joyce, who never escaped from the English atmosphere of green lawns and flowering shrubs, tea on the lawn in the warm August afternoons, gauzy summer dresses like flames in the Victorian garden. Joyce would never have understood all this. Dear Joyce!

'Of course it's true, why do you doubt? He used to wait and then when I used to ignore him—I had to, you know, because the slightest concession would have been so significant to him —he just used to laugh in rather'—she thought it over for a moment—'yes, in rather a nice way, I suppose, and go off with his hands in his pockets, showing a great tear in the behind of his trousers. It was just as though he didn't really care, and yet it never made him give up trying. Come to think of it, I suppose that is why Mrs. Ford was so annoyed. She said she told him off, let him have it, told him all the usual things, and he seemed to take it all as a great joke. That was what Mrs. Ford found more insulting than anything else, I suppose. Yes, I suppose he must have done the same to her, just stuck his hands in his pockets and walked off, whistling.'

'Insolence!'

'Not really. I suppose he really was rather nice. We used to snub him awfully and yet it never had much effect on his spirits and he never seemed to bear any resentment. I'd find him waiting for me the following evening. It got into a kind of joke. I couldn't help laughing when I saw him. And he used to laugh back, so gaily. But I'd never let him walk with me. He was rather frightening really, to be so gay—and a bit simple.'

It pleased Winter to learn that Rider had, if you looked at it fairly, been so natural. He had acted like an innocent, like a virgin. Winter could not understand why Nellie had found him frightening, nor why on the other hand, Mrs. Ford had repulsed him. The picture that he was now preserving in his mind's eye was that of Rider strolling casually away across the sand with a rag of shirt poking derisively out of the hole in the seat of his trousers. That's all I really care for you, the shirt tail would say. What the hell!

CHAPTER X: *Ramadan*

FORD DID NOT COME UP TO THE WELL for nearly a week and when he eventually did return he was as normal as though nothing had happened. He came into the office about nine o'clock, rather like an excited schoolboy who has been given an unexpected holiday, and Winter found it easy to pick up the thread of relationship between them as though the scene of a week before had never occurred. During Ford's absence there had been no mention of him—that he was ill, that he was tired, nothing was said that would cause apprehension to anyone. With Flynn Winter was exchanging few words these days and when they did speak there was always the subject that was on the point of being brought up, always the cavity that was being skirted, the embarrassment, the unmentionable. Winter felt it improper to discuss anything but the most impersonal subjects with the Irishman. They got into the habit of talking more and more about his modelling, for he would talk without self-consciousness and even with enthusiasm about his hobby. One occasion he was even on the point of suggesting that he should model Winter's head. The other could imagine the words trembling on his lips but at the last moment it was as though the Irishman had remembered something and fallen into a silence.

Cator, now recovered, returned to work.

Everything was, seemingly, as it had been.

Everything was the same and yet everything had changed. For Winter the problems, so far from all being at an end now that an apparent calm had been reached, were more real than ever; and the more disturbing for being so vague. He could not put his hand on them. They dissolved before him as he approached and then re-formed behind him when he had passed. The questions that he had put to the oracle of Rasuka had been answered, but so ambiguously that he was suffering from that peculiar kind of desperation that will overcome a man when he has to solve a problem in a certain specified time and he sees the hand of the clock creeping inexorably round. Winter was a simple man. He was no subtle thinker. He was not a brooder. He had been given a certain measure of intelligence which, before the death of his wife, had expressed itself in the usual work and diversions. He thought that he had understood himself. Then Joyce had died, and that was the first inexplicable thing, for no matter how the coffin had knocked against the side of the grave he could not believe that anything of his was being buried. For the first time events were happening to him and he had no sense of actively controlling them. Grief for the death of his wife might one day come bursting out like the pent-up fires of some volcano that had been muffled by sheets of hard igneous rock. There would be a devastating explosion. All this was nascent within him and he feared sorrow and the sight of sorrow, never knowing how much it would release within himself by sympathy. He would be cruel rather than grieve, he thought. Let the widow wail and Hebechi be unjustly executed, for what have they to do with me?

He always had to know where he was going. He liked to feel the ground firm beneath his feet and his love affair with

Nellie, no matter how much he needed her, was carried on in the half-light and there were times when he could hardly see her face for the emotion that was closing his own eyes. There was no reason why he should not ask her to marry him. They were both free and he could not understand the inhibitions that made him walk round and round what he wanted so much, never allowing him to dare to set one foot inwards. He did not like the casual liaison. He did not want Nellie as a mistress and there was some hidden sense of guilt that prevented his taking her as a wife. There were times when she seemed to be waiting for him to say the expected words. At nights, just before parting, he would say: 'Oh, why do we have to part?' and she would reply, 'Yes, why?'—there was no reason why they should not be together always. The expression on her face was an interrogation. Why could he not ask her to marry him? Was it, by any chance, the thought that she had set out to 'get' him? He did not think it was that.

So that the love affair with Nellie did not seem to be leading anywhere and in Winter's life if things did not lead somewhere they came to an end. He protested to himself that he could not give up loving Nellie. Whatever else came to an end this was something that would have to go on. One day, the propitious moment would come, his lips would be unsealed and he would be able to say: 'Nellie, will you marry me?' Until then there was a double guilt. He felt guilty to that sense of order and justice, to that limited logical world that had always governed him: and he felt guilty when he saw Nellie's face in the lights of night, whether stars or moon, and she wanted something more than the kiss or the embrace. He was being strained to the uttermost.

He wondered if he would become unbalanced like Ford and the idea so frightened him that he took to more exercise and read the lightest fiction he could lay his hands on. He adopted temporarily a flippant and teasing attitude towards Nellie—it was surprising how easily he could manage this—until she was at first bewildered and then enraged. She didn't understand him all at once. She struck out.

It was the very first time that Winter went to her room. All their previous meetings had taken place in his bungalow—it was safer—but Nellie said that she did not like the long walk over the sand afterwards in the small hours of the morning, even though Winter always accompanied her. She wanted to lie in bed afterwards and give herself over to thinking. By having him in her room there would be, moreover, the added spice of danger. It was much more exciting for Winter to come to her room where there was always a chance of their being discovered by the Cators. She might even enjoy being discovered. She cared nothing for their opinions and her love affair might even gain added zest from an awareness that others knew of it—they knew of it already, of course—but not that she had spent the larger part of many nights in Winter's bungalow. Winter was not unwilling to come. His sense of fairness did that for him. The walk back over the sand afterwards was rather tiring, and she had to start in the office the following morning at eight. It flattered him, moreover, that she should go to such lengths. She admitted him through the large french window that gave out on to the balcony and the moment that he was inside he felt that he should not have come. So thin were the walls that he could hear the Cators breathing in their bedroom. But what was a deterrent to him was a stimulus to Nellie. She pulled him towards her.

Aware that he was loth, a tiny flame of anger sprang up.

'What's the matter?' she whispered, louder than was necessary. It was sibilant in his ear like the hissing of snakes.

'Quieter! quieter!' he begged and listened to the breathing coming from the next room. He stood motionless, clasping her in his arms, but listening.

'Don't be silly! They won't hear! Well, you knew what it would be like. You shouldn't have come. I'm taking the risk, not you, I was just wanting to make it easy for you. You can go if you want to. But I warn you, if you go you'll never come back.'

'Shut up! Don't be a little fool.' But words would not silence her. He could only close her mouth with his lips. Still the flame of anger burned inside her and she felt a great urge to mock and tease him.

'No need to be frightened,' she murmured. 'If anyone comes I'll tell them it's all my fault. You've got nothing to worry about.'

If he spoke at all he knew that he would say something unforgivable so he looked over her head in silence. That she should have asked him to come and put him in this impossible situation was enough in itself. But that she should now take it into her head to taunt him . . .

'Will you shut up?' he hissed as though he really hated her.

'No, I will not shut up,' she replied as though she recognized an enemy. And he drew her closer to him so that she was resting her head on his chest and gripping his left shoulder with her right hand. She opened and closed her hand on it spasmodically.

'Why are you here? Why do you come?'

'Because I love you.'

'At the moment you sound as though you hate me.' This was milder and milkier and he knew it was an invitation to kiss her but he could not find it in him to deny his feelings. They were both furious with one another.

'No,' she said, still clinging close to him. 'You neither love me nor hate me. I don't think you could love or hate anyone. You're cold, cold as ice. There's no feeling in you.'

He wished passionately that what she was saying was true.

'You're playing false. You're just an—an adulterer,' she reached up and whispered gently in his ear as though it were an endearment. 'You think I'm your wife—like your wife, I don't know! But I'm not. I hate your wife. You'll either love me for myself or not at all. I'm not going to have you looking at me and through me trying to find someone who isn't there. Look at me—not at her! I hate her and you with her.' She spoke with all the bitterness of which she was capable and by reason of her having to express it all in whispers there was an unbelievable savagery behind her words. 'Would you have looked at me twice in England, for example? No, it's just because we're here and you are you. It's all false. It's mockery, horrible. Oh, you're so very unfair, so selfish. All men are selfish.'

She ceased suddenly and listened to his heart beating. Its steady rhythm never altered, a slow, earthy pulse.

Could it be true what she was saying? Suddenly he did not want to be with her any more, nor enclosed in any room. He pushed her from him and, not caring who heard the noise he made, walked out. He found his tongue dry and his face twitching in a way that aroused vague memories. He almost laughed when he realized what was the matter with him. His face was trying to cry and yet could not remember how to go about it! It was true what she had said—he was selfish, selfish, for they would not have been tears for her, but tears for himself, hardly of sorrow either, but perhaps of fear in face of the inexplicable, the strangeness, the chaos of life.

Rider would not have done this, he thought. He would have

laughed and walked away with his hands thrust deep into his
trousers pockets, revealing the tail of his shirt like the white,
bobbing, defiant tail of some retreating rabbit.

But to Winter it was as though, all at once, he did not know
where to go, set down in a strange and unknowable city. It was
already so late that there were few lights about the valley, although behind him the arc lamps at the well were glowing and
making a kind of false dawn in that part of the sky. There was
no moon. The walls of the wadi, the cliffs, took on an oily
blackness against the star-scattered sky but although the
heavens themselves were radiant with these many stars here in
the valley it was as though he were at the bottom of a pit. And
whichever way he went it would not make the slightest difference. He did not think of direction. His legs kept moving,
given energy from a source that might have been outside him
for all the control he exercised over it. Would it matter where
he went so long as it was away from that dark room with the
mocking woman and the heavy sleepers on the other side of
the partition?

The small pebbles at his feet revealed that they had golden
lips. The sand blossomed into golden grains. Everywhere there
was light and shadow, brightness and purple and like a wave
suddenly cast up on the shore came cries and voices from the
area within the compound where the employees of the well
had their living quarters. A man was laughing a great belly
laugh that stopped suddenly as though he had bent his head
down once more to hear the joke out, then he continued, shaking out his great 'Hur! Hur! Hur!' as though ridding his body
of something unwanted. A woman screamed with laughter. A
drum began to sound, softly at first, and then more insistently,
beating on the stretched fabric of the night until each listener's
ear, each listener's diaphragm was a tympanum and the unseen

drummer was controlling them as surely as though they were marionettes and he holding the ends of the strings. Winter felt stirred, in spite of himself, as anyone will feel stirred by the beating of a drum. The natives were celebrating some feast by the light of the arc lamps, some nocturnal feast—of course, the only one, Ramadan, the terrible month of fasting when between sunrise and sunset there was to be no eating nor drinking, the devout not even swallowing their own spittle, nor lying with their wives, until the evening gun from the Sultan's palace was heard. Then, in the night the feasting! To begin with a glass of sweet syrup as a ceremonial breaking of the fast, for after twelve hours one has been so long without food that the appetite has to be carefully treated. The main eating would not come before ten o'clock and this was the aftermath when the younger and more active workers would still have enough energy to caper about the place and sing while their replete elders looked on with chibouks, the Eastern pipes, in their hands.

They were crying and calling to one another like forest birds when the drum ceased palpitating—rather lost, a little dazed. Then when the drummer's hands were once more falling on the tightly stretched skin there were cries and immediately a score of young voices swung into a rhythmic chanting. They were mocking someone. Winter could hear somebody's name, a native name and obviously belonging to one of the workmen, repeated rhythmically over and over again—there was a tremendous joke going on at someone's expense and no doubt he would be good-humouredly running from one to the other of his taunters trying to stop their mouths with his open hand. Or perhaps he would sit in the middle of the circle grinning at them and mocking them in return. An unmelodious, wild, desert pipe

introduced itself into the hubbub and was greeted with shouts.
'Ramzy—amzy—amzy!' they chanted.

Winter passed through the gate of the stockade but they
were far too excited and engrossed with what was going on in
the illuminated area in the centre of the crowd to take any
notice of him. Their eyes flashed with excitement, some tug-
ging at the miserable scraps of hair on their chins that was all
that could be managed in the way of a beard in this part of the
world. Two youths were carrying on a kind of ceremonial
sword dance. But there were no swords. Instead they carried
long staves which they whirled gracefully round their heads
and tapped together—yes, it was even a little like quarter-
staff play. Many of the men and youths were sitting on the
sand with their white robes gathered closely to them for the
evening was quite cool; some of the women were sitting on
stools outside the neat little huts that the Company had built
for them, and some were sitting on the steps. All had given
themselves over completely to enjoyment. It was as primitive,
and as un-self-conscious as the wailing of a baby. Such happiness, Winter felt, shut him out. He was the foreigner, alien
and incapable of entering into these simple mysteries.

He was no longer angry with Nellie and could even see that
as a woman with any sense of pride she could hardly have
acted differently. It was not that he forgave her, for incidents
like this are on such a scale that they are outside the province
of forgiveness. Rather was it that the uncertainty and the guilt
which Nellie had drawn out of the air—as the solitary tree
will draw lightning—had ceased to trouble the clear image of
her face which he preserved in his mind. It was as flawless as
crystal. The stars themselves, these velvet black ravines, those
weary-happy faces under the arc lamps, all these might be in
question—light shot through with darkness, joy shot through

with pain. It was the world itself that Winter was uncertain about, not Nellie. He was sure of her. And the beating of the drum was so hypnotic that he was hardly aware of what was causing him pain—whether desire, frustration or a merciless black punishment.

'Ramzy—amzy—amzy!' chanted a section of the crowd who would not abandon their earlier joke. A wave of merriment went round the crowd; it went round almost visibly, like a wind swishing over a field of tall grasses so that you are astonished to find the grass still there when the wind drops and not piled up against the furthest stone wall where the goats are cropping. The crowd swayed with laughter. Ardently Winter wanted to share it all. If their spirit could have been picked up like a piece of bread from between the feet of the jumping sword-dancers he would have done so. But it was more mysterious than that. By now some of the crowd had noticed his presence and those nearest to him began to adopt a more subdued note of merriment. He was one of the bosses. But this Winter scarcely noticed.

'Ramzy—amzy—amzy! Ramzy Effendi!' Where was the unfortunate Ramzy who had been giving himself such airs that his mates were laughing at him and calling him Mr.—Mr. Ramzy—the respectable one, the professional man!

At first Winter could not understand why he was so carried away by the happiness of these people. He had never known anything so infectious as their laughter and high-pitched excited voices. They threw their hands about, found something wonderful every minute, and when those nearest to him, those who had seen and recognized him and consequently restrained themselves a little only to forget him immediately, when they looked round at him he was elated to see that their eyes were stained with tears of joy. He had to

remember who he was. How everyone would be scandalized
if he forgot for a little while and threw himself into the cele-
brations with as much abandon as they.

As it was they defeated him with their joy, for did they not
have what he was looking for? Nothing can be more holy than
happiness and who can fail to worship it when he sees it? So
that Winter, when he saw this group of wildly happy people,
naturally felt that they had some secret which had been de-
nied him. They were happier than he was because they knew
more than he. And that was why he was carried away, carried
away as much as his nerve would allow him, smiling to himself in the darkness of his corner because these people had a
mystery to which they might possibly admit him. He was with
the right people, the happy people! Happiness needs no justification or excuse. It exists like the coming up of the sun and
the sinking of great rivers into the sea as a fact for wonder
and worship.

The following day he presented himself at the Sultan's palace and asked for an audience, the third and the last that he
was to have. The Sultan received him most kindly and, indeed, contrived the impression that he had been expecting
him. He was seated as usual behind his glass-topped desk,
though to-day, for a change, he was not wearing a turban but
a tarbouche round which he had wound a length of white
silk. But Winter was too intent on the business on hand to
allow his imagination to roam round the palace and smell out
secrets. Coffee was brought in almost immediately, this time
by a girl in a long blue robe. This extraordinary innovation
caused Winter to look up at her sharply, and the Sultan, seeing the expression on his face, smiled and said, 'It is what I
thought. You white people here have no sex life.'

'Your Excellency, it strikes me as absurd and dangerous that a criminal like Hebechi should be allowed to get off scot-free as he has.'

'Scot-free?'

'Quite free—without any punishment.'

The Sultan showed himself to be unsurprised by the turn that the conversation was taking, and his next words almost hinted that he had been turning this very problem over in his mind.

'We must not be savages, Mr. Winter, must we? Please drink your coffee before it gets cold. It loses all its aroma otherwise. No, my reference to savagery was not in connection with your coffee getting cold. What I am talking about is the question of punishment.'

Round, serious, professorial eyes looking at Winter over the tiny coffee cup, no bigger than a thimble, that the Sultan had just fitted over his lips and the end of his nose. It was a very snug fit.

'The question of punishment,' went on the Sultan at last, when he thought he had sufficiently prepared the way by raising a fundamental problem in Winter's mind, 'is not an easy one. We must beware of revenge. It is not dignified to be revengeful.'

'Your Excellency,' said Winter patiently, 'this is not revenge. This is the question of punishing a dangerous criminal. It is my belief that if he is not caught he will make another attempt on the life of Mr. Cator.'

The Sultan's face wore an inane, incredulous smile as though he were a baby just presented with a particularly colourful and noisy rattle. 'Oh, no, Mr. Winter. You will be talking about principles next. Now, I don't follow principles. I follow my nose.' It was as though the rattle had suddenly devel-

oped some extraordinary quality, had changed colour or given
out a surprising squeak. He was delighted with himself. 'I
follow my nose.' He repeated his own joke.

'He'll probably turn into a fully fledged bandit up in the hills
and make a thorough nuisance of himself.'

'Mr. Winter, you are being very European. If he becomes a
bandit, it will be very good, for then he will be killed by other
bandits. However, I do not imagine a clerk going up into my
mountains and becoming—a bandit. I do not doubt for one
moment that he has already had his throat cut. And why
should I send out an expedition to trap one man? One man!
It is not dignified. If there were a group of them . . .'

Winter presumed to interrupt him. 'You laugh at questions
of principle, Your Excellency, but you will find that the British Government thinks of nothing else but questions of principle.'

The Sultan did not lose his good humour for one moment,
but sat perfectly still, his podgy hands folded on his lap, looking across at Winter as though they were engaged in some
intellectual, friendly game like chess. Winter was passionately
eager to take part in this expedition, and though his partici-
pation had so far not been mentioned there was not the slightest doubt in his mind that the Sultan was well aware of his
hopes. They made great assumptions about one another, Winter that the Sultan could be intimidated by any mention of the
British Government—an idea that was completely false—and
the Sultan thinking that Winter had some ulterior motive in
wanting to penetrate to the interior of his little-known country. He was convinced that it was not mere love of justice,
though he was well aware that the European, and the Englishman above all, will do monstrous things if he thinks that it is
—what was the word?—principle. But the Sultan did not

think it was that. He could understand a man making an attempt to catch Hebechi out of a spirit of revenge. When one's brother or friend has been attacked, then, indeed, one's honour demands that some demonstration of vengeance be made. But the Sultan had seen Winter and Cator together and had the feeling that there were no bonds between them. Possibly Winter wanted to make the journey out of a love of being where no other white man had ever been. He might even have heard false legends of treasure-filled tombs. All this or perhaps just European restlessness. Whatever it was, the Sultan did not believe that Hebechi was anything other than an excuse for the trip. He was quite determined, under these circumstances, to make Winter pay for his pleasure.

'Mr. Winter, this is an expedition that I, as head of the state of Rasuka, do not consider necessary. Yes? I wouldn't send it. I would prefer my men to die here near their own sea. But you think, "No." It is more important to catch this man, even if a dozen men die. Well, this is what I say. You can have your expedition—I know that you have the wish to go yourself although you have not said so. But you must pay for it! I will supply you with—men, camels, what you want, all what you want. But you must pay me. And if a man dies you must pay twenty pounds to his family.'

Winter looked at him in amazement. It was an unusual experience to live in a state where the government expected private citizens to pay for the privilege of catching criminals. The Sultan looked at his visitor with as much satisfaction on his face as his dignity would permit. He was quite sure that Winter would turn down the offer.

'On the condition that you give a reward for the capture of Hebechi. You should give a reward of five hundred pounds sterling.'

The Sultan was quite certain that Winter would not see so much as the hem of Hebechi's robe. 'That is a fair proposition. I am in accord.'

'You must tell me what you propose charging—how much a man, how much a camel.'

'For the camels I will charge you ten pounds a month,' the Sultan said immediately, not so much as blinking, 'and my soldiers you may pay five piastres a day. You feed the camels and the soldiers. It is your expedition.'

'Ammunition?'

'We will arrange that.'

Winter took his leave of the Sultan and returned to his bungalow where he lay on the bed. The audacity of the man in asking him to finance an expedition to catch a man who, so far as the law of the country was concerned, was a dangerous criminal, in turn astounded and amused Winter. But he never for one moment hesitated to accept the offer and was eager to begin as soon as possible before the Sultan changed his mind. He worked out the expenses. Not more than four camels—and that would include his own—would mean forty pounds. In his calculations the trip would not take a month. Fifteen piastres a day in pay—say five pounds a month. Fodder for the camels and provisions would cost little in comparison. He counted on the expenditure of not more than sixty pounds for the month, and was elated at the thought of getting away, out of the oppressive valley. He was, now, thinking entirely of himself.

The evening with Nellie, the Ramadan celebration, the inconsistency and confusion of his own ideas, the rising envy of Rider that he was experiencing, were a fierce coil of energy tied down within him and straining to be free. One clear image had stuck in his mind—that of Rider walking away over the sand with the tail of his shirt showing. From that moment Winter had envied him, for it seemed that Rider was free in a way that he could never be. Turned down by any woman he had been making love to, Winter would have sulked, stood on his dignity, assured himself that, after all, the woman was not worth it. But what Rider had signified by the tail of his shirt was that life itself and its tangled complications were not worth it to a man who looked at them from a sufficiently distant point of view. It would be the end of stagnation to move up into the clear mountain air on the backs of the swaying camels. He envied Rider because of what he was sure could be nothing more than his trivial, shallow nature. Rider never gave him any sense of depth. He was too happy for that. A sensitive man would not have taken being snubbed quite as easily as Rider had done, Winter thought. He could not but identify a real sense of human values with his own character. Winter had no humility. He envied Rider as a king may envy a beggar his freedom and quiet of mind. Winter felt himself to be infinitely superior to the rather simple-minded person Rider must have been—or must still be, for it was by no means sure that he was dead. But he wanted to make the gesture of walking away with the tail of his shirt showing. He wanted this audacity.

He was still sustained by the airy happiness of the Ramadan celebration.

It never occurred to him to go to Ford and make formal application for a month's leave of absence. It was rather odd that Ford should have anticipated the expedition by forbidding him to go into the interior, but none of this could be taken seriously, of course, for poor Ford was quite mad. Winter would go up to the office as usual during the few days that would necessarily elapse before his little party could set out for the interior, but he would not discuss his plans with any-one. It did not occur to him that secrets of this kind are quite impossible in Rasuka, and within two hours of his interview with the Sultan interested persons in Rasuka knew all about it.

Flynn would not mention it because he did not consider himself to be quite on talking terms with Winter; by ignoring the rest of the Europeans in making his plans, Winter had, in any case, tacitly implied that what he was doing was none of their business. He sank into a gloomier silence than ever. Flynn even wondered whether Nellie planned to go and de-cided to protest if it should turn out that this was the idea.

Ford hadn't the courage to say anything. He was very much opposed to the expedition, but that fact in itself was enough to make him question the rightness of his opinion. Ford always suspected the things that he wanted and only felt that he was doing right when he was doing something uncon-genial.

Plunkett thought that Winter was a fool, and made a special trip across to his bungalow with a satchel of medical supplies and instructions to put a few drops of iodine in any water be-fore he drank it. That is, if they found any water. He also handed over a bottle of gin, pointing out that apart from all its other qualities it was antiseptic in an emergency.

Nellie alone was angry. She felt that the breach between Winter and her was now too wide ever to be crossed. Even though she had been trying to hurt him she felt that he had insulted her by leaving so abruptly when she had invited him to her room. At least he should have maintained the conven-tions of being ardently in love with her. Yet she did not want the mere conventions. She really wanted his love. It didn't matter to her why he had wanted her embraces, whether it was because of the fortuitous resemblance to his wife sitting

in a characteristic position and with the light coming from a
certain direction; and whether or not he would have made
love to her in London, or anywhere else for that matter, what
did all this matter? She was not romantic. She did not believe
in soul-mates. Love was the occasion and the circumstances
and the person all together. This was as much love as she
thought could be asked. He had always wanted to know about
her past—she had to smile even when she thought how little
there was to tell.

But when she arrived at Winter's bungalow as the evening
was just coming on she found only Rachid sitting at his end
of the veranda. He was at his old occupation of making ornamental boxes, gumming snippets of bone and ivory to the lids
and sides. Nellie made herself comfortable in a creaking
basket-chair and Rachid gave over his pleasures in order to
make her some coffee and bring it in shining kanak to the
small table at her side. She was curious about the task in which
she had interrupted him, but felt that any questions would
bring such a flood of explanations that she would be wearied.
Rachid looked at her in silence. It was evening. The eastern
sky was dark in the face of the sunset. The coffee was sweet.
At any moment she expected Winter to come out on to the
balcony and posed herself in the most effective way to receive him. She did not care what she said by way of apology.
But Winter did not come and the lower levels of the wadi filled
up with darkness. The sky-line of the eastern escarpment was
watery gold. Rachid had returned to his task, but as it was
now too dark to see he sat in silence with the implements and
bits and pieces of his hobby scattered on the floor in front of
him, looking now and again in the direction of the visitor.

She could stand it no longer and asked him where Mr. Winter was.

'Gone! Him gone!' answered Rachid, with a delighted expression on his face. He had feared that Winter would want to take him on this trip and was still bathing himself in his relief.

'What, already?' she said, wonderingly, and looked up the valley where the hills laced their fingers together. There was the purple of night gridded by the gold of the sunset on the higher reaches so that she thought of her own Scottish hills. She had not thought that he would go so soon.

CHAPTER XI: *The Journey*

THERE WERE THREE SOLDIERS AND HIM-
self, each riding one of the cream-coloured Asiatic dromedaries
that were imported in large numbers into Rasuka each year.
The youngest of the three soldiers brought up the rear, leading, by means of a halter, their one baggage camel which carried all their provisions for the journey—a couple of military
bivouac tents, rice, tinned meats, beans, a little flour, and two
large and greasy goat-skins plumped up with water. Winter
had wanted the soldiers to abandon their military uniforms
and adopt the ordinary dress of the country as being less con-
spicuous, but this the Sultan would not permit. Each soldier
was, therefore, wearing a thick khaki tunic of infantry pattern,
white robes which swept down to their ankles, and white tur-
bans elegantly wound round the head and fastened in front
with a large brooch bearing arabesques. On their feet they
wore rough-looking sandals. Folded up, so that they acted as
cushions, were the brown cloaks such as are worn by any
Bedouin in the cold weather. Then a rifle over the right shoulder, swaying and dancing with every motion of the dromedaries.

Winter had more confidence in the youngest of the soldiers

than in either of his two comrades. This youth, for he could
not have been more than seventeen or eighteen, was a great
dandy and contrived to show Winter an ornate, ugly ring, a
thing of brass which he wore on his right hand, within five
minutes of meeting him. He was obviously very proud of this
ring. He had a string of jasmine flowers in his hand and even
found time to tie jasmine to the head harness of his beast, so
that the sickly sweet perfume hung over the little caravan for
the first two days, and after that the flowers were withered
and brown. But Osman was not to be cheated. There were,
even in this aridity, some wild flowers and he was always
leaping from his high saddle to dart among the rocks after
strange-looking blooms, shaped and coloured like moths. He
had a gentle, nasal, singing voice, of the kind so much admired in the east, and even the stiff reserve of the other two
soldiers would seem to melt a little when Osman threw his
head back and sang of the two brothers who loved one another more than man can love woman, or can love freedom,
or can love life itself. His voice would seem to come alter-
nately from the back of his throat and then from the sinus
cavities of his face. To accentuate the sonority he would cup
his hand over his mouth and croon gently to himself, quite
forgetful of where he was.

The other two soldiers were more often silent. They were
afraid. Osman alone had been pleased with the opportunity to
penetrate into the interior, disbelieving or not taking too seriously the stories of the bandits who lurked there. Who could
they find to rob if there were no travellers, he asked ingenu-
ously, and it had to be explained to him that these men were
nomadic tribesmen who lived by their flocks and only took
the golden opportunity of turning bandit when a traveller was
foolish enough to come into their midst.

Ahmed Mansour was a Shawish, that is to say, a sergeant, and as he wore a black beard one knew immediately that he was not a Rasuka man. Possibly there was some strain of the Indian in him. He was a fine man, sitting his dromedary with great grace and looking eagerly round him all the time, his neatly pointed beard seeming to have apprehensive faculties of its own. His skin was smooth and clear like a woman's, his hands long and sensitive. He would very rarely condescend to speak to the boy Osman except to reprimand him now and again for not keeping an eye on the baggage camel. 'See, O boy,' he would suddenly shout, turning in his saddle and giving the impression that he must have eyes in the back of his head, 'the water-skin! Do you think this is a land of streams that you let the skin slip to the ground?' He must have been a very brave man for he alone out of the four was convinced of the menace of the bandits. For hours at a time he would ride with his rifle across his knees.

It was always Aqil, the third of the soldiers and the most graceless, who would bring the caravan to a halt when the evening came, for he would begin complaining, first of all, to the bearded Ahmed Mansour as being more approachable, and then to Winter himself when Ahmed appeared not to hear him, that they had travelled far enough for one day, that the night would be upon them before they could find a suitable place for camping. He would mutter to himself for hours and had obviously been the least willing of the three to come. His imagination had been blunted by an innate stupidity or he would have been more frightened than he actually was by the sheer walls of rock that were now rising all round them, not so much the hostility of this land of rock as its indifference to the humans who were creeping along its corridors and lighting fires against its ribs. When, by the fourth day, they had not been attacked, Aqil muttered less and fell into a stupefied apathy which showed that he had given up thinking about or reacting to his environment. Perhaps it was the only way to contend with the heartlessness of the land in which they now found themselves.

They skirted a hill of flints, having risen from the floor of the valley to follow what had seemed to be some sort of a track, but this only led them down to the wadi again, wider here than at any point they had previously passed. The geology of the land appeared at first complicated and confusing, masses of limestone or granite, alternating with beds of flint, all swallowed up sooner or later by hard, igneous rock that caught the sunlight like glass. But now it could be seen that the original limestone of the country—the granite was more or less localized to a district some twenty miles from the coast—had been overlaid by a volcanic flow, and the black rock was more and more in prominence as they continued their journey.

And yet the land gave the impression of having been populated at one time. The track they were following would be raised up above the general level of the floor of the wadi, and this was obviously the work of some primitive inhabitants who had wished to maintain a passable roadway even when, in winter, the rains filled the wadi with water for a few brief days. Growing out of the side of this causeway were a few ancient 'Ilb trees and they all brightened up at the sight of vegetation once more.

What Ahmed Mansour feared more than anything else was that they should find water, for that would give them the means to continue still farther on their journey; so that after the first pleasure of seeing growing things once more, he lapsed into a gloomy silence at the realization that there was

water, and in all probability they would soon come across a
spring. The wadi spread out wider and wider until it became
a vale suspended as it were between two steep-sided cliffs.
Vegetation there was, of a kind, tamarisk and a kind of thorny
tree of which Winter did not know the name.

And then they came across an old stone fort, of the kind
that he and Flynn had been riding out in search of these
months past. It was probably centuries old and although the
walls were solid enough up to a height of ten feet or so the
upper courses were on the point of collapse. Osman pointed
out that there was no well for the fort, which meant that the
place had been inhabited by djinns who could live without
water. But he did not take his own remark very seriously. No
one descended from his dromedary to enter the fort. Such
signs of human life only seemed to accentuate the desolation
of the valley in which they found themselves, the one-time
home of a people who had moved on, deterred by famine or
internal wars, leaving only these forts and the raised cause-
ways across the wadi floors to show what once had been.

It was a little surprising why the Shawish had picked on
Osman to be one of the party and not someone a little more
like his own silent, bearded, soldierly self. But after one or two
days Winter realized that Osman was justified in the eyes of
Ahmed Mansour simply as a cook. No sooner were the camels easing themselves down in the sand in the shelter of some
overhanging rock than Osman was scouring round for the bits
and pieces of brushwood that could be found even in this
desert place. Once he had a fire going he flung a bit of fat into
the bottom of a tin, allowed it to melt, and added a quantity
of water which spat like an angry cat. This boiling, the polished rice was added and the can stayed over the fire, Osman
swinging it backwards and forwards to prevent it from cook-

ing too quickly, until the contents had boiled dry and the grains of rice were perfectly cooked and yet not cohering in a shapeless, sticky mass. Winter had never tasted such good rice. It was dry and sweet, an excellent base for the tins of beans that he would open after heating and pour over the plates of the three soldiers and finally his own.

But as they continued on their journey there was a growing of emotional intensity as though the wilderness were becoming increasingly aware of them. Ahmed Mansour now refused to allow a fire to be lit unless they could find a cave and hang some sort of covering over the opening in order to conceal the light. As the nights were now cold, for they had reached a considerable altitude, Winter had to choose between the acrid smoke of whatever small cave they came across or staying outside, sitting close up against one of the camels with a rifle across his knees, waiting for the faithful Osman to come out with a plate of steaming rice and a tin bowl of tea. In the desert places of the earth there is a consciousness in the inanimate rocks. In the absence of human life the desolation had a life of its own and though Winter could imagine what his little party would look like from the top of one of these cliffs he had no feeling of being under the eye of any human watcher. The valley had narrowed once more and the rocks, here coloured like roses, folded round them with a curious kind of intentness.

One morning soon after starting the leading camel began crying like a child, writhing its neck first to one side and then to another as though in pain. The other camels stopped immediately and Ahmed Mansour could only get the complaining beast to continue by beating it about the neck with the thin cane he carried for such emergencies. The caravan proceeded but now the animals themselves were unwilling for in their obscure intelligences they knew the uncertainty of their riders and sensed that there was no definite objective in view. They were going more slowly now than they had ever done and only Osman, out of the party, still had any cheerfulness.

It was to him that Winter talked. His lack of Arabic crippled him terribly but somehow they managed a limping conversation for Osman had that intuitive intelligence which seems to know what you want to say before you have said it.

'It is a long way,' said Winter one day, thinking that the boy like the other soldiers had wearied of the journey.

'Not if we eventually arrive,' Osman gave him to understand, cheerfully.

'I hardly think that we shall find him amongst these hills. I did not imagine such a wilderness. He might be anywhere.'

'Certainly, O sir, I do not think that he would have come this far by himself. He had no animal, not even an ass with him. Surely he was picked up by the tribesmen.'

It was only then that Winter realized that the boy was talking about Hebechi, whereas in his own mind there was no one but Rider.

Osman liked to imitate Ahmed Mansour's way of sitting his dromedary, holding his head back so that his beard stuck well forward, changing his rifle from one hand to the other. Osman stuck out his chin, first glancing at Winter to see that he was under observation, and with sparkling eyes shrugged his shoulders and moved his arms in what he imagined to be a caricature of the Shawish. Then in the middle of his performance he would see a peculiarly coloured pebble and hop out of his saddle like a flea.

'Really, O sir, this is not the way to catch a man,' he said. He assumed that Hebechi must be a great personal enemy of Winter's, for the boy knew, of course, that the Sultan was not paying their wages. 'It would have been wiser and more cunning to ask His Excellency the Sultan to summon the chieftain.'

'But that could not be done.'

'Yes, O sir, that could be done. That was done two years ago when there was a robbery. Then His Excellency the Sultan takes a hostage for the man who has run away. That is the way to catch a man who is in the hills. But no doubt you have a wish to catch this evil one yourself. You must have a great hatred for him, O sir.' This was a compliment for it was properly recognized that hatred was the sign of a man of spirit.

It stood to sense that the tribesmen knew that they were there but curiously Winter was unafraid. The possibility was that they would be picked off one after the other from behind a rock, in ambush—and he could feel no regret for himself—curiously enough only a vague sort of sadness for Osman who seemed so cheerfully oblivious of the thickening of the atmosphere through which they were moving. Ahmed Mansour and Aqil, the other soldier, had seemingly come to an understanding and rode as close to one another as they could manage, always in the lead now. For these two Winter could feel no regret although he knew that they were only there because of his own personal whim. But they had adult, coarsened natures, aware of the possibilities of evil in the wilderness, they were like taut strings vibrating in the wind of peril that was blowing. It never occurred to Winter that they were being really remarkably brave. He was not interested in them. But in Osman's character there was something that was very appealing, something feminine that called out for protection.

'I killed a leopard once, O sir.'

'Where was that?'

'In these hills, but farther away to the north, near Ma'awa,

for that is my home. We tie a goat to a stake. Then you wait.
A big leopard, so big you've never seen anything like it. White
as a bone. I shot him when he was in the air—jumping—like
that!' Osman stuck his tongue out to show what happened to
the leopard.

Winter was following this story so intently that Osman
looked sharply up into his face—then grinned. 'No, O sir, you
must not believe all that I say. This is not true. I have not
killed a leopard. But do not tell this to Ahmed Mansour for
I would not have him know.' They both looked towards the
two soldiers who were in the lead by some thirty yards or so
and deep in conversation.

'Wouldn't you like to return?' asked Winter.

'Yes, when the time comes, O sir.'

'I mean now. On your own. You could take your camel and
we'd give you enough water and rice.'

Osman looked at him in astonishment and then in distress.
'You are displeased with me, O sir. . . . What have I done
or not done?' Winter tried to explain that he was far from being displeased with the boy, but Osman could not believe
that there was any other reason behind Winter's extraordinary
question. He immediately began to sulk.

He had a thousand taking, feminine ways, that Winter
found seductive and more and more the burden of his responsibility towards the young man became oppressive. The hostility of the other two soldiers seemed to be growing, and
Winter realized that it was not beyond the bounds of possibility that they would murder him and return with a tale of
having been ambushed. The relationship between Winter and
Osman was now such that they would certainly kill the boy
too.

Ahmed Mansour in the lead came to a sudden stop, but

Winter, in close conversation with Osman, who was trying
to tell him how he planned to come into a certain inheritance,
was not aware that there was anything the matter until his
own beast stopped and began hissing like a snake. Mansour
did not say a word, did not even turn his head, scorning, it
seemed to Winter, a man who could talk so freely to a boy
and be interested in his chatter. Conversation, it seemed, was
out of the question, so Winter urged his dromedary between
the mounts of Mansour and Aqil so that the three of them
were sitting side by side and looking down into a little valley
where a cluster of palm trees and some tamarisk were growing
under the wall of the farther cliff. Here was water. Mansour
made no move. He put up such a barrier of mental resistance
against venturing into the valley that, in Winter's mind, the
group of palms was growing on forbidden and sinister ground.
There was not a breath of wind. The sere fronds of the
scrubby palms and the dusty-looking trunks might have been
painted on the neutral background of the sandstone cliff. Winter's dromedary ceased hissing, champed on its bit, and then
there was a heavy, earthy silence. Even the animals were reluctant to enter this little valley. An extraordinary circumstance, for here was water. But the valley itself, the palms, the
tamarisk, the stained, sandy-coloured cliff, wore the air of
having been contrived and expressly assembled for some purpose. The stage-manager had just left the set and the curtain
itself was only waiting for the actors to enter and take their
places. A warm breeze blew in their faces, suddenly spirited
up from nowhere.

The solemnity of the occasion was too much for Osman.
He began to talk unnaturally loudly, asking what they were
waiting for and why they did not make forward and profit by
the water that Allah had seen fit to put in their way. Mansour

told him to hold his tongue, speaking so savagely that the boy broke off in surprise and looked at Winter as though expecting the white man to intervene. Mansour held his rifle forwards between the dromedary's ears and led the way on to the stage.

'See, O sir,' said Osman as they came up to the well. 'Tracks of men and animals. This is a watering-hole of the tribesmen. But I am not afraid. I have never been afraid. This, for example, is the spoor of a gazelle, so we might have fresh meat soon. Then there is a hyena.' The boy slipped to the ground and walked round excitedly, chattering out the names of the various animals which had left their tracks. There were fresh camel droppings, so the tribesmen had been here very recently. Osman found the skeleton of a horse and insisted on taking Winter over to see it where it lay half buried in the sand beyond the palm trees. Nothing but cleanly picked bones, no trappings, no means of identifying the rider, but the boy said that horses were rare in the mountains, only ridden by a great prince or a foreigner. It was hard to say how old the skeleton was—hard, that is, to say whether it had been there ten months or ten years.

Even if his horse is dead, it does not mean that he himself is dead. It may have died of natural causes. So Winter thought with Rider in his mind.

But the atmosphere of the little valley was inimical to any thought that would lift a man's eyes up from the ground. In spite of himself Winter found himself looking round cautiously with every step that he took, and Osman, who never ceased to chatter, was now only an unnecessary annoyance. Winter had his revolver in his hand, for the lowering sky—an overcast sky was entirely exceptional at this time of year—and the attentive rocks gave warning of an imminent attack, so that when he turned to Osman in order to tell him to hold his tongue, the thought came to him easily and naturally. He could kill the boy quite easily. In less than five seconds the boy would be dead and he, Winter, would be freed. The friendship of Osman was more gratifying than the friendship of any man Winter could think of at that moment. He had such an immense fondness for the boy that the sense once more of being enchained by his feelings almost caused him to groan aloud. Osman had been watching him with large round eyes, like some desert gazelle, and he asked what was the matter with grave concern in his voice. Winter put the revolver back in his holster, horrified by the thoughts of which his mind had shown itself capable, and led the way back through the palms where he was surprised to find that Mansour and Aqil had not yet caused their dromedaries to kneel.

'Come on,' he ordered. 'Down with you! Can't wait all day. We'll camp here.'

At that moment a shot rang out among the rocks and Osman fell silently forward on to his face, the bullet having penetrated the back of his neck, severing the thread of life within the spine and shattering the vocal organs in his throat so that even the air exhaled by his dead body in the force of its impact with the ground made not the slightest sound. He fell with his right hand at his side and the left slightly behind his back as though waiting patiently for an order. His face lay squarely in the sand.

Winter felt a spasm of acute annoyance. That this should have happened! And then his mind was climbing a windy hill of wonder, making great strides and trying to catch up with this appalling event. So far up the hillside had the event been set that Winter, in spite of desperate efforts, could not reach it. Everything failed. He could not force his imagination to reach thus far. He saw everything too coldly and clearly to be able to understand it. The boy's limbs and the scattered sand around him were washed in a thin clear light. In its terrible immobility the body might have been a photograph that Winter had been studying long and carefully and from which he was now vainly trying to withdraw his eyes. Within him there was one chill spot, one centre of self-control, that kept back the fever of the whole body, allowing him to bend down and turn the body over. In the fall the nose had been broken, but Winter could see nothing hideous or distorted in the face. With the soft tips of his fingers he tried to brush away the grains of sand from the boy's lips and eyes. He rearranged his turban. Then removed his own coat and covered the face.

He was quite unaware of anything, for the moment, but the enormous quantity of breath that he was exhaling. He had been holding his breath until his temples throbbed. To his surroundings he was quite oblivious and did not notice that Mansour and the other soldier had hurriedly made their dromedaries kneel along two sides of a triangle so that they could take shelter in the angle provided. Winter had no thought of the preparations that the soldiers were making for defence any more than he thought about the next bullet that inexplicably did not come for him. He stood stiffly on his feet, looking down at the boy, seeing him at a great distance, as though he were looking at him through the wrong end of a telescope, or seeing him at the bottom of a well, yet with stereoscopic clearness. The small, hot wind that had sprung up now fell. There was no rustling among the sere branches of the palms. A heavy silence in which Winter could hear the boy's piping voice telling him once more about the leopard, white as bone, that he had killed among the hills near Ma'awa, north of here. And still there was no further shot.

Ahmed Mansour whispered. He was lying behind the shelter of his kneeling dromedary. He and his companion Aqil had not the slightest doubt that the white man was frozen with fear and they experienced contempt for him in proportion. For some moments they had waited for the second bullet to come, but when there was only this tempestuous silence Mansour whispered to Winter to lie down or at least take some sort of shelter. Although the Shawish had no liking for Winter and now despised him for his fear, it is a natural human impulse to save life. Even if Mansour considered it necessary to kill Winter himself later on, at the moment he wanted him to take shelter and prepare to fight for his life. Mansour even considered the possibility of handing Winter over to the tribesmen, together with his dromedary and that of the boy, as a sort of sacrifice. He realized that they were not interested in Winter as Winter. They would want the clothes he wore, the weapons he carried, the beast he rode and the food on the back of the spare dromedary. They would murder not from pleasure, but even out of compassion, not wishing a man to wander naked and dying of starvation among these hills. If Mansour could have made things easier for himself and Aqil by shooting Winter at that moment he would have done so. The Shawish could see that he was still standing there as though in deep thought.

Aqil pointed out that the night would soon be upon them; and then perhaps there would be a chance to steal out of the ambush, if ambush was what it was. There was the possibility that half a dozen tribesmen were astride their line of retreat, but there was just the chance that their attacker had been alone, a solitary shepherd, who had shot down Osman to try out a newly acquired rifle. An hour after sunset, then, the two soldiers planned to make all speed out of the wadi where they felt like animals in a trap. They would tell Winter what they planned to do. Mansour looked round the neck of his beast and saw that Winter had lifted the dead Osman in his arms and was walking steadily over to the palms where he placed the body in the shadow and then extended himself on the sand at its side. The sun striking through the palms cast sepia stripes across the two recumbent forms as though putting down a carpet for them.

'It is not fear that man is feeling,' said Mansour, turning to Aqil. 'It is grief.'

Aqil was too bitter about the man who had brought them to this needless death to be interested in what he was feeling. He would have liked the satisfaction of being the instrument of Winter's end but felt that the Shawish would, at the moment, oppose him.

'How can it be grief? What has he to grieve him?'

'He is grieving for the boy.'

'But what was the boy to him? A fine boy, no doubt. A fair boy.' Aqil laughed coarsely. 'But not for grieving.'

The act of murder remained anonymous. It was as though the wilderness itself and not some wandering tribesman had struck the boy dead. In its pointlessness, in its futility, the act had that casual quality of nature at its hardest, the boot on the ants' nest, the tree falling across the cottage on a windy evening. The shadows emerged from the cracks and crevices of the rock faces, stretched out dark arms to one another, fighting to overcome the last vivid brightness that burned across the upper strata. Before the shadows of the palms could reach the foot of the cliff they were in turn being swamped by the greater shadow of the cliff that was shutting out the sun. The wadi was filling with sepia. The higher rocks alone were like bright banners.

'One man alone,' said Mansour. He was feeling a rising tide of joy at the conviction that they were not being threatened by a whole band of tribesmen. Aqil was not going to allow himself to be seduced from his contented pessimism by any foolish hopes. He continued to grumble quietly to himself. They were both convinced that now they would escape from the valley, though after that the journey back to Rasuka would be extremely hazardous. It was enough for the moment that they were still alive. This was sufficient to give Mansour a sudden access of happiness. In ten minutes the sun would be gone.

'Mansour! Aqil!' They were startled to find that Winter had walked over from the clump of palms and was now standing behind them. They could not understand how he had come so quietly, and to this fact Winter owed an immediate ascendancy over them. For the moment they felt intimidated. When he spoke to them he did not look at them, but fixedly at the cliff opposite as though fearing to meet their eyes. Apart from this he seemed the same man, to the soldiers, as he had ever been.

'Come and help me dig a grave for Osman,' he ordered.

Mansour refused. He would not give any reason because all he could say in self-justification was that it was foolhardy. They would be needlessly exposing themselves as targets to the unseen marksman. As Winter himself was walking about freely this would be tantamount to a confession of cowardice, even though Mansour was now convinced that Winter wished to die and might even be wishing to draw the fire upon himself.

'Get up, I tell you!' Winter did not touch them, but he turned his eyes upon them for the first time and shouted so that his voice came back ringing from the walls of the valley.

Mansour lay on his side and turned his face away, unwilling to meet Winter's eyes. Aqil sat with his rifle across his knees. 'O sir, let the dead alone.'

Winter spoke in English, forgetting or not caring that they would not understand. 'That is just what you can't do—let the dead alone,' and then in Arabic but more quietly now, but with such a measure of determination in his voice that Mansour felt his own head turning round to look up, even though he himself did not will it.

'Come with me and we will cover Osman up and we will take back some of his things,' said Winter to them persuadingly. His hair had come down over his long narrow face, falling between his eyes which looked out now with inexpressible pain. Mansour felt himself compelled by the eyes, not because of any authority that they had but because the suffering that he saw there distressed him more than he could himself understand. Without a word he got to his feet. He could not bear to look at Winter's weary eyes, but looked round first at the valley that was now almost dark beneath a couple of stars and then down at Winter's arms where the veins looked swollen and black in the half light, down at his riding breeches where there was a patch of blood above the knee. 'Let us go, sir,' he said softly and with compassion; and he drew his bayonet from the frog at his side to act as a tool in order to turn over the soft sand. They left Aqil behind with the animals. Their task was easy for the sand was soft. When they had finished the valley was very dark, but the cliffs reaching up on either side seemed to hold the stars entrapped between their heavy bite. What a radiance in the sky, Winter thought at last, lifting his head when they had piled some stones over the spot where the boy lay, what a suffusion of light as though on the other side of the cliff there were a great city and this the reflected glare of its myriad lamps.

'And now, gather . . .' he began, gesturing towards a samr tree, a kind of thorn, that was growing outside the area of the palms. He did not quite know how to explain himself in Arabic, so as Mansour wiped his bayonet on the hem of his robe, he walked over to the tree and began snapping off some of the lower branches which were as brittle as glass. The Shawish watched him and thought this gathering of wood might be in connection with some Christian ceremonial. Winter returned with an armful of the savage thorns, the arms of his shirt torn to ribbons and his wrists stained with blood. 'Gather,' Winter repeated, making gestures with his arms, and together they returned to the tree, breaking off the lower branches, making many journeys backwards and forwards to the site of the grave where they made a pile of their material. Lying beneath the palms were a number of sere fronds. Winter went round patiently gathering them and bringing them to the pile.

'Sir, you are not going to make a fire?' said Mansour in sudden consternation. It was now getting to be very dark in the valley. The palm fronds and the samr branches made a heap some three or four feet high over the spot where Osman was lying. Winter thought of the young David, eager and happy, setting out to watch the battle, singing and playing on the harp to entertain the mad old king. Just such as had been Osman.

'A fire, sir, would be a madness. Let us take our beasts now and return from this valley. We have been preserved, thanks be to Allah, so far, though how much further . . . You would be seen against the fire and shot. It would be like a gazelle standing against the sky on a high rock. Like that they would shoot you.'

The darkness now was so heavy that Mansour could not see the expression on Winter's face. He was standing strangely still, a black, rock-like figure. Then he spoke. 'You and Aqil go to the end of the valley, where we came in. Leave my dromedary. Take the others. Wait for me.'

This was what Mansour himself had wished for. He murmured some words which might have been valedictory and hastened across the sand to where Aqil was waiting. Winter stood listening to the complaints of the animals, their roaring, like wind in a narrow passage, the whispered consolations of the two men, the creaking of leather, feet sifting through the sand. Mansour was removing the bell from the neck of his dromedary—the tiny tinkle could be heard. There was some delay while the pack-camel was caught and then three enormous shapes moved off into the darkness. All sensations were coming to Winter through his ears for he did not lift his head to look at the night sky imprisoned between the walls of the valley. He found matches in his pocket and bent forward with cupped hands to set fire to the thorns. The match scratched and the little hollow of his hand was brilliantly illuminated— then a gust blew the flame out and he was dazzled by the blackness once more. Looking back, from the height of his saddle, Mansour saw a garnet tongue of flame licking up at the night and the black form of the man they had left behind standing in front of it and intently regarding the passionate striving upwards of the fire.

The thorns crackled. Sparks shot like meteors. So dry and brittle were the thorns and palm fronds that the life the fire gave them would not last more than a few short minutes. The flames scorched Winter's face and arms, for he was standing unregardingly close, and yet the chill within should have been enough to resist the heat of Osman's pyre. The flames would leap up for a few minutes, but the chill would last, he felt, until he himself was taken off in the frost of death. He stood in the firelight like a man of gold, shadows running over his face as the flames swayed and bickered, changing his expression when in reality there was only the most complete rigidity.

He was sorry now that he had allowed himself the gesture of lighting the pyre. It was unworthy, cheap, in comparison with the live memory he retained of the agile boy leaping from his saddle and picking the moth-shaped flowers. The flames, but they would soon be over now, and the valley return to the decent darkness that was more fitting, gave a false illusion of life. They swayed like dancers, they flowed like water, they unfolded like blossoms under the sun, they welled up with their burden of smoke like the heavy thoughts of man that come climbing the hollows and arcades of the body to the brain, yet there was no life in all this movement. Winter could put his arm in the fire and it would bite like some savage animal, but there was no life behind that bite. He could pour on water and the flames would hiss at their destroyer, but it was in the black ashes that the true spirit of the fire was to be found, in immobility, in death.

If he were to scratch back the surface of the sand and uncover the body of the boy he would not have been moved. The youth was immobile in the face of the one great problem, and would lie in silent contemplation of it while the earth closed up its valleys and opened its plains to the sea. Osman had really died. At long last Winter could say to himself, 'He is dead,' and the words had a sense.

Never had the door of death been so violently slammed in his face. The privilege of death, the passing beyond, the acquisition of knowledge which Winter, as a relic from the superstition of his childhood, thought to be one of the provinces of death so that the dead appeared as all-wise and all-knowing, had been withheld so peremptorily. His loneliness was all for those who had burned up their bright lives and now rested in the black ash. But with them he had no touch, no sense of contact. Even as the flames of the fire burned down, the memories of Osman that he had thought to preserve for ever were changing, clouds going across the face of the sun so that to the watcher on the hill the shadows going across the green fields seemed to be changing the contours of the land. It was hard already to re-

member the accent of the boy's voice. There was the story of
. . . what story had he told? Who was this boy? Where did he
come from and where would he be in ten years' time? Ten of
my years, not his! He has not the sad discipline of the years.

The last thin flame was blue. It hovered above a golden twig
that blushed and faded with the breeze upon it. The small heap
of twigs, glowing and black, still heating the night air, murmured as they settled closer to the earth. The dead had their
own province. And Winter had awakened. They were all out
of shouting distance, infinitely far ahead. Naturally he was
thinking of his own dead wife, farther away from him now, it
seemed, than she had ever been. He even thought that some
of the emotion that had welled up over the death of Osman had
rightly belonged to her. It was for her that he was mourning—
and for his own death. If lamentations came up like perfume
into Paradise, he thought, she would recognize this for her
own—but this was silly, vain, stupid! The turn of thought tor-
mented him. How could he allow himself the petty comfort of
an after-world at a time like this when the leaping flames and
the watching walls of this strange valley had been at such pains
to show him otherwise? He had to brace himself for a sterner
comfort. 'You are gone,' he talked to himself as he walked over
the sand to the palm trees. He was talking to his wife, talking
to the boy Osman, talking to Rider, talking to all the dead. He
had discovered death.

He climbed into the saddle of the kneeling dromedary and
gathered the reins in his hand. Ten minutes later he had won
the end of the valley and the voice of Mansour spoke to him out
of the darkness.

'It is you, O sir?'

'Yes, it is I,' Winter replied, feeling an access of bravery.

There was a silence for some moments. The two soldiers had

been waiting for him with the baggage camel under the shadow of an overhanging rock. Here the darkness was so intense that they only communicated their presence to him by the sounds they made, and Mansour's voice coming out of nothingness had an oracular quality about it. He spoke about the dead Osman, trying to comfort Winter.

'He was young and died quickly enough. Who knows what grief there might have been waiting for him round the corner? He died suddenly in his happiness. He might have grown old and a nuisance to his relations, so that they might have cursed him every time they saw him. "Why does not the old one die? Is he to live for ever eating our bread?" Or he might have died in great pain from some disease. He might have been tortured.' All this the Shawish said and anything else that came into his head in order to comfort Winter. 'And what does it matter now that we are all to die together? In the morning surely we shall be attacked. We must remain on watch all night here.'

'There is no point in continuing the search,' said Winter, touched by the man's words.

'Undoubtedly he is dead or with the tribesmen.'

'No, he is dead,' said Winter positively. 'Rider is dead. Of that there is not the slightest doubt.'

'It was of the man Hebechi that I was talking,' replied Mansour.

'We can do no more,' said Winter. 'In the morning we shall try to return to Rasuka.'

'If you had not said that,' said Mansour, 'we should have killed you and tried to make our peace with the tribesmen. But, as Allah wills.' He turned savagely on Aqil, who had muttered something. 'As Allah wills.' And he found some words from the Koran to sustain himself and the two others.

CHAPTER XII: *The Return*

THE DAY AFTER WINTER LEFT FOR THE interior Ford demonstrated in no other way than by going down into his cellar-workshop and starting to break up his machine with the largest hammer he could lay his hands on. It was easy to shatter the glass rings through which the bobbins fed the thread on to the wire. Fragments of green glass spattered into the face of the Arab boy whose normal task was spinning the raw cotton into thread. The boy gathered up his robe and shot out into the sunlight. The more massy parts of the machinery stood up to any amount of hammering, and even at this point Ford experienced some satisfaction at the solid way he had built. Eventually he plucked the bobbins from their pins and flung them into a corner. They went weaving through the air like streamers at a carnival, and Ford, when he tried to move, found that the cotton strands had wound round his legs. He kicked himself free and picked up a mass of raw cotton to wipe the perspiration from his face. He removed his coat. He found a spanner and rapidly loosened the screws that held his little turbine on to its table. Then he lifted his foot and sent it to the ground with a crash. He still held the spanner in his hand, evidently a much heavier weapon than the hammer he had previously been using, and he went to work on the rest of his machine

with renewed vigour. With his hands he tore off the cotton
feeds, breaking them like chicken bones. Within ten minutes
the machine was ruined beyond repair, and Ford climbed painfully up the steps into the sunlight, feeling that he had escaped from his enemies to a desert island; and yet in order to
make his disappearance all the more complete he had burned
the boat that brought him. He was safe but marooned. The
morning sunlight was so strong that he fished in his breast
pocket for a pair of sun glasses and then decided that he must
now go up and tell his wife. She would be pleased, he felt.

'There's blood on your hand,' she said immediately he came
into the living-room. 'What are you carrying that great spanner
for?' Her husband presented an extraordinary appearance. He
was dressed in the neat clothes he usually wore in the office, but
there were streaks of black grease on his face and, as she had
pointed out, the back of his right hand had been torn. It must
have been when he wrenched off the cotton feeds. But apparently there was not enough of the extraordinary in his appearance, or she was too phlegmatic, to be distracted from
the letter she was reading. 'At long last,' she said, waving the
letter in the air. 'May has seen fit to write to us. Proud hussy!'

She was lying on the settee, wrapped in her dressing-gown.
She crinkled her bare toes and her husband found himself
watching them carefully. Then he went to the bathroom and
washed his hands and face carefully. His wife followed him.

'Here, what d'you mean by leaving your great, dirty spanner
on one of my tables?'

'I've been dismantling the machine.'

'Why?'

'It doesn't serve any purpose.'

'It used to keep you quiet. Why did you dismantle it?'

'I've just told you. Well, I didn't dismantle it. I smashed it!'

'Well, come along then. Come and show it to me.' She knew that was what he wanted. She stuffed the letter that she had been reading into the pocket of her dressing-gown and took her husband by the arm. 'I'd just like to see what you've been doing to get yourself into such a state.' She spoke chidingly as though he were a small child.

'All right!' A moment later they were standing side by side and regarding the havoc that he had wrought on the machine over which he had expended so much loving care.

It was more than she had been prepared for. At that moment he was standing meekly by her and it was almost inconceivable that he should have been the instrument of such destruction. She looked at the turbine wrenched from its stand, the bobbin-carrier flung into one corner. He had exerted himself as a man will only under the stress of a great passion.

'Well, it's all over and done with. I don't want to see it any more, so we might as well give the place over to the servant. He can sleep here.'

'Come along upstairs,' she said, 'and stop babbling. You're a fine one, you are. Anybody would think you'd gone out of your mind. You spend months and years . . . and then you go and do this!' She was like a child who has brought up a tiger-cub and now finds it mature and dangerous.

'You're a fine one, you are,' she mocked at him. 'What a man! My God, why did I marry you? Why did I let you bring me to . . .' She flung herself back on to the settee where she had been in the first place, and pulled out the letter once more as if she were half of a mind to continue reading it. Ford stood there in the middle of the floor, watching her, his hands hanging slightly forward, an intent expression on his face. There was a malicious sting in her mockery. It was all the more resented that she did not become angry. But she remained very much in control of herself as though to imply that he wasn't worth losing her temper about. 'Now what am I going to say to people about you? I wouldn't say anything about your machine if I were you. Keep the cellar locked. And stop looking at me like that! What do you expect me to say? It isn't every woman who's burdened with a poor mad husband like you! The least that you can do is to leave me alone. I want to read a letter. Oh, do stop looking at me like that!' His fixed gaze rather unsettled her. It never occurred to her that he would attempt to do her any mischief, for she was twice as strong as he was: in any case, why should he want to hurt her? 'Oh, all right then,' she said impatiently, as though he were a kitten that had been continuously fussing for favours and was at last to be granted the morsel of fish. 'Come here! Come and sit down by me!' She made room by swinging her legs off the settee and her husband came over and sat meekly close up to her knees.

For a moment she looked at him. He was looking straight in front of him, waiting for her to make the next move. She prodded him with her toe. 'Hey! Wake up! Where d'you think you are, anyway?'

He started and turned to look at her. 'Oh, all right,' she said, slithering her legs round. She caught him in her arms and gently folded his head to her, covering it with fond kisses. 'My dear, dear boy,' she murmured. 'What is it? What is the matter? Well, come now, aren't you going to kiss me?' She kissed his ear. 'But look, I can't make love to you if you stop like that. You're sitting so straight and rigid. Anybody would think you'd got frozen.' She kissed his cheek. 'Come, get up here with me. Come on!' She made room on the settee and he wearily extended his length at her side. 'My chick!' she murmured, and at last he put up his arms and allowed his fingers to stroke her neck gently. 'What are you thinking of? Why

don't you say something?' she crooned. They were not really
questions any more than the questions one puts to very small
children. The mildest stimulus and she felt that he was being
soothed by her words. She felt the strain and the rigidity going
out of him. 'I'm warming you, aren't I, my love? I'm thawing
you. There, d'you feel better now? Come closer to me. You
must let me make love to you. Oh, my baby!'

She was suddenly aware that he was weeping, not by any
sound that he made, but by the moisture on her neck. He made
no sound in his weeping. It was as a child will weep in its sleep
for some sorrow it is dreaming, or some fantastic abandonment
while all the others in the party go on singing and dancing, and
you are left in a dark shadow at the side of the road. And when
you awake you forget the cause of the sorrow but the sense of
grief remains, and on the following night you dream that you
are being cast out from all human society, beyond the reach of
spankings and rocking-horses, and again there is the silent
weeping on the pillow.

'Won't you tell me?' she whispered once more, but he could
think of nothing to tell; there were no words to frame his explanation. He was awake and it was daylight. He did not know
why he wept. There was only the desolation of sorrow.

They lay there quietly all the afternoon, she stroking his hair
and even singing quietly until she was aware that he was fast
asleep. Then she rose, left him lying there and went to the bathroom to wash. She felt strangely happy and yet could not put
her finger on the reason. It may be that someone had casually
paid her a compliment and she had forgotten the occasion but
the pleasure remained. She hummed to herself, and when she
returned to the living-room she found that Nellie Leader had
come and was looking down at her sleeping husband. She put
her finger to her lips by way of warning and they both went out

to the veranda. 'He's resting. Of course, I think he's terribly upset by the way that Winter went away in defiance of his instructions. He won't say anything to me, but I'm quite sure that is what it is. If it were me, I'd report him straight away and make no bones about it. How are you, my dear?' She had been exquisitely conscious all the time that she had been talking about Winter that her words were hurting the girl. But now she turned a radiant smile upon her. 'You look pale. You should have a holiday. Why didn't you ask Mr. Winter to take you with him on his little jaunt?'

'Oh, please! I don't want to quarrel with you.' But Nellie was very angry and was wishing that she had not come. Winter's going had left her quite lost. The very sight of Cator and his wife was repugnant, she had no wish to go and see Flynn, and the only other alternative was to call on the Fords. Apparently she had come at a bad moment.

'Quarrel? About what? But we must talk quietly or my husband will wake.'

Nellie could not stand the woman's gibes, her scorn. 'Oh, you're a hard, bitter woman!' she cried, and immediately getting to her feet, walked down the steps and struck out across the sand back towards the other group of bungalows from whence she had come. She felt as barren as a field in winter. Turning over the bits and pieces that went to make up herself, she could not find anything that was bright and new. The very fabric of her nature was faded, and her sudden anger with Mrs. Ford had been the only intense spot that day, or since Winter had last kissed her. She felt as sterile as the sands.

Flynn was sitting on his veranda and was delighted to see her. He rose to his feet with a great smile lighting up his face. 'Nellie, how nice it is to be seeing you in off-duty time. Won't you come in and . . . ?'

She came up the steps and took a seat.

'I've just been to see Mrs. Ford. What a hateful person she is!'

'Oh, really! What is it she's been doing now?'

No, no, no, Nellie protested inside her. Don't sound as surprised as that. If I am right and Mrs. Ford is as hateful as that, then it should be common knowledge and you should have known it beforehand. And if it is not true, then it's me that's hateful and you shouldn't flatter. Her pride made her react in this way, but Flynn had such a great store of comfort to pour at her feet and was so evidently ready to believe anything she said and take her side against the rest of the world that she smiled at him. He was elated. He thought more fondly of Winter now that he had set off on his expedition.

'Oh, it isn't what she does or says. It's the way she says it.'

'What about?'

'Oh, don't cross-question me, there's a dear. Let's just sit here and look.'

'You shouldn't walk about in the heat of the day,' he remarked, and settled comfortably back with his pipe to gaze at his little garden, where a mohir tree was now in its glory of scarlet blossom. It looked as though a thousand brilliant cockatoos had settled on the branches, and if you were to clap your hands the tree would give off its blossoms like a fire giving off flames. There was a smell of crushed geranium leaves in the air. This reminded Flynn of the eucalyptus cutting he was encouraging in a pot close at hand. He broke off a leaf and handed it to Nellie with instructions to rub it between her fingers and then smell them.

'Oh, how nice. It makes me think of sore throats and running noses.' Not quite knowing what to do with the leaf now that she had finished with it, she put it in her pocket and then darted

a quick, shy smile at Flynn only to look away again, quite seriously, at the little garden.

'I'm sorry to be such bad company,' she said.

'That's all right. You couldn't be bad company. It's quite
enough for me just to have you here.'

'You're very sweet to me.' And she meant it quite genuinely.
After all, it must appear to him that she must be upset by Winter's going away. And she was not too much of a fool to be
ignorant of Flynn's own regard for her and what he would
think of her grieving over Winter. Even if it was true, which it
was not. Yes, he was very sweet. He allowed her to sit there,
not saying a word, and he didn't even embarrass her by an in-
terrogative attitude. It might have been the most natural thing
in the world for her to present herself in this distraught manner
and beg him to keep silent.

The scent of the eucalyptus still lingered in the air. Occasional wafts of geranium came up from the bed below. There
was heliotrope growing up against the veranda, putting out its
cloying sweetness on the afternoon air. The perfumes came and
went like music.

She was suddenly aware that Flynn had seized her hand and
was pressing it gently. She made no move to withdraw it and,
thus encouraged, Flynn put his pipe down on to the wicker
table and cleared his throat.

'Nellie!'

A great constriction in her throat seemed to be preventing
her from making any reply. Her 'Yes' eventually came like a
faint croak. There was a silence. She closed her eyes. It was
soothing to have one's hand held.

'When are we going to continue with the modelling of your
head?'

'Whenever you like.'

Flynn just thrilled with joy. 'I thought it was going pretty well. Perhaps in a week or ten days, if you were to sit regularly, we might get it finished.'

'Yes.'

'Nellie!' She opened her eyes and looked at him. 'Nellie— you know that I love you, don't you? I mean, it's rather super-fluous to say it.'

'Yes, I know.'

'Do you—could you? I wonder now, if I were to ask you. Do you love me?' She turned his fingers over in her hand and now looked out absently at the garden. He was filled with a great terror.

'You do love me, don't you?' he asked, although he knew that the question was foolish.

'No,' she said eventually, but still holding on to his hand. It seemed that Flynn was talking of a condition that had never been—love. At that moment, although she had answered no to his question and therefore seemed to imply that she knew what love was, she was experiencing only that feeling of great empti-ness, of unfulfilment. It would have been stupid for her to reply that she could not really answer his question because she did not know what love was. He would have looked at her in amazement for there is a general conspiracy to inform that we all recognize love when we experience it and are able to say, conversely, when we are not in love. At that moment of late afternoon, with a persistent eucalyptus stain on the tip of her nose, Nellie would have been much more honest if she had confessed that she just didn't know. For the time being she could hope to conceal her ignorance by a brave exterior, like a student trying to bluff his way through an oral examination. She had known what love was once. She was trying hard to re-member, but everything was obscure and dark. Love is not a

mohir tree, she thought, flaming in a garden. Oh, it was so hard
to find and recognize when you had found it!

She could almost feel his heart beating merely by holding his
hand. She wanted to say that she was sorry for him—she was,
terribly sorry, but then, she just didn't know what to say to
him! It was amazing that he knew so definitely about himself,
for Nellie did not doubt for one instant that he was genuinely
in love with her. But he was a healthy, masculine sort of person
who would always be in love with someone, always with the
most desperate seriousness.

'You didn't ask me to marry you,' she pointed out.

He shot out his words like potatoes out of a sack. 'But I do,
I will. Surely that was implicit——'

'No,' she corrected. 'You asked me if I loved you and that is
not the same thing.'

'Isn't it? It seems like the same thing to me.'

'It interests me to know why you asked me if I loved you.
It's the sort of thing only one man in a million would say. I
don't know that I like it. It shows vanity. And yet to outward
appearances you are a very modest person.'

He appeared almost over-balanced, profoundly shocked by
her words. If it weren't for the fact that any sort of criticism
of Nellie was a treason in his eyes he would have thought her
a little too bold. He could make nothing of her but made no
move to withdraw his hand although he was aware that it had
ceased to be a link between them.

Flynn felt himself sliding, little by little, into the background.
Nellie was looking out at the garden with as much intentness as
though there were some third person there in whom she was
profoundly interested. Flynn was excluded. He wanted to
assert himself brusquely. 'Don't ignore me like that,' he wanted
to say, but with the sudden realization that she was undoubt-

edly thinking about Winter, a heavy depression fell over him which left him no spirit to demonstrate in any way.

'Nothing seems to be leading anywhere, does it?' she said. 'Day in, day out, and we don't seem to be getting any forrader.'

He knew that she was only thinking this because Winter had seemingly taken things into his own hands and broken the little string of events that made up the life of the European colony in Rasuka. He knew that she was admiring him for it.

They were both on the point of mentioning Winter's name, but somehow that point never came—it was like the large bubble that seems to be just about to burst and then floats down the river and out of sight under the bridge. Each knew what the other was thinking and the knowledge laid a restraint upon them.

Nellie took her leave with difficulty, feeling that she had been ungrateful to him but not knowing, for the life of her, how she could properly demonstrate the real affection she felt for him. Yes, she would come more regularly to sit for the modelling. Not to-morrow, she said, but the day after, and he really was very sweet to her. She did not deserve it, she said. 'You've got much too good an opinion of me. You don't know me. You've just made a fairy princess out of me. I'm not like that. When you talk to me I don't feel that I'm real. The slightest touch, the slightest puff of air and I shall fall to pieces.' She hesitated, not knowing whether what she had said meant anything at all to him. 'You like me too much. You just make me feel that I'm not standing on the ground—but about three inches above it. And I don't like it. It doesn't feel safe. Makes me think I'm going to fall down at any moment.'

Flynn looked at her in complete bewilderment. 'I hardly know what you are talking about, but I suppose it's all right.'

'I'll come the day after to-morrow.' She would not let him

see her back to the Cators' bungalow and he watched her walk off across the sand, her neat little figure mocked by its long blue shadow. On the whole he felt pleased with himself. What he had achieved was considerable. He had told her that he loved her and she had taken it all seriously even though she had said she did not love him in return. She had not laughed at him. As for her not loving him—well, in his heart he did not believe it for a moment. She was just going home to think about it now. He was quite sure that a lot would happen during the next few days of modelling. If he loved her then she could not fail to love him, he felt.

But nothing did happen when she came to sit for her bust during the days that followed. She kept the conversation going like some bright stream that rippled over smooth rock, with no depth, not even enough to distort the end of a stick if you thrust it to the bottom. Flynn was never again to enjoy that feeling of intimacy that he had enjoyed when she had walked over from the Fords' that afternoon. He could have held her hand now but it would have said nothing to him. He was farther away than he had ever been; but, being a very single-minded man, he was able to model away at his damp clay with sufficient ardour to allow him to forget, for the merest moments now and again, the presence of the woman posing for him. She was wearing white shorts and a green chequered blouse but when Flynn set himself seriously to the modelling of her nose she became something abstract at once. It was just as he was coming to the end of that hour's work that he would remember the devotion he had for her: and the reminder would bring a sudden pulse of warmth to him and he was ready to do any foolishness out of sheer light-heartedness. But only for the moment. Nellie was allowing him such a very small part of herself now—the tips of her fingers, the characterless conversation, the frank, open smile of a good friend. On each occasion Flynn was sure that the next time she came the looked-for, the oh, so eagerly awaited moment would come! He was not an imaginative man but the thought of taking Nellie in his arms would excite him so much that his pipe would go out. He was sure that on the next occasion the opportunity would present itself—he was not quite sure how. But that opportunity never came. Though Flynn was trying to do his best to forget Winter the knowledge that he was foremost in Nellie's mind came to infuriate him. He could see her wondering where he was. He could imagine her working out the number of days before the inevitable return.

But in this Flynn was not quite so shrewd as he imagined. True enough Nellie was thinking about Winter as frequently as anyone else in Rasuka—with the possible exception of the Sultan—but it was in no way an obsession. She was never anxious for his safety and did not doubt that within a reasonably short time he would return, though on what basis they would resume the relationship between themselves she did not know. She would not anticipate. But she felt a chill inside her which could not be warmed by sun or any human contact. She liked going to pose for Flynn because she sat there in perfect quiet and stillness. The knowledge that Flynn was looking up from time to time to observe attentively the details of her face was infinitely soothing. It was flattering. She never liked Flynn so much as during those quiet hours when he slapped and modelled his clay in her honour. A woman will grow fond of her hairdresser in the same way.

One evening, she did not quite know how, she found herself near to Winter's bungalow. She had not visited it since that time Rachid had told her of the departure of his master and now felt that there was nothing she would like better than to go and sit on the veranda for a little while. Rachid was very pleased to see her. He had been sitting with his little decorated boxes at the sunny end of the veranda but as soon as she came he went and prepared coffee.

'To-morrow, he will come back,' he said comfortingly, and then stood back to look at her with bright eyes. He contrived the impression that he expected his master back at any moment. There was expectancy in the air and Nellie had to make a great effort to stop herself from smiling up into the lad's face and asking him how he knew that Mr. Winter was returning the following day. 'To-morrow,' Rachid repeated as he moved away with the coffee things when she had finished, and 'To-morrow,' he repeated when she left the veranda half an hour or so after having closed her eyes in the long basket-chair.

She went there on several occasions after that, always at the same time of the day, and Rachid always gave her the same cheerful welcome and assured her that Winter would be returning the following day. But this assurance which had amused her in the first place now became something rather frightening. Every time that Rachid said it there was an implied measure of the long time, the inordinately long time, that Winter had been away. She came to fear Rachid's cheerfulness and the utterance of the fatal word but nevertheless she did not allow her growing apprehensions to prevent her from visiting the bungalow.

'Did Mr. Winter say when he would be back?' she asked the boy one evening.

'One day—two day'—very cheerfully and vaguely. 'To-morrow him come.'

Winter had said nothing, she realized, about the date of his return. He had not known because at the time of his departure such a thing had not had the slightest importance. She was genuinely impatient for his return now and even found little waves of annoyance and spite running through her that he should have thus gone off on what was little more than a stupid jaunt, an affair that did not in the least concern him.

It had been all very well in the first place to be ashamed of taking the side of a native against a white man. She knew that he had been considerably upset by the anger of Mrs. Cator and the realization that his luke-warm championing of Hebechi had to a slight degree caused him to be ostracized by the rest of the community. She remembered that horrid party—the night that Cator had been attacked. What a job she had had to persuade Mrs. Cator to come! And if Cator himself had not been so pig-headed he would not have sulked and stayed behind until the last minute. Then Hebechi would not have had the opportunity of attacking him. Winter certainly had stirred up a considerable amount of resentment in the Cator household because he had seemed to think there was more than a possibility of Cator's having embezzled the money himself. But it was carrying things to extremes, surely, to attempt to make reparation by hunting down the escaped criminal yourself! There was something a little too emphatic in this gesture.

When she woke in the mornings she felt devitalized. She had to wait long moments for the strength to come back to her so that she could move her limbs. She would look up at the brilliantly white ceiling—for she always slept with the shutters open so that the first light of morning woke her—and feel the life in her limbs like the faint washing of an electric current from the crown of her head to the tip of her toes.

If I should never move again, she would think in something like terror, and set her teeth to break out of the spell. She could produce nothing, was as dry as a pip from yesterday's orange. She was stale.

Her memories of Winter now seemed to come from a great distance, faded pictures that made you sleepy to look at them—as anything seen in a poor light—all wan and soporific like in the night the crowing of a cock.

Would he never come? she thought.

She lost count of the number of days that had passed since he left. She was, she knew, getting used to a new rhythm of life; if he did not soon return the days would be passing as colourlessly as they did in most people's lives; tucked away inside her would be the sense of loss, the disappointed hope, the reaching out for the dangerously distant flower—but who is not like this?

There was a patch of rough, broken earth outside Flynn's bungalow—it might even be the site of some previous building, removed because the wooden foundations had been eaten away by ants. Nowadays the broken stones were an ideal breeding place for sand-flies, but they were so tiny as to be almost invisible. The lizards were very much more in evidence, one moment as immobile as death or a stone and then a flick across the sun-drenched earth and the creature was five or six feet away. Such stillness followed by such breath-taking speed! They moved like thoughts. There were perhaps a dozen or so flickering over the rough stones when Nellie, on her way for another sitting, stopped to have a look at them for a moment. Pick them up and their tails fall off, or is that another animal? Lizard, she said to herself, lizard, reptile, and shuddering slightly, walked round the bungalow to the veranda where Flynn was waiting for her.

She felt gay and wanted to amuse him. 'Let's go out and catch lizards,' she suggested. 'Let's see if their tails really do drop off.'

'Yes,' he said, smiling and not moving out of his chair. 'There are lots of them round here but they are quite harmless.'

There he was again! He was not taking her seriously. He did not want to go out and catch lizards himself and therefore it did not really occur to him that anyone else might. It was a royal assumption that other people only wanted the things that he did.

'Well,' he said at last, having looked his fill at her. 'Let's go in and get started, shall we? It's almost finished. Think I could finish it from memory, though I shouldn't tell you that.'

'Why?' she asked, a little bored.

'You might think it unnecessary to continue your sittings.'

'I shouldn't do that,' she said absently.

'It's almost finished,' he repeated, a little sadly, 'and how disappointing it is really. You set out to do one thing, and then you see that you've done another. Your smile—I don't see how I can catch your smile! It's inert,' he went on in depreciation of the head he had modelled, 'such a miserable little thing.'

'I think it is very good,' she said, sorry to see him cast down in this way. 'I'm sure that you've flattered me an awful lot.'

This was the day of Winter's return. They all came back, Mansour, Aqil and he. After being twenty-three days in their company there was such antipathy to them that he was eager to break away at the earliest possible moment. Coming down into the valley of Rasuka, seeing the spindly derrick of the well, the bungalows scattered about the sides of the wadi, the Sultan's fantastic palace, and above all seeing the serene sweep of the sea, brought a peculiar rush of excitement. One was always forgetting the sea and then seeing it again and seeing it for the first time. It was stained like some precious stone.

He vaulted out of the saddle of the dromedary, having flung

the reins to Mansour, and looked round eagerly for someone he knew. There was one person in particular he was looking for, but when it became clear that she was not in sight, his disappointment was as keen as if he had asked her to be there. An Arab youth, probably a servant, was walking slowly over the sand in his direction. Winter was as impatient as a child.

He trotted across the sand to his own bungalow and Rachid, who was sitting on the balcony, started up in horror at the apparition appearing before him. Winter showed his teeth in a tremendous smile. He had not shaved since his departure and a thin, chestnut beard lengthened his already long face. His clothes were soiled and the shirt torn at the shoulders. The patch of blood was a brown stain at the knee.

'Hot water,' said Winter cheerfully. 'Lots of it. Hallo, Rachid, how are you?' He stood on the veranda and rubbed his hands so fiercely together that he could feel the dirt coming off in little pellets.

'Good, sir?' asked the boy seriously. This was in reference to the expedition.

'Yes, Rachid, very good,' Winter said heartily and went into the living-room.

'You catch him, sir?' Rachid had not been so startled for a long time. He had not seen the two soldiers go off with the dromedaries and so there was nothing to explain Winter's sudden appearance. He might have suddenly blossomed out of the sand for all the warning of approach that he had given.

'Catch who?' asked Winter. He was already stripping off his clothes. 'You must go over to the barracks and collect my gear. Left it with 'em. No, we didn't catch anyone. Nobody there to catch.' He hummed to himself out of pure joy. 'I say, where's that water? I shall be on your track. Hot water—can't you see that I'm dirty?'

Rachid got the primus stoves roaring while Winter sat naked in his chair, stroking his beard. There would be no time to shave that off. He would leave it. She would be surprised. Once more he strode to the door and shouted after Rachid to know if the water was ready. Steam was coming out of the kitchen.

'Put out some clothes,' Winter ordered as he went in to take his bath out of a large tin bowl. Handling water in such quantities after twenty-three days was like playing with silk. He ran his hand through the water for the pleasure of feeling its caress. He washed himself carefully all over and then dressed in the clothes that Rachid had put out for him, no socks but leather sandals, white trousers and a linen jacket, silk shirt, open at the neck. He did not care what they were as long as they were clean. He put on the panama with the yellow sash. Before going out he caught sight of himself in the mirror. It was not the first time that he had seen his beard for he had not been without a mirror but it was the first time that he had looked at it with such satisfaction. He decided to keep it. In contrast with his light-coloured clothes his face was dark and un-English.

Then with the excitement of a young man setting out for his first date he went out to look for Nellie. He had no patience to walk and ran lightly over the sand towards Ford's bungalow where, for some odd reason, he thought she might be. He had not felt like this for—oh, when was it that he had run out of sheer delight and because there was so much strength in his limbs that they itched to be in motion? The last signs of his illness had gone away. He had got over the typhoid. He felt like a new man. He had been re-born.

Mrs. Ford was as startled as Rachid had been. She looked at the wild, bearded figure, was struck by the clearness and brilliance of the eyes before she realized that it was Winter. She was so startled that she was polite to him, answering his ques-

tions promptly and eagerly; by the time she had collected herself sufficiently to be resentful he was hastening away across
the sand as though he hadn't a moment to lose. She went into
the living-room to wake her husband and tell him that Winter
was back but looking as though he had discovered a gold-mine.
It was the only thing that could explain to her the distraught
kind of happiness that was radiating from his face. She would
not listen to what her husband was asking but sat in silence,
wondering what had been in Winter's mind when he had so
hurriedly set off for the interior. She was quite convinced now
that it had been an expedition in search of some kind of treasure. It was hard to shake her from this conviction, even years
afterwards.

At last, Winter found her where he had first seen her, sitting at the far end of Flynn's living-room with the light beating
about her face. To a third person, to Flynn, it looked as though
the whole thing had been pre-arranged and expected. Nellie
did not show any surprise. Her movements were too precipitate
for that; no sooner had she heard his footstep than she was
running across the floor to meet him. It was like the return of
the wanderer in a badly acted play. Nellie had just been waiting for him to come in, so it seemed to Flynn, and she had
known that he would come at that very minute. He put his
modelling tools down in disgust.

She was not even surprised by his beard. From the moment
of his return there had never, in Winter's mind, been anything
but the thought of this very moment. He had no eyes for anyone or anything else in the room. He did not know that Flynn
was there. He took her in his arms with such vehemence that
she gasped and he was almost too blind with emotion to notice
that he was hurting her. He felt that he had never understood
anything up to that moment.

'I just didn't know——' he said.

'Oh, my darling.'

It was as though something dead was finally being packed away.

'I just didn't know,' he repeated more softly.

He had mourned and the impediment had been dissolved out by his tears. At last they had come! As any man, young and in full possession of his faculties, should be, he was free and now ready to move forward on that other journey, not forgetting the past nor yet allowing it to anchor him to any salty rock, but carrying the dear burden of his memories on with him— the last up-lifting of his dead wife's eyes, her loveliness, the shot in the valley, the fire in the night, and the missing human man whom he felt that he had known though never seen; all these things he saw that he could take with Nellie into the future.

When he kissed her it was as though he had never kissed her before.

'That you are alive and well, that you are living and breathing,' she cried in triumph, hugging him to her.

'I just didn't know,' he murmured.

'But we never know,' she said, 'about ourselves. That's the last person we know anything about.'